'Wait, this can't be happening,' I thought to myself. I looked at the girl then at the little girl and instantly I knew. Renee, that's the name she gave me, attempted to snap me out of my daze as I stared at her daughter. I regained my composure and looked at Renee again. 'And you are?'

'Renee,' Renee said suddenly confused but then she realized that I didn't know. 'I am Reggie's daughter's mother.'

'Reggie?' I said. This felt like some soap opera shit.

'Reggie,' Renee said again. 'Tall, dark-skinned and he got a bald head. This is our daughter, Nicole.' I could see that.

'He'll be here soon. He called from the airport. Would you like to come in?' I said moving aside. But she didn't move. She just looked at me. I just looked at her, finally realizing that I just met my man's daughter's mother for the first time, a child I never knew about to begin with. I wasn't hurt though, I wanted answers. "Listen, I think we really need to talk.'

'Talk? About what?' Renee said eyeing me suspiciously. 'We don't need to talk about nothing. Who are you?'

'Wait a minute,' I said taking a minute to check myself. I was through with being polite. So I leaned in so her daughter didn't hear. 'I see you need the remix. You fucked my man and you coming off like you are the injured party. Let's try this again, bitch. I said we need to. talk. Can we talk woman to woman? Are you at least woman enough to do that? Or should I skip the preliminaries and just beat your natural black ass?'

Renee looked hesitantly at me again then at her daughter. I guess she thought about it for a second and realized I was serious. So Renee walked in, holding Nicole's hand tight, as I moved aside. I took a deep breath and closed the door. It was on and I wouldn't have it any other way...

Here's What Readers and Reviewers Are Saying About Rasheed Clark and "Stories I Wouldn't Tell Nobody But God..."

"If I had to describe this book in two words I would say, breathe taking..." – April "Lovely" Royal, Poet

"Rasheed Clark has produced an emotionally gripping page-turner..." - The Rawsistaz Reviewers

'I'm not one for reading, but I read this book in two days. I could feel the characters..." - Chris Edwards

'With the turn of each page your heart is taken on a roller coaster ride...' - Carlyn Skipworth

"This novel will make you laugh, cry and sure enough agree with everything these characters have to say..."
- OOSA Online Book Club

'An intricate mix about love, family and just plain ol' reality..." - Christy Davis

"I felt so many different emotions while reading the book...I cried, I laughed, I got angry and that is what makes this book so good..." F. Traynham

"I found myself turning pages to find out what would happen next..." - APOOO Book Club

"A fresh voice in African American fiction, this book is the one book every woman should own a copy of..."
- Barnes and Noble Review

What will you have to say about Rasheed Clark and 'Stories I Wouldn't Tell Nobody But God?'

Stories I Wouldn't Tell Nobody But God…

…Out Of Fear Nobody But God Would Understand

Rasheed Clark

A March Third Project

March Third Imprints

Copyright 2007 by Rasheed Clark

Revised Edition

ISBN: 0-9799302-0-0

ISBN-13: 978-0-9799302-0-1

(Originally Published With ISBN: 1-59916-004-8)

Dedication

This book is dedicated to my mother, Elizabeth and my sister, Jama (that is Jay-Muh). Two of the strongest African American females I have ever known and the first I have ever known to love me for being me. My mother laid the foundation for which I was to build my dreams and my sister has always been there along side me to help me make them come true.

I also dedicate this book to every woman who has faced the challenging task of trying to raise a child in a world that the Lord knows nobody ever asked to come to, like my grandmother Gertrude Barbara Clark. I also dedicate this to the only father I have ever known, my grandfather, the late Robert Luckey.

For decades, he stood by my grandmother's side riding the waves that only a family of eight sons, three daughters and a countless number of grandchildren and great grandchildren could bring. He would walk to the ends of the earth if you would ask him to. We will always love and respect you for the father and friend you were to all of us.

I also dedicate this book to the many people that have crossed my paths and showed me another side to life. I once heard that whenever you meet somebody, you are never supposed to say hello, you are supposed to ask what you are here to teach me. Good or bad somebody will teach you something.

With that said, this book is dedicated to Neil D., Chris, Ms. Gertrude, Carolina, Ms. Pat, Ms. Davis, Mrs. Nhambiu, Jim McNeil, Wendy, Cherenne, Shanda J., Kathy, Ms. Tish, Audrey M., Dr. O, Ms. Perry, Kim, Latifah, Ms. Linda Sapp, Lee Lee and Ms. Beverly G., Grandmom El, Grandmom Lewis and my best friend growing up, the late Brian Thomas, who I promised years ago to never forget him when I made it big.

If I am forgetting anybody, trust me I didn't mean to. There are so many people and so little space. This is for you. Who you are is your gift from God, who you become, is your gift to God. You, in your own way, inspired me to do this...

Introduction

When I sat down and put pen to paper to write this story, I had one of two options. I could make up something totally fiction like a gangster story, which would have been predictable, some off the wall stuff about life, how many strip clubs, gangsters and drug deals can people write about?

I chose to adhere to the first rule of writing and that's to write about what I know. If there is one thing I know, it is a story. There has always been a story.

Anybody that knows me knows that I have been through a lot in a short time. My mother passed away when I was 17, my father was a drug addict who was never there for me.

I raised my sister after my mother passed away, put myself though my senior year of high school and then college, and eventually got myself a good job all on my own and by the grace of God. That's a story unto itself, one that I will tell eventually.

In these times though, I have met many people. In these pages, I can honestly say are many of their stories. Stories that many of them wouldn't have told nobody but God, out of fear that nobody but God would understand. They are stories that deserve to be told the right way. Maybe they can help you.

Now I know what most people at this point are probably thinking something as if 'I know this man isn't putting my business in the street.' Am I?

The truth is somewhere in the world there is someone feeling the way many of the characters' in this book feel and probably have gone through or are going through many of the same things. Trust me, not everything is about you. You may want it to be, but it isn't.

When I started this book, I had to ask myself what gives me the right to write a book about relationships when the people that know me knows that a relationship is the last thing I ever ask for. I am famous for 'firing' my friends and even the girlfriends I had been involved in. I used to just kick people to the curb and I move on. No apologies and no regrets.

In the end, this book has taught me something. A relationship isn't just that, a love relationship between a man and a woman. It can be about friends, family or even just people you know and how you see yourself in that relationship.

With each relationship, there is happiness and there is pain. That is something I know a lot about. Just remember, God can mend all broken hearts. You just have to give him all of the pieces.

I have to warn everybody, this book leaves no stone unturned. I talk about everything and everybody. Everything and everybody. I would have hated myself if I didn't. There are only a few issues in the black community that I didn't touch. That's probably because I couldn't think of them at the time. You will see.

I had to do my homework though to find out many things though, like telling Nikki's story and Day's story. Now people are going to sit there and say, 'Oh, so that is why he asked me that.' You are right. That is why.

I don't know everything. Nevertheless, I had to keep it real. I am not scared to ask any thing of anybody. That has never been my style.

Having said all of this, many of you will probably wonder exactly how I fit into all of this. It is simple. I just wrote the story, what you read is often the way I heard the story. Somebody just told me to tell it from a first person to make you truly feel the character's joys and pain. That is all, nothing more and nothing less. Enjoy the story...

'You better not never tell nobody but God. It'd kill your mammy…' --- Alice Walker's 'The Color Purple'

Sista

It is times like this that made me want to slap the shit out of Nikki for bringing me to this hellhole. It is a quarter to twelve on a Saturday night and I am sitting in a club. Not just any club, I am in Club Escape, a dark, smoky club on Delaware Avenue. With the crumbling plaster and chipping paint, this isn't somewhere I wanted to escape to, more like somewhere I wanted to escape from.

I adjusted my stool so that my back was to the wall giving me the opportunity to see everything and everybody that came through the door. It feels like I have been waiting for the last hour on Mr. Right to walk through it. When I checked my watch, I realized he's late.

This is definitely not a good way to start out the first week in March of 1998; a year that I promised myself and God would be different.

'This is some bullshit,' I said aloud to nobody in particular. It didn't matter because over the loud thumping of the music nobody could hear me anyway.

'What am I doing here?' I wondered. 'I am not the club hopping type. However, here I am. I guess it is either this or another night at home watching 'Mad TV.' At least if I was watching 'Mad TV,' that shit would actually be funny.'

Just sitting here made me realize all the time I wasted trying to read every black romance novel and books about relationships I could get my hands on. I did it with every intention of getting another female, male, somebody, anybody's take on the situation of trying to find a good man or even borrowing him for a minute. Beggars can't be choosers.

Every one of those writers, like Terry McMillan, Eric Jerome Dickey, and Omar Tyree should have known better than to give women like me false hope in their books about finding a man. Who are they kidding with that 'happily ever after'

13

nonsense? Some soap opera fantasy of a man coming and sweeping me off my feet. Forget it. I would have a better chance of waiting on Denzel Washington to get a divorce.

If one thing is certain, I found out the hard way that if I can't deal with a messed up man, then some times, I would be left with no man. Yes, I know, no man is perfect. Who is?

Maybe, I am going about it wrong in my approach to having a relationship. Lord knows that I have tried everything that a woman possibly could, but still the right man eluded me. Maybe he is hiding from me. Afraid of commitment. Coward.

Look, I am past the point of prayer and closer to the point of checking the bible for God's recipe on how to make a man. He made Adam didn't he? I would make a Maleek. He will be 6'2, 200 pounds and chocolate. Shit, let me stop playing. I would settle for 5'5, 160 and named Rufus. At this point, I wouldn't even care if he turned out to be ugly.

Out of all the books I read though, I will not lie; it was Terry McMillan's *Waiting To Exhale* that gave me hope. Maybe I would finally get my chance to breathe. I would finally exhale, knowing I had a good man in my corner. In essence, I soon discovered that Terry McMillan lied about all that exhaling shit too. She lied, you hear me. Go ahead and tell her.

'Well, fuck you, Terry,' I thought to myself eyeing some of the very same men that I eventually would go home without. 'Some of us women will just have to breathe in and out with or without a man each and every day.' Especially when for the last half an hour, nobody, not even one of these sorry ass men, had the nerve to ask me to dance.

'Forget them,' I thought to myself as I adjusted my skirt and slipped my shoes off. 'My feet hurt anyway.'

As the opening bars of SWV's 'You're The One' flooded the club, it took every eligible, and some not so eligible, man and woman to the dance floor. I tapped my feet against the bar stool to the beat. The song fit the occasion. It's a song about cheating that goes something like 'what your girl don't know won't hurt her.' Seeing many of the people in the club tonight, for some, cheating is exactly what would happen tonight.

I am not the kind of woman to get into all that cheating business. I never mastered the art of picking some brother up in a club for a night of sex. Wait, you are tripping if you think it is anything but that--sex. Anybody who thought that that kind of relationship is anything else is sorely mistaken.

How could it be love if most women probably never knew the other person's last name until after their panties drop? On the other hand, they will even accept a man giving out a nickname. What kind of name is Kev? Buy a vowel and give me the rest of it. I like to know who I am dealing with.

If you ask me, women are stupid. A woman will give a man every bit of information he asks for. Most sisters are never bright enough to ask for anything in return. Welfare offices are filled with women who will have a baby by a man and don't even know where he lives.

Knowing a name, favorite color or their mama's name would be a start, but most relationships that start in clubs never get that far. It is always a wham, bam and thank you ma'am. Followed up by an 'I'll call you.' When? Unless the brother is all that, a sister won't even give him her real number. She may never tell him her real name.

Hmm, look at the women on the dance floor. That is right, ladies, do that dance. Go ahead and have your fun now. You are the same women doing the two-step with the same sorry men who a restraining order will keep you 100 feet away from.

Shit, I know there are some other women up for that mess. I saw other women, including my own sister, Loretta, go through the sneaking around, the lying and ultimately the dumb shit that comes with either that woman getting pregnant or the other woman finding out and having to break out the windows to

15

that man's car, house or both.

Then there are the ones that like to act a fool at a man's job. Look at that girl over there with the braids and the blue dress on. No, not her, the dark-skinned one ordering a drink from the bar. Now, she fits that description. If you listen hard enough you might hear the theme to the television show 'Cops' playing in the background.

Why are you playing? We all have had friends like her. The kind of woman that goes to her man's job to harass that man with her hands already pinned behind her back. She will be waiting for the cops to come after acting a damn fool. Wait until her dumb ass gets to the station, she already knows how to demand her one phone call.

Who is she going to call? Not her mother. What mother is going to come get her child out of that mess? No, her mother is probably home watching the kids. A female like that is going to call her best friend to come bail her out.

Now if that girlfriend is a good friend, she has been waiting by the phone since the woman left out. She is waiting on the call with bail money in hand.

If she is a best friend, she already knows how much because she knows her friend, with her dumb ass, has probably did it before. Now the best friend, she should stay her ass home or both of their asses will be locked up.

Hmm, I thought to myself eying the people on the dance floor. I didn't feel up to a guest-starring role on 'Cops' for beating some other woman up for something, or someone, to be exact that didn't belong to me.

No, I would rather be alone. It suited me just fine to be sitting in a club thinking about what if. Nor will I be the other woman. Why is it men always lie about not being with somebody when they are?

I genuinely wanted to believe that the right man would come along for me, if not tomorrow, eventually. When he did, he would belong to me and me alone. That is the way a relationship is supposed to work. I have watched my mother and father build that kind of relationship all my life. That is what I wanted.

Wait. Let me introduce myself. My real name is Clawja Dawn Renee Robinson. Please don't mess up my name. Say it with me: Claw-juh. There you go. For a minute, I thought you were going to act like the other folks who mess up my name. Like, you used to ride the short yellow bus to school.

I am not, let me make this clear, the kind of woman to bull shit you into believing that I am something I am not. Nevertheless, somehow I get through the day. My mother named me after a Jamaican woman she once knew and I genuinely love my name because it is different, like me.

Since the day I was born, I have always been called Sista. My brother Brian called me that and everyone else followed his lead. I weigh a good 200 pounds easily. The same 200 pounds don't always compliment a five feet six frame. So, you know I got to work with what I got. Weight and all.

I try to keep my hair done and my nails polished and styled in a French manicure. I pride myself on picking the right clothes, so that when, okay if, that so called 'right man' did come along I will be worth having.

I can be the woman he could take home to his mother and not have to worry about his mother talking about me after I left, saying dumb shit like 'Where did you meet her?' Or, petty shit like, 'You need to take her back.'

I know how my mother acted towards my brothers and the women they dated and I know there aren't any women that are good enough for my brothers, if you let my mother tell it.

Knowing the third degree my mother gave to anyone that feigned interest in her sons, why should any other mother be any different about the women their sons dated? A mother knows. So I knew to come correct or not come at all.

For years, my mother Lucy Belle has outright lied about my weight. For the first ten years, whenever the conversation came up: 'Sista's a growing girl. That is baby fat.' For the next ten, it was always: 'Sista's just big boned. She takes after her grandmother Hazel.' For the last eight, I am just fat.

The only problem for me is that few men could appreciate a full figured woman. To most men, I am just some fat bitch and I could care less, at least some of the times. It seemed to me that if a woman didn't come in a single digit size most men didn't want me. I am just some fat bitch to them.

'Damn it!' I said aloud. Now that is the fourth time I had to move my seat so that skinny bitch could pass and get through the aisle. Is she stupid or dumb? It's as if hunger is cutting off her common sense. Eat something.

She had better not come this way again. I am not moving. Who, tell me, is she trying to impress by keep running back and forth. Skinny bitch. She probably doesn't even weigh a hundred pounds soaking wet and that's if she is holding a brick.

It didn't help that the club is full of them. Hmm, look at them. The same people that I know will be in church tomorrow asking the Lord for forgiveness for the sins they would commit in the next few hours. I go to church but I also don't profess to be an angel. Some of the biggest devils are in the church.

See that's what you call a fake Christian, a person that does their fair share of evil, and then find God, like he was missing. Then they want to tell you how you are living wrong. I felt like saying you just found the Lord, I always had him. Bible study doesn't make up for the days you were freaking on Friday, sinning on Saturday and asking to be saved on Sunday.

The next time you are in church and somebody is holding their head down and they look like they are in deep prayer, they aren't. They are tired from being in the club all night, then going home with some guy they met up with. Guys many of them barely knew. I have seen it before. You don't have to tell me. I did it. Maybe that is why I am sitting here jealous.

Yes, I have tasted the forbidden fruit of a man that was already in a relationship, married or not. At some point, it has crossed every woman's mind if the man has enough money or looked good enough.

Oh, really, you are saying it hasn't? You really need to stop playing. Money and even looking good enough will make even a faithful woman say okay to just about anything.

Now before you go jumping on that kind of man, just know men like that offered little beyond sex in that kind of relationship. He damn sure couldn't take you home to meet his mother. His wife might be waiting there, ready to beat your ass for messing with her man.

Let's not even talk about the one's that lives with their mother but claim their mother lives with them. If that was true, why do you always have to whisper during the nights you are there? Shouldn't she be quiet?

Going out on a date is another thing. Oh, you could go out, but it meant out of town to somewhere nobody would see you or even know your name. Somehow, Motel 6 isn't my idea of a romantic date. At least not again, I thought. That isn't the kind of love I want. A married man could never truly love you.

How could he when he is living with another woman and vowed to love her until the day he died? No, I need somebody there on a permanent basis to take the trash out, fix little things when they got broke, and just be there to hold on to in the middle of the night.

I am not the kind of woman to play those kinds of games. I have been through that shit before. Twice, if you count this guy named Ted. Ted is one of those married men. Married men must love clubs like this. The loud music should keep unsuspecting women from hearing the sounds of the keys to their cars from jingling against their wedding rings safely hidden in their pockets.

Looking at the women on the dance floor or draped on some man's arm. Half of these women weren't any better. Most of them came here tonight looking for a man. Half of them spent the better part of the night sipping on soda or water, waiting for a man to buy them a drink.

No self-respecting women would allow herself to put her goodies on sale for the price of a glass of Hennessy or something to eat later. Yet, they existed. My pussy is worth a lot more than dinner at Red Lobster. Even then, I would rather split the check.

Damn, I feel good now. The Singapore Sling I ordered fifteen minutes ago just kicked in. The slow buzz filled my mind as I swayed to the rhythms of Beanie Man's 'Who Am I'. Still nobody came up to ask me to dance. I know they see me moving. That is club talk for come ask me to dance.

Looking around, I couldn't help but to eye some of the sisters and brothers coming up in the club. I got to give respect where respect is due tonight though as I realized that most of the women are in fact, dressed to the nines. Some, not all, I thought, as one light-skinned sister walked past me.

I am going to give her the fake smile when she walks by again. Look at her, who does shit like that? She has on a tight, hot pink jump suit and matching boots. That weave looks like a hot mess and that is obviously not her hair. Another case of H.I.B. (hair I brought.)

'She must not have any friends,' I said to myself. 'If she did,' I couldn't help but to think as the sister moved in to hug a light-skinned brother in the corner. 'Her friends would have told her not to wear that shit.' Looking at the brother now feeling on her ass, as I sat here alone, I realized somebody must like it...

Sista and Nikki

I scanned the room looking for my best friend, Nikki. Nikki or Nicole Love has been my very best friend since grade school. She came to live next door to us after her mother died of cancer. A few years before that, Nikki's father was killed in a car accident. Nikki didn't really remember him.

Half Jamaican and half Puerto Rican, Nikki is five feet eight and has a natural mane of honey brown hair that offset her caramel complexion.

Her hourglass figure made most men stop and stare and most women mumble 'bitch' under their breath when they caught their man looking at her. Nikki could pull any man since we were fifteen and for the last 20 years, I settled for being Nikki's fat friend.

It was Nikki's idea to come to the club that night. According to Nikki, it would be fun. Nikki knows I am not a club hopping kind of woman. Nikki was right though. I did need to get out the house. I needed a change of pace from sitting around doing nothing. Maybe that is what made it so easy for Nikki to talk me into coming out.

'I can't even remember the last time I step foot in a club. Why go?' I told Nikki over lunch the first time she suggested it. 'It is just the same people every weekend, disc jockeys playing the same songs, watered down drinks and people doing the same basic two-step. I could watch that kind of shit on *Soul Train*.'

When I finally saw Nikki, she was sitting on Reggie's lap. I can't stand his ass. Reggie is Nikki's on-again, off-again boyfriend; he was a starting player for a basketball team that shall remain nameless. He didn't last long when he got side tracked with an injury and ended up in sports management.

I really didn't care. When it came to Nikki and Reggie's relationship, it is more off than on. Now I understand why Nikki disappeared the minute we got here.

21

At six feet two, Reggie is black as night, bald by choice and according to Nikki her 'Fire and Desire.' At least she like that song when she met his tired ass.

I never liked him. I couldn't count the number of times that I spent hearing about how Reggie was fucking up with Nikki. How he mistreated her and still Nikki kept going back to him. I knew there had to be other women, but I didn't feel it wasn't my place to tell Nikki about them.

Reggie has fallen into a habit for the last couple of years of just disappearing, which isn't easy when you are a celebrity. Sometimes, there are stories I wouldn't tell nobody but God out of fear nobody else would understand. With Reggie, I feel Nikki is better off not knowing.

From what I can see, Nikki was all huddled up on Reggie's lap and rubbing his face. I couldn't help but to laugh. If we didn't come to the club that night, somebody else would have been going home with Reggie.

Some corny chick that probably heard about his reputation and his money. Females are trifling. Some women will fuck anything that moves. Just fall down on the dick.

'Let me go tell this girl I am ready to leave,' I said to myself. I don't feel like another night of watching Nikki chase Reggie. Unlike other women, I will never tell Nikki that she is a fool. I reasoned that Nikki is one of those women that like a lot of drama going on their lives. She must like drama to deal with a man like Reggie.

How many times would it take before Nikki learned to stop pretending she is Jesus Christ? Jesus could turn water into wine, but Nikki would never be able to turn Reggie into a good man. Still, Nikki tried. She got that kind of bullshit.

I slid from my stool and slipped back on my shoes, when a guy bumped into me when I went to move. Damn, can I move? I looked him up and down from head to toe like 'Are you crazy?'

First thing that caught my eyes is that he had on a silk pant set in March, when he should have known it is way too cold. Wait, though, that wasn't even it. Something else is wrong with this picture. It was only when he smiled a smile like he is undressing me with his eyes, I knew.

'Lord, no he didn't.' I said. I looked again and laughed aloud. 'Yes, he did. Yes, the fuck he did.'

The brother is cross-eyed, so he is doing a simultaneous removal of my shoes and my bra. If that wasn't enough, he had the nerve to have on a pair of matching blue alligator shoes that looked so run down and leaning over that he probably has to lay down sideways to put them on. Oh, my God.

'Excuse me,' he began with enthusiasm 'But I have been watching you all night long girl.'

'Go back and keep watching,' I said aloud but almost to myself as I brushed passed him and then headed to the other side of the club like I never heard him.

'Why is it that a guy had to come up to me with some corny ass line to use instead of just saying hello to get my attention?' I wondered.

Then there are the brothers who thought because I am a big girl that the mention of lunch or dinner at an 'all you can eat' spot would pull me the same way. Some men want to believe if you look at them or even smile that you want to fuck them.

'Please,' I thought to myself.

Having to deal with that fool, by the time I reached where Nikki should have been, she was gone. I looked up in time to see Nikki on the landing near the exit, pointing at Reggie. He was talking to someone as they both headed out the door.

I mouthed the words 'fuck you' to Nikki, as Nikki waved back and pointed at Reggie again. Nikki then shrugged.

Just then, Reggie turned and looked at me. He smiled. It became obvious to anybody who saw that, that somebody would fuck Nikki tonight--Reggie.

'Shit,' I wanted to scream. 'There goes my ride.'

I turned to get my coat and paused briefly to dig into my purse for a bus token. Once I found it, I looked up and just standing there was Mr. Gators with his pearly white teeth smiling back and holding his car keys. I thought to myself, 'This just isn't my night...'

Nikki

I woke up Sunday morning and looked at Reggie wondering if I should wake him or let him sleep. I decided to let him sleep, giving me a chance to take a shower and then make breakfast for the two of us. On second thoughts, we could always go out for breakfast. I don't feel like cooking.

Instead of talking about our future, as I planned, all we ended up doing was having sex. Not that I am complaining but there is a lot on my mind. I made a mental note to call Sista again and find out how she made out. Just not right now.

Reggie is the reason we went to the club in the first place. I thought it would be fun to get Sista out of the house to have some fun too. Lord knows that Sista never really went anywhere. I knew that Reggie would be there with his friends. There's nothing like showing up looking good as hell to make your man remember what he got at home.

Usually, I don't spend any time around his tired ass friends, a bunch of ball players, a few who were his clients and having to spend the night tripping over their big ass feet. I get tired of them staring at my tits and my ass.

Shit, if I have a dollar for every time a man undressed me with his eyes, I would be a rich bitch. However, one of them was having a birthday party last night, so he gave Reggie a few VIP passes. Shit, free passes to a club are free passes. Sista never did come up to the VIP lounge. She didn't miss anything.

'Who's going to be there?' Sista asked me with every right to be suspicious, when I mentioned going out.

'People,' I lied realizing that Sista wouldn't go if she knew Reggie would be there. I damn sure didn't want to go by myself.

'This smells like a set up,' Sista said with caution. 'You know I hate being in a club with a bunch of tired ass people. You sure you want to go?'

'Yes. Look you will be there with me,' I lied again. 'Girl, it is going to be fun. You and me. We haven't had a girls' night out in a minute. Don't you get tired of sitting in the house moping? Try something new. I heard Club Escape is the place to be on a Saturday. The club stays popping'.'

'I hope so for your sake,' Sista said giving me that look like she was still suspicious. Sista dropped the conversation after agreeing to go. I know I am never going to hear the end of it now that I left Sista in the club to be with Reggie.

Look I had to do what I had to do. Like right now, I need to get my dress off the floor. I paid too much for that thing to let it stay there. I really need to take a few days off and really clean this place up. My place gets dirty fast.

Reggie suggested that I let the housekeeper that cleans his place do mine, but I passed on the idea. I just didn't feel right unless I cleaned it myself. Like my Nana always say, even if you only got a box and a bed you need to keep it clean.

Since Reggie got drafted to play professional basketball years ago, the money has always been there. He played for a few years. Then he got hurt, but his contract was guaranteed. Now he works in sports management. On what Reggie is making he could have easily afforded to buy a mansion on the hill, but I chose this apartment. That is until…I just smiled.

What was I thinking though to decorate everything in here in cream from the living room to the bedroom though? It is mine though, even though it never truly felt like home. As I slipped into my robe, I suddenly felt sick.

As I made it to the bathroom, I couldn't help but to smile at the image staring back at me. I looked good. Running my fingers through my hair, I silently thanked my mother for giving me that good shit.

'You go, girl,' I smiled. If I wasn't me, I would--. Shit, I just threw up. I squeezed my eyes shut and began to do the math. Two months, six days. Lately, I found myself counting off the days, trying to figure out when I will start showing. It would be then when I couldn't lie any more to the people that I loved most.

By then, when the baby came, there would be one more person to love me. The best part is that Reggie already knows and wanted the baby as much as I did.

I looked at myself again in the mirror and then looked back through the open door to see Reggie was still sound asleep. Reggie slept too soundly for me. I watched Reggie sleep. I couldn't help but to think, 'A serial killer could get him the way he slept. Snuff his ass right out. Damn fool.'

As his girlfriend, I know, I know. I would have to play my part. I know for a couple of days, I would have to go on the news crying, falling out and carrying on because his dumb ass didn't get up. I laughed at the thought. No, I couldn't let our child grow up without a daddy.

Now that I am pregnant, I know I will never hear the end of it from Sista or my grandmother. At least until after the baby is born. Sista especially since I know that Sista never liked Reggie. My grandmother hated him. A mother knows I guess.

I couldn't lie to my grandmother. She knew Reggie and I used to go through it all the time. She heard the fights even back when we were younger. Some times, I would go days, weeks, and then even months without seeing him. I tried to see other people but I always went back.

Sista always questioned why I keep going back. It was something that I can't explain. I just know how I feel. Maybe I am so deeply in love with Reggie that I couldn't see that he isn't right for me. I just don't know. Even when things went wrong, something in me still made me want to try.

I know he was seeing other people when we broke up. Hanging around all of those basketball players, guys like that always do. Shit, I did. I dealt with a few people too. This last break up had lasted months.

When he came back, I was always acted like I haven't been seeing anybody. Men are stupid they can't tell if their woman has been cheating. Guys claim to be able to tell if their woman has been cheating. That is bullshit.

They say dumb shit like 'I know my size.' Dummies, we can push babies out of our stuff and it still goes back to its regular size. Unless you can lift a lip print, a fingerprint, or a dick print from a pussy, a man will never know what we are doing. They won't.

Reggie is big though, I must admit. He definitely buys his underwear in the men's department. However, when he start all that 'Who's your daddy?' shit or that shit about 'Am I hurting you?' I have to keep myself from laughing at his ass. As I said, men are stupid. What can they really do?

Unless a man's dick is the size of a baby's head, he can't do shit. Like I said women push big ass babies out every day. They say when a woman has a baby she has the strength of ten men, what can a man really do with eight to nine inches? If even that. I will not lie; the sex with Reggie was still good though.

Still, I can't help but to wonder what is going to happen now. Yes, Reggie still disappeared on me at times. Yes, he lied about where he has been and who he has been with. The worst part about him lying is that I knew it. He knew it.

Like I said, I know there were other women, Reggie dealt with. There had to be. There is always some chick on the side to make a man feel like he can still put it down. Nevertheless, he came home to me. That is what counted, right?

I suspected every man has other women, no matter how good things are at home. Any woman that believed he didn't is

28

blind and a fool. No woman wants a man that other women wouldn't want. It takes all the fun out of things. Other women and the shit they do are not my concern though. They just don't matter right now. My first concern is my baby.

I lingered in the mirror for another two minutes before stepping into the shower and turning on the water. The immediate stream of cold water before it became warm woke me up. Reggie was still not awake. I smiled again feeling good, thinking to myself, 'I must have worn Reggie out.' I put my thing down.

If Sista called wondering what happened last night, I am going to let the machine pick up. Church isn't on the menu for the morning and that is something that God would understand.

Who told every black church choir to always have to turn one song into a twelve inch double album remix version that won't allow you to sit down for a half of an hour? Church services always seemed to get longer and longer.

Right now, I need to talk to Reggie about the future. We need to talk about the baby. I never had been good at expressing my feelings. I won't lie when I am hurting about the only person that I talk to is God.

Right now, I needed to talk to Reggie. We need to talk about what is going to happen to us. Would he keep his place or my place? We need a house. Reggie can afford it.

I have already started leafing through magazines and books picturing how I wanted my daughter to be. I hope it is a girl. I planned to dress her in so many cute sets. I rubbed my stomach longing for the day when my daughter would call me--Mommy. There are some big changes ahead. Big changes.

I rested my head on the wall as the water washed down my back. I tried to relax. I will not lie. It hit me hard that I am pregnant. Me. I am going to be a mother. Scariest part is without my mother around; would I know how to be one? I know I

29

should be happy. Some times, like at this moment and the night before, I just didn't know what to feel.

In the back of my mind, the questions still lingered about Reggie. Whenever the conversations come up about children before he always seemed so apprehensive. Now that I am pregnant, something in him changed. Still, I can't shake the feeling there is something else. He has always made excuses about having a baby.

'Why mess up a good thing right now?' Reggie asked when we first got back together after a bad break up two years ago.

'But, we need to talk eventually,' I sat up and looked at Reggie. 'How can a baby mess up what we already have? I thought we were stronger than that?'

'Look, I am always on the road. Right now, it's just not good, I have my contract negotiations coming up and it's just bad timing. I want to be there for my child, Nikki. Not somebody that comes home long enough to kiss my child goodnight.'

I looked at Reggie long and hard before I spoke, 'But it's something I want, a family, a dog and the house. The whole nine yards, that's what I want. Can you understand that?'

'Hey, I do,' Reggie said smiling at me, 'I'm going to give you all that. Just not now, things just aren't right. I got a lot going on and I needed to focus my attention on that. Just not now--' His cell phone rang interrupting the conversation. Reggie got up from the bed and walked away.

I couldn't hear what he was saying but he was obviously upset. He looked back at me as he walked out the room. I tried to listen, but I didn't hear anything. I figured he was upset with work, so I left things alone. I'm pregnant now and he still clams up. I don't think why. That's just Reggie, I guess. I dismissed the thought and the questions in my mind as Reggie stepped into the bathroom and then into the shower with me. I started to speak but Reggie put his fingers to my lips…

Renee

'When are you going to come get your daughter, Renee?' my mother screamed into the phone. She can be so loud when she wants to.

'Could you please stop yelling Mama? I told you last night I'll be back in the morning,' I said trying to pretend she woke me up. 'I hate coming into the projects at night.'

'Well, it is almost one o'clock in the afternoon. You're safe, the muggers, rapists and killers clocked out at five this morning. Renee, get up. You didn't hate it when you used to live here. Get your black ass up and come get your daughter. You didn't leave her a change of clothes or anything. That's nasty Renee. I didn't raise you like that. She's a little girl. I will call her daddy on you or child services.'

I hated when she started yelling like that. I especially hated what she said about calling my daughter's father.

'Call him for what? You can call child services; I take care of my daughter. You also know I wasn't coming into the projects last night. It's not safe. That is why I don't live there any more, Mama. I'll be there, Mama,' I said looking over at the clock. I wanted to say to her, 'See if they still have your picture up in the wanted section.'

I guess she wasn't trying to hear it because she hung up on me. I was ready to go back to sleep when I felt it. Long, hard and black. The remote was jabbing me in my back. I went to grab it when I realized he was up.

'Sup, girl,' Mike said with his breath smelling like what the fuck. 'Can I get a little something before you got to go?'

'Fuck no. Why don't you talk that way?' I said rolling out of bed. If I wasn't up before, I am up now. I can't believe I slept with Mike last night. Mike is nothing more than a corner boy. A small time hustler that isn't good for nothing but somebody to fuck if you are desperate.

31

Last night, I was desperate, lonely and sick and tired of being sick and tired. I spent the better part of the night trying to get the attention of my so-called man. I guess he is my man. We were back together for all of a month, I think, before he disappeared again. As I looked at myself in the mirror while putting on my robe, I saw Mike's reflection in the mirror.

I watched his big ass feet sticking out of my covers and I realized all I wanted was for him to go home. He laid there playing with his manhood under the covers like he was willing it to life. Nope, sorry, player, the sandbox is closed. I pulled the covers off him and waited for him to get up.

Mike definitely isn't the guy you could take around your friends. He is tall, light-skinned, and kind of fat and has the biggest lips that you could ever see on a man. Lips that served one purpose and one purpose alone and that purpose wasn't to cool soup off. Trust me. There is no soup on my body.

'How many times do I have to tell you, I got a man,' I said picking up his clothes and throwing them to him. 'If I wasn't drunk I would have put your ass out last night, Mike.'

'Ma, how come you have to keep playing that man card,' Mike said as he got dressed. 'I never saw a dude roll up in your spot. Why are you fronting? Last night was cool but I am not pressed. If you know what is good for you, you would let that cat ride out and get on this dawg.'

'What are you stalking me? How do you know who comes to my place? That is why I don't fuck with you like that now,' I said staring at him with disbelief. 'My man and I are going through some shit right now. You don't hear me talking about your daughter's mother.'

'Don't give me that dumb look,' I said, 'I know about her. On the other hand, I should I say any one of your baby mothers. I saw all three of them over there fighting the other week. You need to deal with your own shit before you start talking about mine. You know what, just get out. Go home, Mike. Just go home.'

'You didn't say that last night. You were on some other shit last night. I don't think you really have anybody, or you

32

wouldn't keep calling on me,' Mike laughed. 'I'm going to be back again. Watch. All those nights you call yourself getting lonely. If dude don't want you, I got you.' Mike said slipping his shirt on. He stopped and started making gestures like he was having sex with somebody.

'Let me explain something to you,' I said tossing Mike his wallet that fell from his pants across the room. 'I got this. I can handle my man. You handle your children's mother.' I said tired of the whole conversation. Mike stopped and looked at me. He walked to the door and opened it and laughed.

'You sure he's your man?' Mike asked.

'Just get out,' I said tired of the whole conversation. I guess that was enough for him. Mike left out the door. I picked up my cell phone and didn't see a missed call. There wasn't even a message. I was looking for one from my daughter's father.

I didn't plan on going to the club last night. However, when I heard my ex-boyfriend, well, the guy I had been messing with was going to be there, I had to. I figured if I got my hair done, my nails polished in and brought a new dress he would see something in me. You know fix myself up. I got my hair braided and brought this nice ass blue dress.

I am not going to lie, the best thing I got going for me is my body. My face is kind of average. As long as my ass is fat and my breast stay a 36D then I am going to handle something. Shit, he didn't pay any attention to me. He was too busy with some other girl. I can't lie. She was cute.

Up until last night, I haven't seen his ass in weeks. I called him, his house, his cell phone and even his mother. You know how mothers are they play that dumb role with their kids. I think I called him about a good twenty times and he didn't answer. He kept letting the answering machine pick up.

I should have just walked right up to him and his 'girlfriend' last night and said something. I wasn't going to cause a scene and risk being put out after paying $10 to get in the club. I was jarred by the sudden ringing of the phone. I answered.

'So what happened,' my girlfriend Shirley asked me without saying hello. 'Did you see him? I heard they were having a party last night for one of his clients.' Shirley works in a law firm that did a lot of business with one of my ex's clients.

'Yeah, he was there. All hugged up some girl in the VIP section. My damn feet hurt. I spent the better part of the night trying to get his attention by constantly walking back and forth. Then that fat girl acted like she had an attitude every time I went over to where he was.'

'I would have hit her and ran,' Shirley laughed.

'Aren't you big too?' I asked. 'You wouldn't have gotten far. Listen, he knew I was there, but didn't even act like I was alive. The minute I turned my back though, he jetted out of the door. I should have chased his ass down, but he left.' Sometimes I feel stupid for doing all of this dumb shit, but I want him. I will not front. He is the type of man I have been after for a minute.

'Renee,' Shirley said 'You need to say something. Do something. Tell somebody about that sorry son of a bitch.'

'Who am I going to tell? He pays child support. He doesn't get high. Plus I don't want him starting any shit that is going to affect my daughter,' I replied looking for something to wear. My mother was right; I need to go get my daughter.

'You are right,' Shirley said. I heard a pause then I listened to Shirley start yelling.

'If you don't sit your black ass down, I am going to send you to your father. Let him deal with your ass. Latoya, come get your brother before I snatch him within an inch of his life."

'Shirley,' I yelled into the phone. When I heard her say hello, I continued, 'Let me go get my daughter from my mother and I will stop by.'

'Alright,' Shirley said. As she hung up the phone, I heard her yelling at her kids more. When she got like that I wondered who is she yelling at, her kids or their father who both the kids looked like. I promised myself that I would never get like that no matter what my daughter's father did.

I wondered where he is at now. I keep thinking back to that first time, I thought we were through and then he showed up one night drunk as shit at my place. I knew I could get him. For a minute I did. He eventually even accepted my daughter and everything. I couldn't complain about that one.

When I met him in the club the first night, I didn't have a clue as to who he was. I don't watch basketball. How was I to know what he did? I didn't care. I just wanted to go out and have a good time. I deserved it back then after dealing my ex-boyfriend Ron's tired ass for all those years. So I went out and was having fun and then I saw him.

He wasn't like the other guys in the club. Other guys act like they wanted to jump me the minute I walked in the club. He didn't do that. He didn't treat me like a back up plan if he doesn't get what or who he wanted.

Sometimes, I get tired of all of those guys coming up to me in the club with their pre-printed numbers. Guys will actually write out their numbers a couple of times to give to different women all night long. He will try to talk to you and your friend.

Then, here he comes. He was looking good and dressed nice. He even smelled nice. After we had sex, normally I would have put him out like any other guy. But something about him was different. As he slept, I figured out what it was by going through his wallet: a Platinum American Express card. He had money. I felt like I hit the jackpot.

We started dating. Okay, he'd stop by for sex. Something told me he was on the rebound but I didn't want to believe it. When we did go out and he did run into somebody he knew, he never introduced me. Still, I stayed with him because he is good to my daughter. I would settle for being his side girl.

Lately, I can't lie to myself any more, the phone calls have dropped off and the visits came less and less. He was seeing her again. I didn't even know who she was until I saw a picture of the two of them together at his place. I was pissed. I called my best girlfriend, Shirley, and was ready to go bust out his windows. But I forgot her dumb ass was on probation for doing the same shit to her daughter's father.

That is why I ended up fucking with Mike tired ass last

night. I was lonely and he was there. Don't let independent women fool you, independent means lonely. Mike was just something, or should I say, somebody for the moment.

I didn't even tell my mother that I am single again. She met my ex a few times. I got tired of her saying 'I told you so,' when things went wrong in my life and they usually did. She said it when I got pregnant; she said it when I told her the situation with my daughter's father.

When I got pregnant again, I thought about having an abortion. I have been through that shit before when it came down to my first pregnancy by a guy named Ron. Ron and I were good up until I told him I was pregnant. After that, it was all down hill. He just changed on me.

Things weren't great from the beginning but when I say they went from bad to worst, they did. I honestly don't know what I saw in him in the first place.

Ron is the kind of brother that the minute you suggests you two go out and do something different, he would holler 'Didn't I just take you out last week?' Then it was only right that I had to remind him, 'That was to the market so I could fix your trifling ass something to eat and that shit don't count.'

So, I had the abortion. I didn't even tell my mother about that pregnancy to this day. Why so she can call me a 'Super Saver Ho?' My mother said it when my cousin kept getting pregnant by all those guys?

'Super saver hoes,' according to my mother, are able to have three kids by a man she barely knows. I am realistic no woman can change a man from being a dog just by laying down with him. I couldn't before or afterwards.

When my daughter came though, my life changed. Suddenly I found a focus, somebody else to believe in. Somebody to live for besides the tired ass guys that I met. I was about to get into the shower, when my cell phone went off. Shit, it wasn't him. I got into the shower and wondered, 'Where are you, Reggie…'

Sista

I slept late and missed church. It was wrong, but something in me wasn't up for watching Sister Ethel in church precisely at 10:32 in the morning catch the Holy Ghost and start in on a tirade that would send her gray, curly wig flying into the third row. Brother Edwards should have been a wide receiver the way he caught it every Sunday.

I am definitely not up to Brother Basil telling me 'Sister, it is so good for the Lord to bring you to me.'

'Actually the 33 bus did it,' I replied and then like a Jehovah's Witness knocking on your front door on a Saturday, I would sit through the rest of the service and ignore him.

Basil has offered to give me the world one too many times. It is just too bad that he was forty and everything he "owned" is in his mama's name. The fool even had the nerve to call my house once collect. I laughed at the thought. Sometimes, I can't help but to look over at him. When I did, he waved. Damn fool.

I looked around my small walk up apartment I rented in West Philly over a store. It isn't much, just a bedroom, living room, tiny kitchen and a bathroom. It isn't much, but it is mine.

I lived with my parents through college. When I got the chance to get a job and make enough money to move out, I jumped at the chance to get away from Lucy Belle, my mother.

My mother, Lucy Belle Robinson, could be sweet as pie some days and on others, I wondered if the devil is mad at my father for marrying the woman that should have been the devil's wife. My father, Earl, is just as nice as any man could be.

I love my father because he is as warm and giving as a man can be. He offered me the money to move but it was something I wanted to do on my own.

37

I have two brothers, Brian and Eric and a sister named Loretta. Brian and Eric are the splitting images of my daddy. Brian is about five feet eleven, a little taller than my father, with caramel skin and wavy black hair. Some people said he looked younger than he was. I don't see it.

In my mind, he was still the same person that used to scare off every boy that used to like me when I was younger. Brian was always over there helping my father or running errands for or with my mother. Being born after Brian, we are very close.

'Mr. Five Hundred' is what my mother called Brian. He has a good job with a Fortune 500 company. He went to Drexel University. He drives a Lexus and has a nice apartment, better than mine. He is the man, the perennial bachelor.

No woman has snagged him yet for that faithful trip down the aisle. Brian is only 30. Then again, maybe it is because most women never lasted more than two weeks.

Eric is something else and I shook my head when I thought about that boy. Growing up, Eric has always given my parents problems. He barely went to school and when he did, he was a disruption.

Unlike other fathers, my daddy knew early on that his sons would never amount to anything unless he put his foot down. With Eric, he could never let his foot up. Eric needed the constant attention and my father wasn't afraid to give it.

I hated that my mother chose to baby Eric because he is the youngest. Despite my mother's lies that her 'baby' is away in Atlanta, anybody who watched Action News knows he is doing five years for armed robbery.

One night after getting high with his boys, Eric went into a convenience store to buy something. The lady said something he didn't like to him and he decided to take what he was going to buy. He took that and everything she had in the register too. He has been in jail for over two years.

Then, there is Loretta. Loretta is twenty-four. To be blunt, I don't understand my sister. Yes, she is my sister but I don't always have to like her. My sister is the kind of person, a real woman would hate.

Loretta Destiny Robinson Brooks has everything any woman would want when it came to material things. I think the only reason why some people stayed cool with her is to find out how the other half, those that have material things, lived when they need to get their own life off of layaway and go get themselves the same things. Go figure.

Loretta married young, at 19, to the first person that asked. Clifton 'Cliff' Brooks was 27, when he asked to marry Loretta. Cliff was already out of school with a good job at as a management consultant, having graduated from the University of Pennsylvania with a Master's degree. He gave Loretta everything, money, clothes, a car and a home.

My number one concern is that he didn't look like the type of man Loretta would go for. He was kind of short, kind of thick and already going bald that didn't look too good or compliment somebody that wore thick, black plastic framed glasses. He is the type of man that all you can really talk about is how nice he is. He is though. He was too nice if you asked me.

To see Cliff and Loretta together would make anybody take a second look. They looked ill matched. Cliff was good to her though, even put her through Temple University. She has a nice house. She has a car in the garage and a good job. But she isn't happy. She repeatedly sneaks around on her husband.

Sometimes, I wondered if Cliff knew, but when I thought about the way Cliff looked at Loretta, I know that even if he did, he isn't going anywhere.

Cliff is what anyone would call a good man. He went to work every day, cooked, cleaned, went to church and came home

39

faithfully every night. What he saw in Loretta, I just don't know. Nor would I ever try to understand. Loretta had a thing for those bad boy types. Nothing Cliff is or will ever be.

What I suspected in Nikki, I knew about Loretta. Loretta liked drama going on all the time. I have seen first hand the number of times that Loretta called Cliff 'stupid' and 'dumb' and tried to provoke a fight, but he would simply walk away after telling Loretta he loved her.

Loretta knew he won't leave her permanently. Loretta had the one thing from Cliff that other women would kill for in a man: his love and devotion.

* * *

It was about eleven when I got up, took a bath, styled my hair and departed for my mother's. I brought a copy of Omar Tyree's book 'Fly Girl' to reread on the Elevated Subway Line. I got off the train and went through the free interchange to catch the Broad Street Subway.

After getting off at Spring Garden, I walked the three blocks going west to 17th Street to my parents' three-story row house. My parents have lived there for over 25 years and raised my brothers and sister in that house.

I opened the door of my parents' house about one thirty and smelled the cornbread my mama baked every Sunday for dinner. My dad was sitting on the couch as usual.

My father, Earl, gave up on going to church with my mother a long time ago. It isn't that he didn't believe in God. It was the fact that the reverend had a better car than my father ever had. According to my father, Earl, it isn't right for a man that only worked one day out of the week.

Now my daddy's favorite past time is watching old westerns on the Sunday cinema. When he saw me, he smiled and held his cheek up for my kiss. From the kitchen, I heard my

40

mother singing along with the gospel singer, Yolanda Adams, and I smiled. I settled down onto the couch next to my father. My mother is one of those mothers that still had the plastic on her couch for when company comes.

Over the years, the furniture has changed, but two things always remained, the plastic on the couch and the cornbread my mother fixed every Sunday morning. I seemed to dwarf my father's small frame sitting next to him on the couch. Damn, I need to lose some weight. My father looked like a little boy sitting next to me.

My father, Earl isn't very tall at all. He is about 5 feet eight, and maintained the same slightly muscular build he developed working for the railroads. His complexion is a caramel brown shade that matched our complexions, my brothers', sisters' and mine exactly.

I don't think I was even there for a good two minutes when the phone rang. I heard my mother yell for my father to answer the phone. I looked at my daddy. He grunted and I went back into the hall to answer it. Like any other Sunday, it was my youngest brother, Eric.

Every Sunday, he 'blessed' my parents with a phone call from jail. His telephone calls are to either to beg for money or a visit. I have visited him about six times. That shit gets tired. I always leave feeling like I did something wrong.

Usually, Brian, when he is there, would answer the phone. He and Eric would talk for a while. I rarely have time or the strength to talk to Eric. Eric has been in trouble on and off, since he was around 14 years old. He has a broken nose as a constant reminder of his bad temper.

At 22, to say Eric is a career criminal is premature. When he was locked up this time, he swore up and down that it wasn't him. Just hearing his voice again made me wonder, why is it when a person goes to jail, that is the first thing they scream? Everybody can't be innocent.

Some people may be innocent, but in the case of my brother, I know him. Four people, a store video camera and being picked out of a line up should count for something. I am just too tired to talk to my brother and the conversation didn't even start yet. It was the same shit every week.

'Hey, Sista, what you doing over there?' he started in cheerfully enough.

'Visiting my parents,' I sighed, not really up for the conversation. 'And you?'

'I am chilling. Did Mommy and Daddy show you the pictures I sent back?'

'Yes, the orange jumpsuit is you.'

'Why you always have to be so smart?'

'Because you do dumb shit, Eric. Why do you call up here every weekend with the same shit?'

'That ain't what I asked you though.'

'Anyway, what else is going on with you,' I asked trying to be polite.

'Nothing much,' he paused. 'So, what are you up to, still looking for a man?'

I quickly lost my patience as I looked at my father who grunted again. 'What does it sound like I am doing? Negro, I am free which is more than I can say about you. Better, yet, that's what your ass should be.'

'I just asked,' Eric replied bitterly. 'And ay, you know I didn't do that shit.'

'Whatever. Every weekend you call up here asking what we are doing. If we say going out, you ask where like we can stop by and pick you up too. You ask what we are eating like we

42

can make you a sandwich to go. You know Mommy and Daddy don't need that shit--'

'Look, I don't have much time. Where is Mommy?' Eric asked cutting me off. I heard the anger in his voice building. Don't get me wrong, I love my brother dearly, but I am not up for his shit. I called my mother and settled in on the couch next to my father again. He looked at me and smiled knowing that I was right.

My father, even though he loved all of his children equally, Eric is Eric, a pain in the ass. One of things I loved about my father is that he is the strong silent type. He rarely said much, but when he did, it meant a lot more.

Suddenly, Yolanda Adams was replaced by the banging of a pot in the kitchen. It isn't even a few minutes before my mother, Lucy Belle, came out of the kitchen. I am not stupid; she was pissed, so I pretended to watch what was on the television.

My mother wiped her hands on her apron and pushed her wig back on her head straight. I felt my mother look at me with a disapproving look that only a mother could give her child. I felt that shit. It is the kind of look that you can feel even if you are not looking directly at your mother.

For my mom to only be like five feet three and a pretty, light-skinned woman, her mouth made her seem much bigger and uglier than what she is.

Though she has shoulder length hair, my mother always has it tucked under a wig, that she thought made her look like Patti Labelle or Whitney Houston. If you asked me, she was still trying to kick it like she is twenty. She needs to let that thought go. Today was no different.

'Now, child, why did you have to go and upset your brother like that? Now, I told you Sista about starting your mess on a Sunday.'

43

'Me?' I said defensively. 'What did I do wrong this time? You keep getting mad at me for speaking the truth.'

'The boy got to learn Lucy,' my father interceded, 'to stay his ass out of trouble. Sista was just telling the truth.'

'That is no excuse, Earl,' my mother countered. 'He is my baby and I think we should support him in his trying times. You don't know what he is going through. He's away from his family and the people that love him. They got him locked up like some kind of animal.'

'Then tell him to stop sending pictures home like he is in a country club. All that smiling and stuff, woman, you are crazy,' my father said turning the sound to the television up. My mother wasn't having that. She walked over to the television and turned it off. Oh, shit.

A fight was about to break out. Lord, all I wanted to do was get through dinner without ending up on the news trying to explain why my mother had to be pried off of my father. I hated when she got like this. Shit, I prayed as a child to never end up like her.

'Now look, Earl,' my mother said slowly through clenched teeth. 'The boy is going through some trying times and I think we need to support him. He is our son too.'

'Trying times? Trying times?' Earl stared at his wife with disbelief. 'The boy has been in trouble so much in the last couple of years that the cops got our phone on speed dial. Drinking, getting high, and causing confusion. The boy couldn't keep a job. Now he got your wig all in knots. I love my son but when he's wrong he's wrong.'

'Earl, now see that is where you are wrong. That is where you're wrong,' my mother croaked in what I call my mother's angry voice. When my mother got this angry, her voice was high pitched and then sounded like a frog.

My mother put her hand on her hip like she did when she was ready to argue and threw down the dishcloth she held in her hands. As it hit the coffee table, I wondered if she was more upset about the crack on her wig or what he said about Eric.

One time my mother got angry with my father after she came home and made the comment that the man at the dry cleaners kept losing her stuff. My father quick as a flash said, 'Maybe if you stop changing your wig he would recognize you next time you come in.' my mother didn't speak to my father for a week. Now this.

My father looked at my mother rolled his eyes, and then looked back in her direction. He knew if she was still standing, there she was up for a fight.

'Lucy, we raised two sons in this house and two daughters and none of the others have given us as much trouble as Eric. Not one. He takes after your brother if you ask me.'

I flinched when my father mentioned my Uncle Joe. Joe is the uncle and reason that every family that had to have a lock on their bedroom door for when the family was over for dinner. In his eyes, if he took something from you, he is just borrowing it. You'll never get it back.

The only pictures of Uncle Joe that my family owned came in a state prison envelope. Uncle Joe was doing three years for robbery like my brother, which made the crack about my uncle painful to my mother and my father, he knew it.

My mother left the room just as abruptly as she came leaving my daddy mumbling. She was upset. She spent the next ten minutes banging pots and pans around. When she set the table, I helped but she didn't even look at my daddy.

With Loretta and Cliff not coming for dinner, it was very quiet during the meal. Brian came just before the meal started and kissed my mother and hugged my dad. Brian tried to ask what was going on, but my mother just mumbled and my father just grunted and kept eating.

Brian offered to drive me home. Good that way I could explain to him what happened. I could tell by the way he looked at me during dinner, I know he was going to ask. As we left, my mother simply held up her cheek to be kissed. She gave in and finally hugged me. My father hugged us both and saw us out.

Before he closed the door after us, he winked at me to let me know everything would be okay. My parents have been married for over thirty years; I know they would be okay in the end. They always were. It would take more than a fight to break up Lucy and Earl…

Brian

All it took was one look at Sista to know why there was enough tension in the house that you could cut it with a steak knife. Things were quiet in the house. It was a little too quiet except for all of the grunting going on. I knew that whenever my parents 'grunted' through dinner, something was wrong.

'Pass the peas,' my dad would say and my mother would cut her eyes at him and then grunt. Then my mother would say, 'Pass the pepper' and my father wouldn't even look at my mother. He would just grunt and slide it across the table.

I looked at Sista as we pulled up outside her place. She tried to give me a quick peck on the cheek and was about to get out of the car when I locked it.

'Why do you keep starting shit?' I asked.

'He is your brother,' Sista said looking at me and pointing her finger. 'It is the same shit every week. I don't know about you, but I get tired of it. I am not Loretta, I will tell Eric about himself.'

'Lighten up, Mom. You know you are starting to sound like Mommy. You know Lucy Belle and Earl aren't going to break up over the shit Eric does,' I said resting my head on the head rest. 'Lord knows I am too old to have to decide if I want to live with my Mama or my Daddy.'

'I am living with my daddy,' Sista said with a smile. 'Your mother be tripping all the time.''

'What did Eric say that got you so pissed?'

'He asked me,' Sista said as she rolled her eyes, 'if I have a man? When will that child ever learn that I don't need a man to validate me as a woman?'

'That is bullshit and you know it,' I said looking at my

47 .

sister with what I called the 'dumb look.' The look on my face reminded her that she was lying. She knew she was.

'I know you aren't talking. You run from relationships.'

'Oh, really? I am just not good with relationships. There is a difference. Women want more than I can give them some times. Like they expect me to be an end to everything that hurts or ails them,' I said trying my best not to agree with her. Sensing that Sista didn't believe a word of this conversation, I changed my tactics.

'Look, most females can't deal with a smart intelligent brother like me. I got the looks, the car, a master's degree and some change in the bank. What I look like messing with a hood rat,' I said smiling. Sista couldn't help but to smile back.

'You do kind of favor Loretta. You know what your problem is you need to stop holding out for somebody that thinks like you and find somebody that thinks like them but respects you,' Sista said. "Then you might have a chance to be happy.'

'Here you go,' I groaned. 'Why didn't Loretta and Cliff come to dinner? Or Day and Nikki?'

'I could ask you about Day. But who knows? Loretta and Cliff must have gone to see his mama. Nikki disappeared on me again. We went to the club and she left me some half-ass message on my machine. She left me in that hole in the wall for her some time boyfriend.'

'Day didn't call me all weekend,' I replied but my mind wasn't on him. I was thinking about Nikki. 'Why does Nikki still deal with that guy? What is his name? Ronald?'

'Reggie? Who are you asking? I guess its love. But, sometimes I wonder if she is in love with him or his money,' Sista said rolling her eyes. Sista kissed me on the cheek again and this time, she got out. She looked back into the car and said, 'Call me and let me know you got in safely.'

I watched Sista disappear into the building before I drove off. My mind drifted back to Nikki. Sometimes, I wanted to tell Nikki she was wrong to keep messing with that guy Reggie, but it wasn't my place.

I met the guy, Reggie and he just seemed phony to me. Like somebody that tried too hard. But again, it isn't my place. I got my own shit to deal with.

I know that Nikki's grandmother and Sista didn't like him so I didn't want it to seem like I was jumping on the bandwagon and dumping on her too. It is Nikki's life and Nikki's decision. Who am I to decide who Nikki should be with?

As I pulled up to my building, I suddenly felt tired. I spent the day dealing with some left over work. All I wanted to do was take a hot shower and then go to bed. As I opened the door to my apartment in the darkness, I could see his answering machine blinking. It flashed '21' in the dark.

'Shit,' I said aloud. 'Why does she keep calling here?' I called Sista briefly and then pressed the play button on the answering machine. Damn. Sabrina.

'Brian, I know that you are probably wondering where I have been, I left you a message before, but I don't know if you got it. I love you--, 'I deleted the message. Then I proceeded to delete the others.

Her name is Sabrina. I messed with her on and off since high school. She isn't drop dead gorgeous like some of the other females I messed with. She was all right, a little short, thick joint and kind of reminded people of Kim from the show, *Moesha*.

My friends used to ask me what I used to see in her. To be real with you, she gave me the best sex I have ever had. She used to sex me any and every which way I wanted. I used to hit that from the *Price Is Right* came on at eleven in the morning until *The Oprah Winfrey Show* went off at five.

Recently, we hooked back up and I was trying to see what she was about until I called her house one night. Instead of the warm friendly voice I was used to, suddenly Sabrina was trying to cut things short. That caused me to wonder.

Here is the same girl who had asked me what I am getting her on her birthday. Yet, she just cut me short. No goodbyes, just a click.

Something is definitely up. With Sabrina, every time I talked to her it is a quiz. Where are you? Where are you going? Where have you been? Now she was hanging up on me like she was in a hostage situation and couldn't talk. I decided to call back and wasn't surprised to hear a brother answer.

'Yo, who is this? We trying to get into something over here,' the male voice said.

'I don't give a fuck,' I responded to the brother's lack of respect. That isn't his house for him to be questioning whoever is calling on the phone. Second, it isn't his phone.

'Where is Sabrina?' I asked.

'What you two mess around?' the brother asked.

'None of your fucking business. Put Bree on the phone.' I said. I was waiting for him to play 'Tough Tony' over the phone. 'Tough Tony' is the person some guys try to act like, a gangster or bad guy that always want to tell you how he is going to fuck you up. It didn't come. I heard a pause and then listened as Sabrina got on the phone.

'Hello,' she said. She knew the truth. She got caught. The guy over there probably is thinking the same thing I was. Why is she acting so funny over a phone call? Bree was tripping and we both knew it.

'Who is that?' I asked.

'My boyfriend,' Sabrina answered shakily. 'You met him before. Can I call you back?'

'No, you go earn your money. That is what tricks like you do,' I said and hung up on her. Since then, It is been one call after the next. Just what I needed another female with a guilty conscious. It was good I am not sleeping with her. Then I would have to kill her. In a world with AIDS, that is the last thing I needed a cheating ass female.

Sabrina was obviously 'on the clock.' That is what I call a girl that had to work to get certain things, but being a whore is a second job to some females. Females like to call guys dogs but never stop to realize there are reasons why guys call girls bitches. They do the same shit.

After all the things I have been through with some females, I feel like I could write a book about females and the things they do. Give me a chance to put their shit out there for the next clueless brother that came along and have to put up with that shit. Probably make a fortune too; I'll call it 'Run Fool Run.' Who has time to write a book though?

These days some times you don't find out everything about a woman until maybe the second or third week of talking to her. My game must be slipping.

Trust me, you will find out every thing, but some of it might take a minute. For the first week or so, she sends in her representative. Some classy chick that you think she is supposed to be and not the hood rat that she really is.

I thanked God for Caller ID. With Sabrina, it took years to find out she was a mistake and Caller ID to keep from continuing to pick up my phone and answering for those mistakes by taking her calls.

Now Sabrina left no doubt 20 messages on my phone a day. Most of the time, it was just Sabrina talking to the machine like it was me. I could be many things but a sucker for a female I

51

never was. My dad taught me that. I promised myself four things, never date a female with children, never go broke, never be a sucker for a female and never get put out of a place by a female.

If it was one-thing for certain two things for sure, a female never put you out at a decent hour. Females like to get crazy at three in the morning and start throwing a brother's stuff out, knowing damn well a man's mother is sound asleep. That is to make sure he wouldn't have no place to go.

I stepped out of the shower, dried off and flipped through the channels on the television trying to find that right thing to put me to sleep but couldn't find it. I wasn't really watching what was on. I was thinking about Nikki. Every time I thought about her, it only made I think about all the mistakes I made in the past with some females.

My problem is that most females didn't really have anything to talk about. If a girl has kids, that is the number one topic of conversation. That would be cool if one of the little kids is mine. If they didn't, they always wanted to talk about how somebody did them wrong.

I couldn't grasp how females felt a need to talk about their ex-boyfriend to their next boyfriend. What for? Then if they weren't talking about their kids or their ex, they are talking about what they want. I hated the materialistic ones.

The materialist ones cut right to the chase telling you about all the places they have been to and what they wanted out of life, all on your time and with your money. Yet, they couldn't wrap their minds around the fact that I am already what I set out to be in life. I am already what I want to be.

A woman at this point can only compliment what is already there. Not to say that we can't grow together, but damn, at least respect what is there. Most women don't want a man for what he is but what he can become to her.

A couple of my mother's friends asked me when I'm going to settle down. Why because I'm 30? In truth, I didn't know. I am not the type to settle for one female.

I once had a dream that I am all set to get married and discovered the bride's maid is the one I truly loved. Commitment is like chaining a collar around a dog's neck to me. I am not ready for that one. Not now. Maybe not ever.

What I need is a good woman. I know there is a difference between a girl, a woman and a lady. A girl no matter how old still acted young. She couldn't think past the things you stop doing at 18.

For some females, they couldn't think their way past getting drunk, high or both. A woman is grown but lacked the class of being a lady. Most females got upset when I called them girls. Hey, if the shoe fits, they have to wear it.

I started to go 'the white girl route,' I said I started. I figured I needed to get with somebody on my level financially. Not to say that messing with a white girl would be perfect but at least she wouldn't have to tie her head up at night to keep her hair in place.

Damn, who wants to fuck with a girl who wakes up looking like a Crip or a Blood gang member? Who wants anybody waking up in a bandana? Black women look fine with or without make up and if need be, sporting a Black Panther afro. But did they know that?

Miss Mary, one of my mother's close friends, told me that what I needed is to meet my match. A woman that would tell me she didn't need me.

Somebody to turn the tables on me. Make me want her instead of women chasing me all the time. Like that would ever happen. Look at me. If she exists, I'm not saying she does, but if she did, she can't be just anybody.

She has to be somebody with her own house, her own car, her own money and a damn good job to make me feel expendable. I laughed at the thought. I know that when God made me, he made only one. You can't get this close to perfection that many times in one lifetime. Then there is Nikki.

Nikki is far from the type of female I would lie to. I know I am a liar at heart. Out here in this cold, cold world, here I am playing that liar's game that all men play. I thought about all the lies I told girls over the years and even still what I heard other guys and my friends say. Lie after lie after lie.

Yes, girl I am going to call you. You know I love you. Damn, girl, I will never leave you. You know that was the best pussy I ever had. No, I will not leave you if you suck my dick. Your mom is nice as hell. You dad is cool as fuck.

You really got a nice place. I love spending time with you and your four kids. No, I don't have it. My phone was off. I didn't get the page. She is my cousin. She is my sister's best friend. You didn't see me at the club.

I can't give you any money this week; I got to pay my car note. It is cool you don't cook. No, I like things floating in my water because you can't do dishes. No, your breath don't stink that bad. Girl, I am at my buddy's house.

That is my sister you saw me with. I will not leave you. I love you. I want you. I need you. I respect you. I was just thinking about you. I got to get up early tomorrow.

All lies. But any guy will tell any female what she wants to hear to get some pussy and women fall for it every time. Every time with me that is. Some brothers can't lie.

Nikki is different, though. I wouldn't lie to her. Unlike the other females, Nikki knows me. I wouldn't know how. She is one of those females that you look at and say to yourself that you can't have her. You assume she got somebody.

In Nikki's case, she did. I didn't want to end up the odd man out when that other brother come running back. My heart can't take it. I truly do love Nikki. I do.

Other girls were different though. Pussy is good but it isn't that good to be all pressed up on a female. But then again Nikki is different. I have seen Nikki from all sides and maybe that is what made me love her more.

Nikki would never be the kind of girl that I would end up calling a bitch. The only way a brother would ever call a sister a bitch is if she broke his heart, she was caught doing some foul shit or she rejected him.

Nikki isn't like that. She may act like a bitch. Stuck up, arrogant and selfish maybe, but she isn't a bitch. There is a difference. With some females, being a bitch is like being a fool, it is better to act like one than to actually be one.

I think my mistake with Nikki is that for years I treated her like a sister. Shit, she is my sister's friend and we grew up together. She practically lived at my house. In my heart, I loved her. Not the way a man loved just anyone.

Shit, I cared more about my car than I cared about half the chicks I met put together. With Nikki though, she is different. Then when I came home from college and found out she was seeing that Reggie cat... I don't even want to think about it.

As I drifted off to sleep I wondered where Nikki was and what she was doing. I turned over in my bed. Just then the phone rang. After three rings, I heard the answering machine pick up and then 'Brian...' Sabrina began. I couldn't help but to think to myself, 'This bitch...'

Sista

I knew I was late when I stepped off the bus at the corner of the block of my office building on Market Street. I prayed it wouldn't rain. Since I was running late, I forgot my umbrella. I didn't even realize what day it was. The weather report said it would rain in the afternoon on Wednesday. Just my damn luck, today is Wednesday.

Now I don't have an umbrella and I am late too. It wasn't my first time being late, in the almost year and a half that I have been working there, so I thought to myself, 'oh well.' I am the administrative assistant at Medco Insurance and to blunt I am good at my job. The office was busy as usual as I stepped out of the elevator onto my floor.

The phones rang constantly on this floor. As I walked past my supervisor's office to my desk, I looked in and saw that it was empty. My supervisor's name is Walter Fischer. He is a really nice guy that looked the other way sometimes for the shit I pull at work, like being late like today. This wasn't my first time being late and this is definitely not going to be my last.

I work in the Customer Relations department as an Administrative Assistant to Walter, as he prefers to be called, who ran the department. I have a good job considering I only have my associate's degree.

It was while working at Medco that I met Paul last year, one day when I was on my way to work. Who is Paul? Paul was somebody that I used to know. At least, I thought I knew who he was. When I met Paul I thought that I finally had it all, a good job and a good man.

Paul was about five foot ten with a light brown-skinned complexion. He always kept his haircut close and a well-kept moustache. Looking back, Paul rescued me from years of feeling sorry for myself about my weight and my size. At the time, I wanted to believe that he loved me and I loved him. Even if he wasn't in love with me, there was something. That is until I

56

received what I like to refer to as 'the call.'

My relationship with Paul started out innocently enough. Every day, I would see him on the bus and he seemed like a nice guy. But, I was shy and unsure of how to approach him.

I wondered if he was a student because some days he had on blue denim jeans and a pair of Timberland boots and the next a nice shirt and a pair of slacks. He always had on his headphones, listening to music.

I called Nikki after a week and told her about him. I wanted Nikki's take on the situation. I told her about all the eye contact. The smiles, the careful glances he made. Was I making a fool of myself? Is he for real?

Nikki being Nikki said, 'Talk to him?'

'Are you sure? I'm not the type of person to walk up to a guy and speak,' I said over dinner that night at Nikki's place. 'What if he has a girlfriend? He could turn out to be crazy.'

Nikki looked at me and nodded. I thought she might say something profound like it wouldn't hurt to try. Instead she said, 'Fuck him first.'

I was scared to death. I am not the type to jump on a man like a white girl does an NBA player. What if he has a girlfriend? What if he didn't? What if he turned to be crazy? What if he was on drugs or something? He might be a sex fiend. Maybe, we could be friends. At that point, it has been a minute.

I kept second-guessing myself. This went on for weeks until finally; I got up the heart to ask what he was listening to. I rung the bell to get off and casually walked over to him as he prepared to get off the bus.

'What are you listening to?' I asked as I leaned into him, realizing the headphones weren't all the way covering his ears. 'It sounds good.'

57

'R. Kelly,' he replied. He smiled and licked his lips and began again staring into my eyes. 'So is the morning I finally find out your name?' he asked.

'Sista,' I said almost stunned by far I had gotten by just asking one question. In a lot of ways he reminded me of a guy named Rasheed that I went to college with. That's all Rasheed did in school was walk around with his headphones. He has a thing for his music.

'Paul,' he said as we exited the bus.

In the next five minutes before he went about his way, he managed to get my name, number, birthday, and favorite color and how old I was. 'Damn, he is good,' I thought, and then I realized that I knew damn near nothing about him, just his name. Damn, he is good.

Later that night, I would find out that he is an Aries, born April the 10th just like my brother Brian and a couple of years older than me. He worked for the state of Pennsylvania and because of the lack of a dress code; he pretty much wore what he wanted. He had a home of his own and was college educated and I knew he had possibilities. Definite possibilities.

I settled into my desk and looked at the phone, trying hard, but not succeeding, to end my trip down memory lane. I couldn't. I thought about the lunches, the dinners and the long walks where we talked about everything from my views on God to the fact that tights and stretch pants on a woman are a woman's way of telling the world that she doesn't have anything to wear.

And when we made love, I knew he could be the one. Who was I kidding? During that time, he was. Paul wasn't like Robert or Kevin, another one of my ex-boyfriends. No, Paul was always straightforward and direct. One of the things I could appreciate in a man. Robert though had a girlfriend at home and a baby on the way and like all women, I eventually found out.

Let him tell it, he never put a ring on that woman's finger, so he was free to mingle. I should have put a ring around his eye. I felt like there would never be a man that I could trust then I met Paul and all of that changed.

The sudden ringing of the telephone again startled me out of my trip down memory lane. It rang exactly as it did the day that day. Exactly a year to the day, I now knew looking at the calendar. I looked at the clock. I remembered it was about 10:15 then, I thought it was probably Nikki wondering what I was doing for lunch. But, it wasn't, it was Paul.

I remembered picking up the phone to discover Paul's voice saying hello. I knew Paul would be sitting at his desk and probably rearing back in his chair and thinking of me. But, something was missing. There weren't any ringing phones in the background, nor was there the voices of his co-workers like usual. Just silence.

'Good morning, Mr. Thomas,' I launched in my sexiest voice that I could muster. The kind of voice that Paul said made me sound like a sex line telephone operator. 'How are you today?' When nothing but silence came back at me, I began again, this time with concern creeping into my voice, 'Hello?'

'I am getting married this morning,' Paul responded.

'What?' I was shocked. Let me stop lying to you and myself, I felt like I had been sucker punched.

'I didn't know how to tell you,' Paul began again. 'I met up with my ex-girlfriend and one thing lead to another and we're getting married this morning and I just wanted to call you and tell you.'

'No, Paul. You buy a car. You have sex. You get pregnant. You don't just get married. This is about the most fucked up way to break up with a person. When was this? When did all of this happen?'

59

'I didn't want to hurt you. What we had was good, but Angela and I--,' he paused. 'I didn't want things to end like this. I didn't want to hurt you. It happened.'

'No, I am not hurt,' I snapped. 'Angel or whatever the fuck her name should be happy. She got you. She can have you.'

'I am sorry,' Paul said unsure of what else to say.

'You should be,' I said not holding back the venomous rage in my voice.

'Look,' Paul ventured.

'No, you look you low-expectation having mother fucker--''

'I thought we could be friends,' he said cutting me off. 'I thought you would better than this. We went out and it was nice, but what I have with Angela is something more.'

'How was I supposed to take this shit? Sit and say it is okay. No, Paul, let me call what it is. It is fucked up. I have been with you for months and you pull some shit like this. I thought you were a better man than this. I thought you were a real man, but I guess I was wrong.'

'What is that supposed to mean?'

'Exactly what it meant,' she said. 'I thought you were better than this.'

'I am not going to argue with you.'

''I am not. Look I can only wish you well.'

'I still want to be friends,' he ventured cautiously.

'Oh, we can, your new wife and I can even do lunch. Let her know how truly fucked up you are. But I guess she already knows that, you are an ex for a reason,' I began again regaining my composure. 'But, before you go, Paul, I want you to do a little something for me.'

Paul felt some relief for the first time since the conversation began. Paul realized what he was doing had hurt me more than he planned to. I guess Paul would do anything to help ease my pain. He claimed he really did care for me. He just didn't love me.

'What is that?' Paul ventured.

'Die slow,' I said. 'You should have married me. I wish you had. Because you know the part in the vows where they said until death do us part, Paul? I would definitely want you to die first.' I hung up the phone and went home and spent the next week in bed.

Nikki got so scared she sent the police to my apartment. They found me with the help of my landlord in bed, eyes red from crying and my refrigerator empty of everything. I felt like if I lost my man, fuck ten pounds. That was fifty pounds ago.

Since then, the relationships have become the last thing on my mind. Falling into like, lust or love is that last thing on my mind. I still wanted somebody to love.

Maybe that is why I was sitting up in a club on Saturday. But, I know the next time I get involved in a relationship; things would have to be on my terms. I thought aloud, 'Whenever that will be.'

After getting settled, I finally answered the phone on what seemed like the millionth ring and instincts told me it was Nikki. It was.

'Girl,' is all I heard. 'Look,' Nikki began again. 'I am so sorry for leaving you at the club the other night. But, Reggie wanted to spend the weekend with me and girl, it was good.'

'So you didn't call me until Wednesday?' I snapped. 'I hope it was good. You know you are wrong, Nikki.'

'Sista, you really need to stop.' Nikki said sensing my mood. 'You need to realize that Reggie and I are together and things are good for us right now. Can't you be happy for me?'

'I am. Remind me to put that on my list of things to truly care about,' I breathed into the phone, irritated at the mention of the Dark Knight as I called Reggie. Something in me wasn't up for hearing about him. That's all I ever did, hear about Reggie.

I heard all about how Reggie had a good job and Reggie had money. Or who Reggie knew and where he went. I still don't like him. Fuck that, I downright despised him. Hate took too long.

'We did our thing. He brought me a lace gown. It is pink and white. Sista, it is so cute.'

'Did it have a price tag on it?' I asked nonchalantly.

'No, but it is new, bitch,' Nikki hissed.

'I was just asking. I just wanted to make sure that you weren't picking up some other trick's bad habit.'

'You know you need some.' That is Nikki's answer for everything. But, having sex isn't an end to every problem. Some women think that can sex a problem away. Bad fight, fuck him. Money problems, fuck him. Suspect he's cheating, fuck him. Feeling lonely, fuck him.

'Whatever. Look call me later,' I said hanging up the phone but not waiting for a goodbye…

Nikki

I hung up the phone and laughed knowing that Sista didn't understand what it is like to love somebody like Reggie. Reggie is just it for me. Maybe Sista is just jealous. It has been a while since Sista had a man.

I decided to lie back down on the bed, having chosen to take the day off again. I just didn't feel like another day of petty office politics. I didn't want to tell Sista that Reggie had left that very morning. He spent every night since the one at the club with me. I needed this time with Reggie.

Sista had to know this isn't my first time messing with him since I decided to stop dealing with Reggie months ago. Nor would it be my last. We are back together and things were the way they were supposed to be.

After we had sex again this morning, I thought about it again that I still haven't talked to Reggie about the baby or the future. I swore to myself and God that my feelings for Reggie were gone. They had to be. He isn't right for me.

Reggie has done his share of dirt and while I did my fair share of mine, I kept going back. This last time though after that earring, I was done. What would have you done if you found another woman's earring in his jeep? Nothing, that's right why would you care? He ain't your man. He's mine, so I dealt with it.

While I never caught him in bed with another woman, I knew it wasn't my earring. He claimed it was a friend from work that needed a lift who left the earring. I still told him that it was over and made every effort not to return his telephone calls.

Then, one day I was at work and a dozen long stem roses came. It softened me up to see him and things went from there. Oh, the bitches at my job were jealous.

I reached for the remote to turn up the volume on the television and some girl was telling all of her business on a talk show. I reached down and rubbed my stomach. I am almost nine weeks pregnant with Reggie's baby. I wanted to believe that it is what I wanted. It is apart of Reggie. I just wish...

I thought about my mother and father and my eyes instinctively went to the large picture that my parents had taken before my father died. I momentarily wished they could have been there to share in the moment. My grandmother, my Nana, Mae raised me, put me through college and made sure that I had everything a child could want for.

At times, all I ever truly wanted is a family again. As I looked around my apartment, I realized that is why it never felt like home. At least, not my home. If I could help it, it wouldn't be my child's home either. I planned to start looking in the sixth month of my pregnancy.

I rubbed my stomach again realizing this is only the beginning of my family. Over the years, Sista's family has always given me that sense of family when I was growing up. My grandmother often worked two jobs, which left me home alone many nights. My greatest fear is being alone.

I was never truly alone. There was always Aunt Lucy and Uncle Earl, who were my grandmother's neighbors and good friends. They were my family, everybody except Brian. I never looked at Brian as a brother or even in the play cousin type of way. He just wasn't. I used to love him. In a lot of ways, I still do. I won't lie, but I'm with Reggie.

For years, I had a crush on Brian. But every time I got up the heart to tell him how I felt, Brian always had a new girlfriend. When he finally left for college, I gave up all hope that we could ever be together. I decided it was time to give up a schoolgirl crush for something more. I guess that was Reggie. Since then, all it's ever been is Reggie.

Even after going away to the same school, being

involved in a relationship with basically only Reggie since I was 17, I realized that marriage is about the last thing on my mind. Sometimes, I wondered if I was just scared of reliving what my parents went through.

Before my father died, my mother suspected that he was having an affair with a woman at his job. My father died in a car accident when I was nine. Rumor had it that my father was with that woman when he died.

I also knew about the other women that people claimed to have seen Reggie with. Women are always trying to get with my man. But, I am the only woman that he loved. They could try to get him, but I am the one he is going to come home to. The thought of that turned my stomach. I didn't like sharing. Not now or ever.

I remembered the night that Reggie came over. That night we conceived our baby. I had it all planned out: the fine wine, the candles, scented bath, dinner in the oven and the smooth sounds of Marvin Gaye playing on the CD player. I wanted him. He showed up in a pair of baggy jeans and a shirt that I brought him for his birthday.

It was a little after nine. He smiled and licked his lips when I realized what shirt he was wearing. He kissed me and slowly allowed the robe I was wearing to fall to the floor.

He looked at me with an intense hunger when he saw that it was all I was wearing. The CD in the CD player changed to Keith Sweat's song, 'Make It Last Forever.'

Slowly, I undressed him and as we went to the bedroom, I blew out the candles on the table. Dinner would wait. In bed, I was so in the throws of making love that I almost forgot to go into my stash in the shelf built into the headboard and grab some protection. When I did, Reggie stopped me and threw the condoms on the floor.

'I want this,' he said kissing my neck slowly. Against

my better judgment, I gave in. I cried when I found out my period was late and cried again when Reggie sat beside me and the doctor confirmed that I was pregnant.

I opened my eyes from my daydream. A guy came on to the stage on the talk show I was watching and confessed to his girlfriend that he is having an affair with her best friend, who was now pregnant. Who does stuff like that? Some things you really need to keep to yourself. I turned off the television disgusted. I didn't need to hear that.

This past weekend had been about Reggie and me and I am happy. I felt bad for ditching Sista, but Sista understood. She had to. Reggie just brought certain feelings out of me that I couldn't explain. Neither of us wanted to get married right now, we might after the baby is born. I wanted to be Reggie's wife.

I rubbed my stomach again and hoped in time that Sista would love Reggie and this baby like I do. One day. So would my grandmother, she'll come around. First, I'd have to find the nerve to tell her I was even pregnant to begin with...

Sista

I switched my radio onto the local radio that played rhythm and blues and soul and began to delve into my work. R. Kelly was asking for some 'Honey Love' as I finished up a report. I was trying to get a jump on the afternoon.

Before I knew what was going on it was lunchtime. With my supervisor in a meeting all day, I knew I could pretty much do as I pleased. I had to catch myself from being startled when Day Shawn poked his head into my office.

'Get up girl, I am hungry,' he said with his jacket already on. I rolled my eyes at him. I shut down my computer and was pulling my coat off the rack. Day Shawn Madison is about the only person I talked to at my job on a regular basis.

Day, as most people called him, is gay by choice and never allowed anybody to tell him how he should act. Though he acted and dressed the part of a straight man, he is very meticulous. He is masculine and even played basketball with my brother. His clothes were always perfect and his desk didn't even have a paper out of place.

Day shot the image of how a gay man is supposed to look and act to hell with one shot. Meeting Day, I learned gay men didn't have to be finger popping fairies.

Gay people were regular people. Shit, there are times when I had to remind myself that more than life touched Day because I know I probably would have tried to fuck him. When you are a single, lonely woman, any man has potential.

Day is about five feet eight, with a low curly Afro with a goatee and weighted about one fifty easily. He had a very light-skinned complexion, light enough to make you think he is Puerto Rican, offset by natural hazel eyes.

We met in college. I was a freshman and he was junior or a senior, I think. He introduced himself again after he made his rounds with his friends, and I knew that we were going to be friends. Day told me he would never ask me my real age when I got old and he wouldn't take no for an answer. It feels like we have been friends forever.

Unlike most women, I never felt threatened by Day. After all, most women would, we both like the same things: men. Most women will swear to the high heavens that they don't have a problem with a gay man.

A real woman like a real man won't have a problem with anybody. But for some women, they'll treat that gay friend like a girlfriend until that gay friend meets one person: that woman's man. Then all hell will have broken lose.

At that point, it's okay for her to be friends with him. Not her man. With all this dl or down low, bisexual thing going on with some men, some women were afraid. People always seemed to be wondering and guessing. As my father once said, who gives a fuck? Some women did though. They had to.

You see when that gay man becomes friends with a straight man, the focus moved from that man as a person to him as a homosexual and gay. It wasn't a problem before of what was inside of him as far as personality.

It became an issue of who may have been inside of him. Maybe it was a fear on some women's part that it might have been her man that was inside him? Who knows?

Maybe some women just didn't trust their man, when they should have had more confidence in themselves. Now every woman has a girlfriend or a friend that she doesn't trust. If she doesn't that gay man is it. God forbid if her man and her friend become buddy-buddy.

Now he's a suspect? Was he after her man? Before you can say amen, her gay friend goes from a good friend to being every faggot, sissy and homo in the book. Listen, if somebody, man or woman, can take what you have when it comes to relationships, then that person was never yours to begin with.

'Personally, I didn't understand straight people's fascination with gay people,' Day told me once, 'or an openly gay's person decision to always make it known. It isn't like you could put being gay on a resume.'

'What so an employer can go, oh I see you like rainbow colors? Who truly cared what a person did behind closed doors? If they did,' Day suggested, 'then people need to check themselves. Especially guys that feel a need to call another man a faggot. Wouldn't it take a faggot to know one?'

That's one of the reasons I valued my friendship with Day, he made sense. But I will tell you, being friends with Day has had its benefits. Under his curly afro and high yellow, light skinned complexion, beats the heart of a human bullshit detector.

With Day, I can get an honest objective opinion that I can't get from Nikki. Day never pointed fingers. He knew the rules, whenever you point a finger at anybody you have three pointing right back at you.

Day saw through the clutter, maybe because he has been through it. From what I gathered his time living in New York wasn't a good one when he found out the person he was living with had a wife and children that blamed Day for the break up of her marriage. She claimed she didn't know. She was lying to herself.

If people lie to God, what makes you think they won't lie to you or themselves? She knew she just didn't want to lose him. Some woman will deny themselves, their children and God to hold on to a man. When it truly isn't worth the effort.

I found, most women, these days, because of the whole DL, Down Low, hype and attention had to have asked herself at least once, is her man gay or at least bisexual?

If he is, what were the signs? Is it because he spent more

69

time in the bathroom than her? Is it because he dyes his hair and gets manicures? How could you tell? It was enough to make anybody crazy. Especially a woman trying to hold on to her man.

Listen, people will tell you who they are. You choose to see and hear what you wanted to hear. But with the DL issue the current rage, Day and I thought it is ironic that most women always thought the worst if their man is cheating and never even suspected that it could also be another woman. Some other woman could very well be pushing up on him and doing all the things that his 'wife' at home will not do.

With news that DL men were supposed to be leading to the rise in AIDS and HIV cases in women, I wondered how any woman could turn a blind eye to it. Most women couldn't bring up the topic of AIDS and HIV with their man.

It might end their relationship to suggest a man take a test for AIDS or HIV. Some people honestly don't want to know. But, how would that woman feel having to explain it to their kids that she had it?

In all of the conversations, articles and stories coming out about black men and sleeping around, the fact that black men have been ravaged by AIDS and HIV for years and nobody bothered to care, that never came up. People didn't even want to talk about it, praying it would just go away. It didn't.

In truth, people simply need to check who they are sleeping with gay, bisexual or straight, man or woman and how you sleep with them? Women need to stop believing the bullshit that comes a woman's way, via misinformed conversations, rumors and overblown hype. Above all that, women need to stop sleeping with just anybody.

In truth, too many women are dying but it is their responsibility to protect themselves. All you ever hear is that sisters are dying of AIDS and HIV with plenty of finger-pointing at the men but never about the women. Women are equally guilty about not educating themselves and sleeping with men

70

they barely know unprotected.

Most women are so caught up in the idea of being in love that they will take anybody. Desperation is a lonely woman's best friend at times. For some women, they figure if he got a big dick and could leave her walking bow legged then he's good.

She will have fucked him within a week and cooked him a dinner in two. Within a month, he'll be laying up in her house and after two months she'll be wondering what she ever saw in him in the first place.

As we walked to lunch, I saw the sideways glances at Day from other people. Guys and girls looking trying to get his attention but scared to do it outright because they wondered if I was his girlfriend. Other people gave me that look like 'why is he with you?' People are trifling males and females. I just shook my head and kept walking.

While most women want to blame themselves for the lost when things are found out, they shouldn't. They should move on and thank God for moving another obstacle out of their way. Don't make it hard on your or them. Why?

There is no need. Don't fight him. Don't call the other person up. Calling the other person is something I still couldn't understand. They don't want to talk to you. Just let it go. But make sure you aren't just trying to mess up a good thing.

Some women and men will do that. Find little dumb reasons to start something. That's just their insecurities talking. They think that man isn't good enough for them or at times, too good so they do shit to end the relationship. Don't believe me? Ask yourself why some black women will break up over a phone number?

Now a white man will have to kill his woman to get rid of her. But a black woman will end things real quick and it could be the number to a pizza place. It's at that point that that woman's insecurities really kick in and suddenly he's accused of sleeping with the girl behind the counter. Some women are crazy.

A woman will actually sit up at night, watching her man sleep and thinking of ways to catch him in a lie. Shit, I have. Other women, with no tact, will actually call up the other woman and ask if the woman is fucking her man. Wouldn't the man have to fuck the woman; it isn't like she could have slipped and fell on the man's dick repeatedly?

There are good men and women out there though. But people always want to talk about the negative shit or scream it from the rooftops. They never applaud the faithful men who stay home and take care of their families. Don't mention father's day. What about the good men that don't have kids? I know I went on a rant again. Sorry, back to Day.

As we walked into the restaurant, Day started to tell me all about his morning, I thought about the first time we met when Day told me his life story back then as he called it. He is only 32 years old now. Day came from a small southern town and a very religious family.

'Very Christian,' he emphasized over lunch the first day we talked. 'My father is a hard working, God-fearing man and my mother kept a Bible in her purse. She is so close to God that when Moses got the Ten Commandments from God, she was there to take it down in short hand. We were close. Very close.'

All that changed when Day realized he was gay. From that point forward, Day had been so deep in the closet; he was sitting next to Christmas gifts. All it took it was a weekend with his cousin's best friend, Monroe, and it was over. Day knew what he wanted. He didn't chalk up his homosexuality to genes or even perversion, just a lifestyle choice. Of course, his mother was crushed and his father disowned him.

'I saw this great card for your parent's anniversary,' I said sitting down to eat. Every holiday and special occasion

72

since Day left home, he sent a card to his parents.

Every time, the card is marked return to sender in his father's handwriting. Still Day kept trying. Rather than tell him he was wrong to try to reach out to his parents, I just listened. That was my way of offering up support.

'I was just thinking about that,' Day replied half heartedly. 'Some times, I don't know why I keep doing it. They are never going to accept me.' I knew the story and wondered if he was right.

It seems that the Day realized he was gay; he had brought Monroe home with him. They had been dating. He thought that nobody was home after he came home from college before his graduation. His mother, as it turned out, was in the laundry room and when she came to put some clothes in his bedroom; there he was half-naked with Monroe.

She walked back out and closed the door. She didn't utter a single word. When Day and Monroe got the heart to come out, Monroe said 'goodbye' and left. His mother sat with her Bible open praying.

When his father came home, she told him what happened and his father called him every name he could muster but the child of God. He was a faggot, a sissy, a queer, and worst of all; his father told him that he wasn't his son.

Day came back to Philly long enough to graduate and then moved to New York after graduating, following another friend who had moved there after college. Day lived in New York for five years before coming back to Philly to work at Medco with me. I needed him here.

Lunch with Day became an everyday thing, I was happy to be able to give and be able to receive a shoulder to cry on. He is a part of my family now. He became a fixture when he was free at my mother's dinner table and my family genuinely like him. My father even called him another son.

Day had even become the best of friends with my brother, Brian. Though Brian would become friends with a rock, if he had to. Brian is that kind of person. Brian could care less one way or another about the fact that Day is gay and frequently gave him advice on his relationships about which I could only laugh, knowing my brother's track record with women. What did he know about relationships?

I guessed with Eric away, it gave the family a feeling of completeness. Another thing I like about Day is that he clicked with Nikki and Nikki rarely like anybody. As I listened to Day talk about his morning over lunch, I thought about Nikki.

I knew that Nikki didn't even tell me she was taking off from work. Her job said she called in sick, when I called to invite Nikki to lunch. That's three days in a row. She's up to something.

As I sat picking over my salad, Day started to tell me on about his plans for the weekend. I know I should have been listening but, my mind was still on Nikki. I was tempted to call her house or her cell phone. But, something in me wasn't up for hearing anything about Reggie again. But still my concerned showed. If Day noticed it but he never mentioned it.

By the time I got back from lunch, I was still wondering what was going on with Nikki when I walked into my office. I should have asked her when she was on the phone earlier. I'm going to call her back.

I said goodbye to Day at the elevator. Several of my co-workers just looked at me as I entered the office. Damn, did I get fired and nobody told me? It wasn't until I got to my supervisor's office that I knew my world was about to fall apart. Walt was supposed to be in a meeting. Something was wrong. Walter looked at me. He shakily handed me the message.

'Clawja, I don't know how to tell you this, but call your brother at Thomas Jefferson University Hospital. Your,' he paused. 'Your father had a heart attack…'

Sista

Within 15 minutes, I burst through the doors of the Emergency Room. If you asked me later how I even got there, I would have been able to tell you. I saw my brother, Brian, talking on a pay telephone in the lobby of the waiting area. He stopped talking and leaned in to give me a kiss.

'Where is Mommy?' I asked squeezing his hand. He motioned with his head towards the waiting room. I looked back at Brian as I immediately went over towards the waiting room. Brian looked tired.

As I walked into the waiting room, I found my mother there with my sister. Loretta was rubbing my mother's shoulder and my mother was sitting like in a state of shock rubbing her hands together. For the first time in my life, my mother was as quiet as a church mouse.

I went over and kneeled down to grab my mother's hands and my mother began to cry. She went to speak and I silenced her. No words were necessary. Now wasn't a good time to talk about what happened.

I knew my mother was already replaying things over and over in her mind. To say the words would only upset the both of us. I looked at Loretta who looked shaken. She was even quiet.

Slowly, the door to the waiting room opened. I turned to look at my brother. His tie was removed and he reached out to take my hand. I stood and took his hand and he gave me a hug. I felt my brother shaking as I let him go. Brian was always the calm one out of the family.

Suddenly, I realized that I had been there for fifteen minutes and nobody had said a word. I left my family to talk to the doctors several times, another time to get something for my mother to eat and drink and twice to pray. All I learned from the doctors is that it was a wait and see chance that my father would recover.

When it was time and the family was able to visit my father, Brian and my mother went in to visit my father. Loretta went in next just as Cliff showed up. I went in to see my father last. Brian decided my mother needed to go home to get some rest and something more to eat. She had been there all day. I told Brian I would stay a little longer.

After the family left, I went back into the Cardiac Care Unit to be with my father. I sat down in a chair that someone placed next to my father's bed and took his hand in my own. He seemed so small. I began to cry and I rested my head against his arm. I felt a slight squeeze and I looked at my father.

'Not now, Daddy,' I whispered leaning into my father. 'We need you here. We can't do this, not right now. I am not strong enough to go through this. Who is Mommy going to argue with? I can't do it like you do. Who is going to check Loretta? Who is going to stay on Eric's case?' I stopped as I felt my father squeeze my hand ever so slightly again. I started to cry again. I couldn't help it.

It was almost 11 when I got up to leave and stopped for a moment to ask the Lord to watch out for my daddy. When I got home, I found a message from Brian on my answering machine that my father died not long after I left the hospital. I sat in my living room in the complete darkness and cried myself to sleep...

Day

'He passed away a little while ago,' Nikki said. Nikki had called to tell me that Sista's father died after Brian called her. When I heard, I sat back down at my desk because I was still at work which seemed typical most days. I ran my fingers over the picture of my parents I kept on my desk. The picture was definitely one of better times, a time when my family was happy.

Even though it was late, I began to wonder what my parents were doing. My mother is probably reading while my father watched television, usually the news. I remembered this scene from growing up. I smiled. Looking at the picture, the smiling man in the picture didn't seem anywhere near the mean, hateful man my father became. His painful words that had hurt me so deeply echoed in my mind.

Somehow, I know my father, being that I am his only child, felt responsible for the fact that I was gay. I know my father was still embarrassed even after all these years. It didn't help my cousin, Melvin, turned out to be gay. We always knew but he was very effeminate and it could be down right embarrassing the way he came off at times.

Since I left home, I haven't returned once and maybe that is for best. Of all the cards, pictures and letter I sent over the years, I never got one in return. Not even a phone call. I guess I shouldn't have expected one either.

That's when I decided to do it. I immediately picked up the phone and dialed my parents' house and let the phone ring. It was late, but I knew my parents would still be awake. The phone picked up on the fifth ring. I started to speak, but once again, I couldn't. I couldn't.

I heard my father say hello several times and I quietly placed the phone back on the receiver and said a silent, 'I love you, Daddy.' I just wanted to hear my father's voice and know that he was okay. I got up from my desk and grabbed up my belongings and turned out the light...

Sista

My father was dead and I couldn't cry any more. I have cried for three days straight. I moved into my mother's house with Brian. I was on leave due to a death in the family and told my supervisor that I had vacation time and would take it if I needed it. I just really needed time to think.

I helped my brother and my sister make funeral arrangements. I sat talking and joking with them about my father, more Brian than Loretta and my mother laughed along with us.

Stories about my father flew fast and free about how cheap my father was. He used to lie about our ages when we were kids to get them into the movies half priced. Or how he has never thrown anything away and how there wasn't an episode of Bonanza that he didn't already know by heart.

I know still something was missing in the conversation. I couldn't lay my finger on it, but it was there all along. Everybody would laugh so hard about things father did and then there would be silence. No words, just silence.

It was like nobody knew what to say. Sometimes I looked at looked at the front door hoping he'd walk in but he never came. Out of respect nobody even sat in my dad's favorite spot on the couch. It was as if he had been sitting there all along.

We even pulled out my daddy's old vinyl albums and listened to Al Green, Sam Cooke or the Temptations. My mother wanted it that way. My mother smiled a few times and laughed hard at the stories. She told us all that you cry when a person comes into the world and laugh when they go out. But, I could see the hurt in my mother's eyes when she went off to bed. It was there and she couldn't deny it. She didn't even try.

That was the moment, I knew. The moment when silence seems so loud and you notice the little things. That is the moment that I instinctively felt what was missing: my father. My father is dead and not all the calling, begging or pleading to God could bring him back. I found comfort in the fact that what happened is the Lord's will. God didn't make mistakes. I knew as well as the others that he had a bad heart. We all knew we just didn't know it would be this soon. I guess it hasn't really hit me yet that the man I knew all my life as my father is dead.

When I walked into my mother's bedroom I found my brother Brian sitting there holding my father's suit in his lap. We would deliver it to the funeral home at noon. I sat down next to my brother and rubbed his shoulder.

'You think Daddy would want to be laid to rest in this,' he asked avoiding my gaze. I took the suit from him and ran my fingers across it remembering the day I helped my mother buy it for Brian's graduation.

'Yes, he would look fine in this.' I said smoothing out imaginary wrinkles.

'It was so sudden, Sista. I didn't get a chance to say goodbye. To say I loved him. It has been a while since I really talked to him, like when we went to go play pool and...' Brian just got quiet.

'He knew we loved him. Even Eric. We all stayed on Daddy about his health. It is a funny thing about death, Brian.' I said taking my brother's hand in my own.

I closed my eyes remembering the times when I was growing up, Brian held my hand just to cross the street and now I was holding his and offering words of encouragement. 'Death comes when we least suspect it. When we don't ask for it and been too busy taking for granted that tomorrow will come.'

Brian looked at me and once again, I saw my father staring back at me. My brother looked just like my father. 'You were always his favorite,' he said with a slight grin.

'Take that back,' I said 'Daddy said he didn't play

favorites.'

'Yes, he did and you were it. Daddy's little girl. Growing up I used to be jealous of that. But when I have a daughter of my own, I hope she turns out to just like you. So I can be the father to her like Daddy was to all of us.'

I smiled at the thought. I looked at my brother, hugged him and smiled, 'Then, I guess I can forgive you.' Brian took the suit from me and walked to the door. Brian turned and looked at me. Brian smiled and walked out.

I stood up and looked around the room thinking about my father. Just then a sudden chilled through me and I wrapped my arms around myself. I wanted to cry but I just couldn't. At least not yet, there was too much to do. In my own way, I felt my father watching me...

Sista

The funeral began as the family made our way to our seats in the tiny church my parent were married in, I saw Day and Nikki not far away. I smiled before sitting next to my mother. Brian was to my mother's left. Loretta, then Cliff, sat next to me. Reverend Graham got up to speak and lead a stirring eulogy about my father.

'Earl can't be with us now. He has gone on to a better place. He isn't suffering and his soul was at peace. He is found a place where the world's worries no longer rest on his shoulders.'

My mother nodded as Reverend Graham went on, 'We miss him but our time will come when we see the glory of the Lord and sit in his company once again. But right now we got to wait. Be patient and serve out the purpose the Lord has for all of us on this green earth.'

'Patience is a virtue' he continued. 'But people got to learn to be patient. That is why we've all of these young girls running around with a hair weave because they can't wait for their hair to grow.' Everyone in the churched laughed and on he went in similar fashion for twenty minutes. The choir sang my father's favorite song 'I Love The Lord.'

One by one my father's friends went up to speak. They told stories about growing up with my father and working along side him. The choir sang 'Silver and Gold' another one of my father's favorite songs. In the midst of it all, I thought about Eric who was brought to the funeral home the day before to see the body.

I thought about my brother now more than ever knowing he took it extremely hard and then to have to be brought in handcuffs to see my father, who was now dead. Brian learned the prison put Eric on suicide watch a little afterwards when a guy called the family to say that after seeing the body, Eric tried to kill himself. Nobody could believe it.

It wasn't until after the choir sang 'Amazing Grace' when Loretta leaned over to me adjusted her Chanel Suit and whispered in my ear, 'Now don't your big ass go falling out because I am a little too small, a size four if you must, and I will not help to pick your thick ass back up.' Loretta then looked at her husband, Cliff and smiled. Loretta can be a nasty bitch.

After the funeral, everyone would go back to my mother's house to eat. My Aunt Mabel, my father's only sister, stayed up half the night to cook with my mother. Aunt Mabel left earlier from the service to get things ready and Loretta left to help with Cliff.

I met Nikki and Day outside briefly before riding with my family to the cemetery. I began to cry when we laid white roses on my daddy's casket. I found it hard to watch the lowering of the casket. On the ride home, we, Brian, my mother and I rode in silence.

Once in the house, I went around exchanging hugs with long forgotten family members and friends. My father only had one sister. Mabel never married and my mother's only brother Uncle Joe was still in jail, so most of the people that came are cousins of my mothers or father's side or friends of the two.

I saw Brian and Day standing in the corner talking. Loretta was all in Nikki's face telling her about some pocketbook that Loretta saw in New York. I thought about what Loretta said at the funeral and had to muster all of my strength to keep from slapping the shit out of my sister.

Seeing Aunt Mabel and my mother huddled in a corner talking to two of my father's friends, I stood alone until the next person came up to talk to me.

Nikki found an excuse to leave Loretta and walked across the room to where I now stood. Nikki put her arms around me and rubbed my shoulders. Brian walked by and I gave him maybe his tenth hug of the day. Nikki hugged Brian too before he went into the kitchen.

'You okay, girl?' Nikki asked rubbing my arm.

'I am as well as can be expected. But I am here.'

'You know if anybody understands any of this,' Nikki said looking around the room. 'It is me. I didn't understand it when I was younger but now I do. So if you want to talk, you know I got your back.' Nikki smiled and I responded. I hugged Nikki.

When the house was quiet and everyone left or gone to bed, I went down stairs and found my mother sitting in the near darkness illuminated only by the streetlights coming in from the window, holding a photo of my daddy.

'I loved him more than any man I have ever known, even my Daddy,' my mother said through her tears as I sat beside her. 'And now, he is gone and I feel all alone,'

'You're not alone, Mommy,' I told her. 'You have us. You still have daddy. He'll never leave you.'

'You kids are grown. Your daddy wasn't supposed to leave like this. Not like this. Sista, it was so sudden, he was sitting there watching some show like he always did and he leaned forward and just fell. I dialed 9-1-1 and everything seemed to go in slow motion.'

Tears began to stream again down my mother's smooth light-skinned face. I rested my mother's head on my shoulder and my mother began to cry harder. My father always seemed so strong and to hear for the first time how he died, I saw him for what he really was, a man.

I got up and grabbed the big family album off the shelf and sat down to look through it again with my mother. My mother laughed at some of the pictures and in that moment told me in all seriousness, I realized my mother lost her sparring partner and her best friend.

83

That night long after my mother went to bed, I sat in the living room and pulled out one of my father's favorite albums and as the opening bars of 'Joy In Side My Tears' by Stevie Wonder began to play, I allowed myself to cry again.

I went back to work only a few days after the funeral, I realized that my family would never be the same. My mother decided to go back to working to occupy her time and Brian and Loretta got on with their lives. Without my daddy, I knew something would always be missing, a strong man in my life.

Something deep inside of me knew I was willing to risk losing a man to fate the way my mother lost my father, but only if God made it a good ride along the way. I now knew he was out there. But where…

Paul

'Call her, Paul,' I told myself at least twenty times. I sat staring at the phone because for the first time in my life, I felt like a complete fool. I heard that Sista, my ex-girlfriend's father died a few weeks ago from a friend of Sista's. I could have sent a card or something but I was sitting here looking at the phone.

I don't know what it is but I couldn't pick up the phone to call her. I didn't know what to say. Sorry about how things ended between us, but I heard your father passed away, so sorry again. She told me to die slow. Plus, if I did call her, what would I say after that?

I picked up the phone looking at the clock and realized that it was only 3:15. Good she might still be at work, so I'll just leave her a message. Yeah, that is what I would do, leave a message and she would hear it and maybe in the end, we could be friends. Why am I playing?

I reared back in my chair and began to think about last year. I met Sista on my way to work and here she was a woman that could honestly understand me. But, then Angela, my ex-girlfriend, called me and I couldn't resist. I met Angela in high school and I didn't know what it was but it was something about her that made me want her.

Angela, I guess, is my first love. I stopped and picked up her picture off his desk. I looked at the Angela with her pretty shoulder length hair. I love my wife. I do.

I couldn't see it in the picture but I thought about her soft, sexy body with the firmest breasts that a man could ever ask for. She called me and like a dummy I answered. Just years ago, she kicked me to the curb. Then she was on my phone acting like nothing ever happened.

High school was one thing. Angela and I were always together. I loved her, she loved me. Now when she decided to go to Virginia State University, I wasn't ready to give up my

85

scholarship to Penn State, so we went our separate ways. Maybe that was for the best.

After Angela, relationships had been easy to come by, but somewhere along the line I was fucking up and I knew it. It wasn't that I set out to mess up the relationships I had, it was just the women I was meeting are messed up. There are always some issues there.

Nine times out of ten, most women have a baby by some guy that has done them wrong and they are either afraid of a relationship or acted like they were too good for me. Then there are the ones that are so career orientated that they didn't have time for a man. Then, I met Sista. She was different. She was a real woman after all the girlfriends I had.

Here was a woman that knew what she wanted out of life and it didn't begin with some man's wife. She was funny, smart and she has a good personality.

For a minute, I stopped and wondered if I did the right thing by letting her go. I thought about the first time my friends saw me with her and I felt bad because they all later joked how fat she was. Now I felt even worst. She is a good person.

We were together and everything was cool and then here comes Angela. I was thinking with the wrong head. She made my dick hard just listening to her over the phone. I was kind of surprised that she called.

The feeling of surprise subsided when I found out that she had gotten my number from my brother, Bernard. He needs to mind his damn business. She could have been trying to kill me and he would have helped.

'Hey, Boo,' Angela said as if she was whispering.

'Who is this?' I asked. Who knew my job number?

'Angela. Paul, stop playing Boo. You know who I am. I

just wanted you to know I am back in Philly and I want to see you?'

'Look, I have somebody right now, I don't think she would like for me to see you,' I said trying to pass it off on Sista and how she would feel. Sista, in truth, didn't have to know. Nor would I tell her if she asked.

'Paul, this is me. I am not trying to break up a happy home. I am just trying to see you. I thought we were friends,' Angela cooed into the phone. I hate when she does shit like because now I couldn't get up from my desk for like a good 20 minutes. I was hard as hell.

'When and where?' I asked. Angela was staying with her Mom. I agreed to pick her up at nine. We would go out, catch up, do dinner and then I'd drop her off. Let me stop playing. She came out the house wearing this little black thing.

It wasn't really a dress. It was more like a sheer body wrap that left little to the imagination. I was thinking with the wrong head. Suddenly, she was at my place and the panties came off. She was looking too good. I think I rubbed and caressed every inch of her light-skinned body.

I sucked every last one of her toes and just when she thought it was over, I sexed her to sleep. Had her catching forty winks. The shit was good. I tried to chalk it up to the fact that my feelings for her had never died.

I had to ask myself if she was truly the one. In the end, I was just scared she would leave me again. Just walk out of my life. So I did the damn thing and asked her to marry me. She said yes. Until I called Sista, I forget all about the fact that I had a girlfriend. It's not cheating if she didn't know about it, right?

Now, most nights, I went home alone any way. About three months ago, Angela's college roommate, Vanessa, turned up in town. Now Vanessa had her attention. It was always Vanessa this and Vanessa that. Vanessa is one of those people that believed that the world should kiss their ass and at times, I had to bite my tongue from telling her to get the fuck out of my house out of respect for my wife. Vanessa is always there, though. Why is she always at my house and in my face?

A couple of times, when Angela wanted to be intimate, I wanted to tell her to go fuck Vanessa. She looked like a man as is. She is a light skinned Dominican chick with a Caesar hair cut and she dressed like, well, me. She dressed like a man. I couldn't see what Angela saw in that mannish bitch. She was so manly, she was damn near handsome.

I know. That is my wife's best friend and I should respect her but I don't. I still wondered though what did I get myself into marrying Angela? Now that I heard Sista's father passed away, my heart went out to her. I had met Mr. Earl a couple of times and he seemed like a nice guy. The kind of guy that every guy wished was his dad. I did.

I looked at the clock and realized it is time to go home. Angela had taken the day off to go shopping with Vanessa. Just the thought of her made my blood boil. If she wasn't at my house, Vanessa was on the phone, dragging Angela around to meet her flaky friends or going off on some weekend retreat.

Then, they went to their old school for a homecoming weekend. Things changed after that. Angela grew distant. Cold even, at times. Just the thought of Vanessa made me sick. I hated her guts. Was it because she was taking up Angela's time?

I couldn't help but to compare Vanessa to Sista's friend Nikki. Nikki was cool, but Vanessa with her almost militant attitude made me sick. She acted like a dude. There was something about her that I just couldn't put my finger on.

While Nikki could be sweet and classy, Vanessa stayed in my face with some dumb shit. I stepped off the bus near my house and was surprised to find Vanessa's car still parked outside. Damn, I wish she would just go home.

It is my house. I owned it a nice four-bedroom row house. My mother, when I first brought it, insisted on furnishing it herself. It is a nice house on a quiet block of mostly elderly women. I waved at several as I walked by on my way home.

I stepped into the house and put my backpack down. Vanessa was coming down the steps and when she saw me she rolled her eyes. Typical dumb shit lately. I don't know why she hates me. I didn't sleep with her ass last night. Then she smoked, I smelled that shit in the air the minute I walked through the door.

I was checking through the mail when I realized that Angela was sitting on the couch wearing a robe. She was flicking through the channels when I came in the living room and didn't even look up at me.

'You feeling alright,' I asked still sorting through the various bills. Angela didn't even respond. She mumbled something and this made me wonder. I leaned over and kissed her. She hesitated.

'You sick or something?' I asked. 'You got on a robe. It's like the late afternoon. What's up? Then no kiss? What happened?'

'I'm fine,' Angela said now looking at me. 'I just needed to get out of my clothes from earlier.'

'I was concerned,' I said leaning in to kiss her again. 'So, I asked.' I guess that was Vanessa's cue because she began gathering up her stuff. I noticed Angela's hesitations as I moved closer. I dismissed it. Then I kissed her, long and hard, more for Vanessa's sake as a show for her than because I really wanted to.

Wait a minute. What is that smell? I rubbed my lips and smelled my hand. Angela flinched like I was about to hit her. I don't know what it was but I smelled something else on her lips. I stopped and licked my lips wondering what Angela's lips tasted like. It was a familiar, like I tasted it before. But when? Why?

89

I realized for the first time that Vanessa was just standing there with this dumb look on her face. It was like a sneer or a smile on her face. What was that shit about? When I rubbed my lips the second time, Vanessa grabbed her jacket and got ready to leave. No goodbyes, she just left.

'Good,' I thought. Can't stand her any way.

'I'll be down in a few,' I said as I went upstairs to take a shower. I looked at Angela again as I went up the steps. She was now shaking. I stopped and came back down the steps and walked back over to Angela and kissed her again long and hard. She was stiff to my touch. I shook off the negative vibe and headed for the shower upstairs.

Once fully undressed, I turned on the shower. I ran my hand over my lips again trying to catch the smell. I know I smelled it before, I just couldn't figure out what it was then or now. It wasn't the first time. The smell was strong too.

Damn, what was Angela eating? I know she didn't eat pork. So what was it? It smelled like, like, like something. But what? I smelled my hand again, nothing. When I undressed, I tossed my wallet onto the unmade bed of my bedroom. It was only then that it hit me like a ton of bricks, what I just wiped off my lips. The room smelled just like it and I just licked it off my lips--pussy...

Nikki

The last couple of days felt like a nightmare. I was tired, moody and easily irritable. Reggie called me a few times, but I didn't even bother to pick up the phone. I called Reggie back but our conversations had been very brief. I didn't feel like talking to him just now.

Right now, though, I don't know if it was the funeral or just life in general that had me feeling some type of way but I was tired. I was in pain too, but I didn't want to take anything because of the baby.

I spent so much time worrying about Sista and her family; I don't think I was taking care of me right. I was tired. Then it happened. I don't even know how to put into words what I was feeling. All I know is I was scared. You would be too if you were pregnant and your period came on.

Then the pain started, I didn't even want to think about it. Somebody once told me that her sister got her period for six months while she was pregnant, but I am not her sister. I thought I was having a miscarriage.

That's why I wanted to talk to Reggie. I didn't want to scare him, so I decided to wait until I knew for sure. Damn, I couldn't tell even Sista the real reason why I couldn't meet her and Day for lunch today. I had a headache just thinking about what was going on with me.

My first thought after I got the message from my doctor that something was wrong. He didn't actually come right out and say it, but I knew that something was wrong. Something didn't feel right. I know that I did everything I was supposed to when I found out I was pregnant. I even took the countless numbers of vitamins. Horse pills are what I called them.

I tried to remember the last time I have been to the doctor's though about myself. But, why when I had so much to do? I'm perfectly healthy, I walk, I run, I jog and I even go to the gym with Reggie. I didn't even feel sick. You are supposed to feel sick to have to go to a doctor. Right?

I was scared. Do you hear me? I was scared, shook. Not for me, but for my baby when that damn doctor told me that they had to run some tests on me and the baby. As much as I wanted to believe that everything would be fine in the end, I knew it wouldn't. I shook my head at the thought that anything bad could happen now. Not now. I could barely drive to my appointment.

I was so sure everything was going fine until the day my doctor called because he found something wrong after one of the test. I thought I took care of myself. Now it has been almost a week since I went ahead with the other test the doctor wanted to run and today I would find out the test results.

I felt nervous because I prayed for this child. I tried not to think of the worst. I promised myself that as soon as the worst was over I'd call Sista and Day and let them know what is going on. I wanted to wait until after everything was over and things were going to be okay.

I didn't want them to worry too. Damn, I even wanted to call my grandmother but I knew she would only worry. I knew my mother and father died young and in the back of my mind, I know she feared the same for me. I am her only grandchild. And now...'What do you mean?' I said unable to process what the doctor just said. 'You can fix this, right?'

'Ms. Love,' Doctor Ingram interjected. 'It is just a precaution.'

'You don't understand I don't get sick. I want this baby,' I said getting up to go get dressed. I looked at the doctor who looked at the nurse.

'Ms. Love, we need to run a few more test to be sure,' the doctor said attempting to gather up his files.

'I don't need shit,' I said still in disbelief but I soon felt my anger growing. 'I took your damn vitamins; I did every damn thing you asked. I took care of myself and you are going to tell me that something is wrong with me and my baby. '

'You don't understand, Ms. Love,' Doctor Ingram tried again. 'We are trying to make sure that everything is okay. Is there somebody we can call for you? You are clearly upset.'

'You call me in here to tell me some bullshit about my baby,' I yelled no longer caring who heard. 'I intend to get a second opinion. I am going to get it and prove you are wrong. I know my body. I know me.' At least, I thought I did.

'If that is what you like,' Doctor Ingram said as he watched as I pulled on my jacket. Doctor Ingram was ready to offer me the name of a doctor when he should have realized I was out the door. I was down the steps and nearing the front door of the lobby when, deciding to not wait for an elevator, when suddenly everything the doctor said clicked in my head.

All I wanted was a little of Reggie to have and to hold. I felt my stomach. That is all I wanted. I needed this child. I wanted it. This is my baby. My family. They didn't know this was my second chance at one. That's when it hit me why I wanted this baby so bad. When I left the doctor's office, I realized it had begun to rain and I began to cry.

As I stood in the rain, I felt dazed and confused. People seemed to race by oblivious of my pain. I thought to call Sista or Day, but they would only ask more questions than I was ready to answer. I stopped myself when I remembered they didn't even know that I am pregnant. I suddenly felt alone.

It was only then that it came to me who I could call. Reggie was out of town and out the question. He will be back soon but right now, I need somebody stronger than even Reggie. Somebody that knows me. I said a silent prayer as the rain came down harder as I got into my car and dialed the number on my cell phone. I hoped he was home...

Brian and Nikki

I arrived home at three in the afternoon after a pick up game with Day and my boy from high school named Shawn. When Nikki called me, I wasn't expecting it. I checked my Caller ID thinking it was the girl I met two days ago at the supermarket that gave her number to me calling. Instead, it was Nikki's number. What happened now?

When I called Nikki back to find out what was wrong and she didn't sound too good. I hung up telling her I was on my way. It had to be serious if she was telling me she didn't want to discuss it on the phone and not with Day or my sister.

I didn't plan on going back out into the rain, but Nikki is like family and I had to be there for her. It took me less than twenty minutes to get to her house. I was already upset that it was raining. Seems like every time I washed my car it rained.

When I pulled up to Nikki's apartment building, Nikki buzzed me in then left the front door of the apartment open for me. Nikki had obviously been crying. More importantly, I immediately saw that she was soaking wet and in tears still.

'What's up baby girl,' I asked removing her wet jacket and then her shoes. Nikki just shook her head. I had to think fast before she catches her death.

I had to get her out of those wet clothes. I put two and two together and suspected that since Nikki couldn't reach Sista or Day that she must have called my place looking for one or the other. It's cool. I'll deal with things myself. It's only right.

She knew I was going to play ball with Day. But right now, even that didn't even matter since she had me here. Then the phone rang. Should I answer it? Suddenly, Nikki did something that surprised me, she turned the ringer off.

'Damn,' I swore to myself over and over again. I didn't know what to do now. Nikki is upset. She's crying. I am lost. I

94

needed to call somebody, but who? My sister and Day were out. I could have called my Mom but I didn't even know what was going on. I walked into the bathroom and grabbed Nikki's robe as she regained her composure.

Nikki walked into her bathroom and I handed her the robe. I looked in the kitchen and seeing the kettle, I decided to make her some tea and riffled through her refrigerator for something to eat as well. I knew things were getting better when I heard the shower come on.

Nikki came out as I put the finishing touches on her sandwich and tea. I can't cook, but I can make a mean sandwich. No words were exchanged but I sensed something was definitely wrong, something that I couldn't do anything but to keep quiet about. You can't talk about something you don't know about.

I didn't want to push, that's my style to go easy with people. So I sat in the living room quietly looking for something to watch on cable. Nikki ate and I was glad. 'She'll talk when she's ready,' I told myself.

'Maybe I should call my sister. She'll know what to do. She's better at this shit,' I thought. But it seems like every time I looked at Nikki she looked at me and I changed my mind though. Damn.

Maybe that was for the best; knowing Sista she might overreact and want to go fuck Reggie up with Day in tow to bail her out. But still Nikki is her best friend. Sista should know though. I would want somebody to tell if I was in trouble.

I thought about calling Reggie. I have met Reggie only a few times, but this is his girl. Maybe Reggie is the reason why she is so upset. It caught me off guard that Nikki wanted me to stay.

I know one thing, deciding what to do is giving me a headache. I got up to go to the bathroom and went and looked into the medicine cabinet for a pain reliever. Nothing was there but a bunch of vitamins. I lucked out.

'Nikki, I got a headache. What do you have to get rid of it?' I yelled from the bathroom. 'A Tylenol, aspirin, an Aleve, Advil or something. Wait, I don't want anything y'all use for cramps. My sister's cabinet is filled with that kind of stuff.'

'Check my pocketbook in the bedroom,' her voice was barely above a whisper.

'Damn,' I said to myself, 'I hate going through a woman's purse.' I was all set to pick up the bag and take it to her when I saw the letter that lay next to it. *Cancer Center?* Oh, shit, what was that about...

Nikki

Last night, Brian was a blessing to me. He came when I needed him to come and he was there for me. He must have stayed until I fell asleep. I woke up to his note and realized why I fell for him the first place. He straightened up my place, put my things away and even did the dishes even from what I ate. He took care of me. That's what I needed.

Reggie called this morning to say he'd be home today around two. I called out sick from work. It wasn't like I am lying. As I drove to Reggie's place, I felt like I was putting off the inevitable decision I knew I would have to make. I also realized why I wanted to talk to Reggie.

I guess I wanted Reggie to know what is going on and why. He has a right to know. He would support me. I guess. He would take care of me and the baby. I called my grandmother and told her about the doctor and what he said but not the whole story. Not yet.

'What are you going to do?' my grandmother asked.

'I don't know Nana. I am scheduled to take a few more tests to be sure, get a second opinion. Then, I'll know.'

'You know I love you,' my grandmother said. I knew that my grandmother was on the other end crying.

'I love you too, Nana.' I said trying not to cry.

'Nicole...,' my grandmother started to say but then stopped. "We'll get through this too. We can deal with this too.'

'I know Nana,' I said before I hung up the phone and began to cry. I once again couldn't even bring myself to tell my grandmother that I am pregnant. I guess because that would mean more explaining than what I needed to do right now. I know how my grandmother felt about Reggie and this definitely wouldn't help. I didn't realize how truly alone I was until I woke

97

up and found Brian gone.

I called Brian three times already today. A lot more than I should have, I know. We talked but not about what I wanted him to. I didn't even know what to say when Brian came back from getting something for his headache.

Last night, for a minute, I had hoped he found the letter from my doctor saying that I am sick and needed to see the specialist I saw yesterday. If he did, I would have had somebody else to talk to.

When Brian did walk back into the room, he acted like he had not seen it, so I didn't say a word. I never mentioned the situation again, nor did I tell him why I am so upset. Or even better, why I called him and not Sista or Day. That had not been an accident, I wanted to tell him.

I needed somebody to talk to that wouldn't judge me or question me. Brian has, in my mind, always been someone I could trust. For a minute, I honestly didn't want to believe that shit the doctor told me, now that I had time to think. I couldn't because that would mean...

I didn't want to think about it. I couldn't. Not now, like it was supposed to go away. Pulling up in front of Reggie's apartment complex, I checked my watch; I knew Reggie's flight was just about to land.

Reggie must have sensed something was wrong because he suggested we meet there later when he thought I got off work. I never went to work. This was more important.

I would have gotten Reggie from the airport but he already had a ride planned. With my key to Reggie's place, I let myself in and made myself at home. It is times like this that I realized why I lived apart from Reggie; some times I just didn't want to deal with him. The spare key is for times when I did.

I immediately took off my shoes and relaxed on the

couch. I was about to call Sista but I realized that she'd know I took another day off from work.

I was glad when Sista said she was swamped with a big project, some audit and wouldn't be able to see me for lunch for a couple of days. I wanted to think that it was good she had something, anything to keep her mind off of things and me.

I suddenly felt tired and decided to lie down on the couch. It was too quiet so I turned on the television. Another talk show. It got me how some people felt obligated to put their business in the street.

They aren't sitting in their living room talking about this. It is national television, which is even worst. Watching some girl on television, I laughed that she brought two men on the show to determine who the father of her child is. She is a fool.

I wasn't there but for a few minutes when the doorbell rang. I figured it was a delivery or something. Maybe Reggie forgot his key and he knew I was going to be there. This is going to be a surprise then.

As I opened the door, I realized that in that brief moment everything in my life was about to change. I looked at a young woman in her twenties, she isn't even cute. I know that is wrong, but she wasn't. She was holding the hand of a pretty little girl with a dark-skinned complexion.

'Can I help you?' I asked, believing the girl and her mother, I think that's her mother, might be lost.

'I'm Renee and this is my daughter Nicole. Is Reggie here?' the older girl asked.

'Wait, this can't be happening,' I thought to myself. I looked at the girl then at the little girl and instantly I knew. Renee, that's the name she gave me, attempted to snap me out of my daze as I stared at her daughter. I regained my composure and looked at Renee again. 'And you are?'

99

'Renee,' Renee said suddenly confused but then she realized that I didn't know. 'I am Reggie's daughter's mother.'

'Reggie?' I said. This felt like some soap opera shit.

'Reggie,' Renee said again. 'Tall, dark-skinned and he got a bald head. This is our daughter, Nicole.' I could see that.

'He'll be here soon. He called from the airport. Would you like to come in?' I said moving aside. But she didn't move. She just looked at me. I just looked at her, finally realizing that I just met my man's daughter's mother for the first time, a child I never knew about to begin with. I wasn't hurt though, I wanted answers. "Listen, I think we really need to talk.'

'Talk? About what?' Renee said eyeing me suspiciously. "We don't need to talk about nothing. Who are you?'

'Wait a minute,' I said taking a minute to check myself. I was through with being polite. So I leaned in so her daughter didn't hear. 'I see you need the remix. You fucked my man and you coming off like you are the injured party. Let's try this again, bitch. I said we need to talk. Can we talk woman to woman? Are you at least woman enough to do that? Or should I skip the preliminaries and just beat your natural black ass?'

Renee looked hesitantly at me again then at her daughter. I guess she thought about it for a second and realized I was serious. So Renee walked in, holding Nicole's hand tight, as I moved aside. I took a deep breath and closed the door. It was on and I wouldn't have it any other way...

Reggie

When I walked into the apartment with my luggage and flowers in hand, my first thought was to check my messages. I haven't talked to Nikki since earlier. I knew she would be coming by after work. She seemed upset every time I talked to her. I didn't know why and didn't want to really ask if she was mad at me for some reason. That probably was the case.

Honestly, I am tired of fighting with Nikki. She's having my baby and I didn't want to stress her. I stopped to pick up a dozen roses, her favorites just to surprise her when I see her.

Nothing was too good for Nikki, nothing in this world. I promised a long time ago to do everything I could to make her happy. For the most part, I succeeded. She was beyond anything I ever expected in a woman.

What I wasn't expecting to see was Renee, sitting in my apartment, with my daughter, Nicole. Nicole was asleep on the couch. I thought Renee broke in for all of a minute.

Lately, I kept our contact to a minimum. She would drop my daughter off at my mother's and I would get my daughter from there. She is nutty like that until I saw Nikki walk back into the room.

Damn, I thought I was about to piss on myself. You know the feeling of being caught. Three years of lies came to an end. I felt like a little kid caught with his hand in the cookie jar. I wanted her to yell, scream, curse, or something.

'Nikki, talk to me.' I said to her, dropping my stuff. She just looked at me and walked to the door. I went to grab her, which I shouldn't have and Nikki pulled away. 'Nikki?'

As she walked away, I looked at Renee who now was helping our daughter put her shoes back on. I knew it was useless right now to run after Nikki and try to reason with her.

Damn, I felt stupid. If I had just told her the truth, shit might be different right now. She could have given me the chance to explain why I lied in the first place. But she just left without even a word. It was too late. I knew it. She knew it. I sat on the couch and buried my face in my hands.

My daughter came over to me and rested her head against mine and I just held her. That's all I could do. I didn't even pay attention to the fact that Renee was still standing there.

'Get out,' I said through clinched teeth. When she didn't move, I stopped and looked at Renee like she was crazy. Another bitter bitch. I knew that Renee is secretly doing back flips that she fucked up the best thing that I had in my life: Nikki.

Here I was planning on waiting until after the baby is born, until after I surprised Nikki with an impromptu wedding. I planned to tell her that good shit about how I want her to be my wife before the baby came.

After we were married, when I knew she wouldn't walk away, I would tell her about my daughter. I kept thinking maybe then Nikki would accept her. Maybe because Nikki would soon have one of her own, a son or daughter. Our baby. I took a deep breath and looked at Renee again.

Renee tried to take my daughter away from me but I moved away. I looked at my daughter, afraid I had scared her, and realized she had fallen back to sleep in my arms. I took her and laid her down in my bedroom.

Renee started to get up but I gave her that look that told her to stay where she was. Once, Nicole was sound asleep again, I returned to the living room, walked to the front door and opened it wide.

'Get the fuck out.' I said not even bothering to look at her. I just wanted her as far away from me as possible.

'What for? I did you a favor,' Renee said showing her

ghetto mentality. 'I told you I was coming. You should have checked to see if she was going to be here. Don't worry, though. I told her everything. She has a right to know.'

'Whatever,' I said not wanting to hear what she had to say. I really wasn't listening, 'I thought I told you just don't show the fuck up at my house. Call me first. My daughter is welcomed here, if she needs anything for you to call my mother.' I said each word through a clenched jaw.

'I am not leaving my daughter here with you,' Renee snapped. "You aren't thinking straight.'

'Why not, I am her father,' I countered. I will take her to my mother's when she wakes up. Right now, I don't want you here. You can get the fuck out.'

'I was good enough when you fucked me.'

'That,' I said nodding my head, 'was a fucking mistake. You were somebody to fuck, not somebody to fuck with. In the end, it was never about you. It was about my daughter. What she needed. I don't love you and I never will. I'm sorry I ever fucked with you. You are another one of those women that believe what you want to believe and only see what you want to see. I fucked with you so what. You are about a dumb bitch.'

'That's why I hate your black ass now,' Renee countered. 'You are a sorry ass man. You need to stop thinking with the wrong head. And I am not going to be too many of your bitches either. '

'Then pick one to be. Don't hate me,' I said laughing, 'Hate your damn self, Renee. You called me your man. Who were you trying to convince me or you? The woman I love just left and she is more woman than you will ever be.'

Renee looked upset as I looked at her. Good. She folded her arms and glared at me. I looked at her like 'What?'

103

'I don't know why you treat me like this,' Renee said obviously trying to play the victim. 'I was good enough for you to have sex with but not good enough to be with you. I tried to do everything I could to be with you and you treat me like messing with me was a mistake.'

I laughed, 'Why lie when the truth will do? You were. You got to stop trying to show your body when you want to show love. You need to learn how to leave men alone until you learn to be by your damn self. How many times we got to go through this shit before you realize I don't want you. The only thing good about you is my daughter.'

Man, if you could have seen the look on her face. She was heated when I said that. She grabbed up her stuff and was ready to storm out. She stopped turned and looked at me. If looks could kill I'd be dead. Fuck her. I didn't care.

'You are just like all the rest of them no good niggas out there. I know I should have never dealt with your tired, black ass,' Renee said turning to leave. 'You have my daughter back by tomorrow.'

'Just get the fuck out,' I said slamming the door behind her as she stormed out. I checked in the room again to see if Nicole had awakened. She was still sleep. I went back to the living room and sat on the couch. Nikki's scent was still in the air. It felt like she was still here.

I was so close to being happy. Then Renee had to fuck shit up for me. I had Nikki, things were going good at work, and I have a baby on the way and then this. Maybe I should be happy the shit is out in the open. I'll give Nikki a few days to calm down and then, she'll be back. She always comes back.

I went to my bedroom and looked at my daughter. She was still asleep. I hated what was going on between me and her mother. I love my daughter. I just don't love her mother. I was just stringing her alone, like the time she threatened to take my daughter and move away so I made her think I wanted her back.

I even offered to marry her dumb ass.

I love Nikki too much to be with any other woman. At least, I wouldn't mess with anybody right now. This shit with Renee was fucked up. You don't know how many times I replayed in my head how I was going to tell Nikki about Nicole. It just never was the time or the words didn't come out right.

I know I should have. Looking at Nicole sleep, I pictured her running around chasing after her little brother or sister. She was going to be a good big sister. I leaned over and kissed her forehead before going back into the living room to pick up my stuff of the floor and the flowers I brought Nikki at the airport.

Damn, what am I going to do now? I picked up the phone and called my business partner and my best friend. It rang twice before he answered. 'Yo, Jay, you are not going to believe what happened. Renee was here, while Nikki was here. Nikki knows about my daughter man. Renee was over here and everything. I don't know what I am going to do...'

Nikki

I was still reeling from meeting Renee. Renee as it turns out is the girl Reggie met like three years ago, when Reggie and I had a falling out. He slept with her and when she told him she was pregnant, Reggie didn't believe her.

'So what did you do?' I asked as I sat on the sofa opposite of Renee.

'I took him to court for child support. If he wouldn't accept her outright, I figured, I'd make him,' Renee said.

Thinking back I realized that Reggie never said a word. If anything he was attentive as hell to me around that time. But it did explain all those angry calls to his lawyer, the ones when he always had to get up and leave the room. I thought it was always about work. If I only knew. Maybe that's why he didn't want to have a baby, he already had one.

'He was proven to be the father and pays regular child support,' Renee continued. 'We all went out a few times. He is nice to me around my daughter, so I used to want to think the three of us have a future.'

In my mind, I was thinking, 'So that's where he disappeared to.' Then the earring in his jeep. That was his daughter's earring. I wondered how long he would have waited to tell me. When Nicole was in college? He obviously didn't plan on saying anything to me any time soon. Why should he? He got away without telling me this long. Damn, he was good.

Nicole is already two and she looked just like Reggie. She has those eyes, eyes that I have seen many times before. They were exactly like Reggie's.

I started to beat her ass after my little chat with her at the door. But, I'm pregnant and her daughter was there. So I kept my cool and waited. I decided we would wait for Reggie to come home. I told Renee to make herself at home. I didn't know if it was fear or boldness but the story just tumbled out of Renee. She just wouldn't shut the fuck up. Yeah, the bitch was scared.

'I really didn't plan on keeping the baby,' Renee said coolly. I wasn't sure if I believed her. What mother would want to kill her child? I started to ask her when she finished. 'I mean I barely knew Reggie. But then after I found out I was pregnant, I was like damn, I can't kill my baby. His dad and mom love my daughter. They think she is so pretty. It was Reggie's idea to name her Nicole. He always calls her Nicole though. Never Nikki, always Nicole.'

I looked at Nicole. Nicole had fallen asleep shortly after her arrival, now stirred in her sleep. As I watched her sleep, I wondered why Renee made a point of telling me it was Reggie's idea to name the baby Nicole. Why name the baby after me? Was he trying to soften the blow? I held my stomach realizing I was going to be sick.

I went to the bathroom and splashed water on my face. I had just come from the bathroom when Reggie walked through the door. I was all set to confront him. I wanted to curse him out. I wanted to hit him. I wanted to hurt him as much as he hurt me.

Let me stop lying to you and myself, I wanted to whip his ass. Then, when he looked at Renee, Nicole and then me, with that dumb look on his face, I wanted to say close your mouth. Instead, I just walked out. No words, I just left. I didn't have the strength to fight him.

In that brief instance, everything between us changed. I knew I couldn't be the other woman. In a case like this, a real woman wouldn't or shouldn't get upset, she should just go find another man. I really didn't fault Renee because I know that Reggie didn't tell her that he had a girlfriend. What man would?

Even if he did, why beat Renee down, Reggie is the one that fucked her? Without a condom, no doubt. When I looked at Nicole, who I have to admit is a very pretty girl; I felt any hostility towards Reggie melt. Don't get me wrong, the hurt was still there. But you can't get mad or upset with a child.

The next day, I walked up the steps of the inconspicuous building and for the first time in my life I was afraid. All I knew was that I was looking out for my child's future. Something in me wished I had told Brian what was going on or more importantly Sista. I didn't know what to say. I had made a mistake.

As I walked across the room to the intake desk, I said a silent prayer thanking God no one was there that I knew or had seen me go in. They just wouldn't understand. I looked at the woman behind the desk that gave me an encouraging smile. Thank you but it's going to take more than that for me to get through this day.

I was told to take a seat and someone would see me. I tried to leaf through the magazines but I had other things on my mind. My child's future is at stake. I thought I had everything all planned out. Now I wondered how it came to this moment.

'Miss Love,' an older Asian lady called my name. I followed her down the hall into an office. It was brief, the visit. I didn't know what I would do afterwards. I just wanted to get through right now. We talked about what would happen in the next couple of hours. In a brief instance, my life had changed so much. After everything I learned about Reggie, maybe it was for the best.

I wanted to talk to Sista. I needed to. I just didn't know where to start. First, I guess I would have to tell her about the baby and then this. I barely listened as the lady explained the procedure. We were through in few minutes.

Then she came, a nurse that is, came to get me. I needed to do this right away before I lost my nerve. You would have. I was about to lose mine. There weren't any ifs, ands or buts about what I was about to do. I needed to do it. I didn't have a choice. I collected up my things and followed behind the woman. I rubbed my stomach and said a silent prayer...

Sista

I spent my lunch hour at the bookstore, Barnes and Nobles, by myself. I don't know where Nikki is. Day, I knew was running late, so he couldn't make it for lunch. That left me by myself. I really need to get used to being by myself. Lately, that's how things been for me.

I talked to Brian that morning. All he really talked about was Nikki. He kept asking about how she was doing and if I talked to her. When did he start calling Nikki? I brushed it off. I haven't even seen Nikki and didn't bother to call to find out why. This week was so crazy at work.

I guess I could spend the day by myself. I am going to the prison Saturday to see Eric with my mother. Eric called me a couple of times and I have tried to stop being so hostile towards him. He has been so depressed that it had my mother sick worrying about him. So whenever he calls, I am nice as hell.

Sometimes, I wonder if I am getting soft. I can still be mean if I wanted to. Things have changed so much in such a short time that I don't know where to begin to feel normal again. I guess that's what brought me here. I figure I could find a good book to take my mind off my own blues. I didn't find anything.

I was ready to leave the bookstore, when I turned and saw that Omar Tyree had a new book that I have neglected to read. In turning to grab the book, I knocked the book off the shelf. Damn it. I went to pick it up and saw it wasn't there. Some tall, light brown-skinned guy already had it and was returning it to the shelf. That was nice of him. Oh, he works here.

He looked about 24 years old with a caramel tone to his skin. He looked more like a basketball player than a bookstore employee, like Rick Fox of the L.A. Lakers with shorter hair. He was dressed in slacks and a shirt and tie. For a minute, I thought I died and gone to heaven. This was not happening.

'I hope you don't treat all of our books that way,' he

began with the warmest smile that I have ever seen. I read his name tag and knew instantly that his name is AJ. I wondered if there is a Mrs. J. If there is, she was a happy woman.

'No, I wouldn't treat any book like that. Especially if it belonged to you,' I said coyly. I know I am tripping playing that shy role.

'Actually,' I said eyeing his tag again for effect, 'I was just looking at it and it fell. You work here?' I said quickly not wanting him to leave despite the fact that he shown no inclination to go. 'I see your name tag, but I never saw you in here before.'

'Actually, I am the assistant manager. Six months into it. But, uh, now that you know my name, can I catch yours?' He flipped through the book in his hand then looked at me sensing my hesitation. 'If you don't--'

'I just saw you in here,' he began again, 'and something in me made me want to know you.' He paused again.

'That sounded corny,' he said and was ready to turn and walk away when I reached out to touch his arm.

'Sista,' I said. His gaze met mine and I sensed something pass between the two of us. I said a silent prayer and thanked the Lord for allowing me to meet this man. Then I asked for forgiveness because suddenly I felt like throwing my tongue down this man's throat and he didn't even know me.

'Actually my real name is Clawja. Clawja Robinson. But everybody just calls me Sista.'

'AJ. Alexander Jamison,' AJ smiled. 'Actually I am about to go on break and if you don't mind, I'd like to buy you a cup of coffee or something.'

We talked for a little more about my name and where we both were from, exchanged numbers and promised to call each other. That was how it began. Suddenly, I went from alone to meeting what I felt was the man of my dreams. He told me he would call me at 8 and when I picked up the phone it was 7:58.

The next day, AJ invited me to dinner. We took in a movie and then spent the following evening at his apartment discussing what he loved most--books. For even that brief instance, Nikki was the farthest from my mind.

I felt bad, but I figured she was off with Reggie somewhere. I finally met somebody that I could care about. In the back of my mind, I hope I wasn't jumping the gun. But, I needed this and unlike Paul, this felt right.

AJ proved to be an attentive listener. I can't lie. He seemed genuinely interested in me and I returned the favor. Until that point, I wondered where all the good men are in the world were.

I had experienced the club scene, but to have met somebody in the bookstore is another thing. A couple of times, I caught myself just looking at AJ wondering if he was real. But, here in the living flesh is Mr. Alexander Jamison and he is real.

'What's wrong,' AJ asked.

'Nothing,' I said as we walked through Rittenhouse Square the next night when we went out for drinks after work.

'Then why do you keep looking at me like that?' AJ asked. 'Did I say or do something wrong?'

'No, I'm trying to make sure you are real,' I said sitting down on one of the benches. 'I won't lie, I have been through my share of bad relationships and I am not sure...'

'You are not sure if I will break your heart. Trust me I can't. I don't know how. You opened up to me. let me return the favor. I was in a bad relationship months ago with this girl and I thought she was the one so I kept holding on. That was my mistake. I gave up on the thought of a relationship after her, and then I met you.'

I laughed.

'What's so funny?' AJ asked.

'You don't strike me as the romantic type. Charming, but not romantic.'

'Trust me,' he laughed, 'I am real man. Real men are sensitive and romantic. My ex-girlfriend didn't appreciate that...' He stopped. 'It don't matter, I won't put her out there like that. She was a mistake.'

'It's funny,' AJ stopped shook his head and started again. 'I once wanted to marry her. She was spoiled and turned into a bitch. I guess it was because she is her dad's only child from one of his three marriages. But that's over, she wasn't right for me. I am ready to test the waters again.'

'What if she came back into your life and tried to change?' I asked. AJ paused as if he was considering it.

'She is an ex for a reason,' AJ said. 'I don't go backwards. I found what I want.'

'So why now?' I asked AJ as he moved closer and took my hand. 'Why me?'

'Honestly?' AJ asked.

'Honestly,' I replied.

'You look like that confident type of sister. Strong with a good head in your shoulders.'

'I could be a serial killer, 'I laughed.

AJ laughed and looked at me 'How many female black serial killers do you know?'

'I'll be the first.' I laughed and grabbed his hand. AJ smiled and rubbed my cheek with his other hand.

'Most of women, I dealt with,' AJ began again. 'They weren't right. Sisters always give guys a bad rap. According to sisters that all the men in the world are either gay, married, in jail, on drugs, selling drugs or only like white women, but I am here to say that not all men are like that, especially black men.'

I looked at AJ. 'Maybe, that is because most women never take the time to look. I never got into all that stereotyping shit when it came to the people I have dealt with. If I did I wouldn't have met you,' I replied and then smiled.

AJ smiled. 'I like that. Even better, I like you. You make me smile and I don't know why. I guess It is because I think I finally found the woman that will be there when the chips are down.'

'Well,' I said in response, 'I just want a man that can appreciate a sister with some meat on her bones.'

AJ smiled, 'I like a woman with some meat on her.' I laughed as AJ leaned over and kissed me. AJ rode with me back to my place and kissed me good night at the door before heading home. He'd be perfect if he owned a car. I wanted AJ to meet Nikki and Day.

As I walked into my apartment, I checked my answering machine for messages hoping that I would get one from Nikki, but found nothing. When I tried to call Nikki, the phone just rang. Oh, well.

It is kind of weird though. Nikki doesn't even know about AJ. When have I had the time to tell her? Day knew. Not Nikki. Something was wrong, I could feel it. If anything, I bet I know where the problems would have started: Reggie. It wasn't like Nikki not to call me. It wasn't...

Reggie

'She hasn't called me or anything,' I told my dad.

'Boy, haven't I taught you anything about women, they are emotional, unstable creatures. Look at your mother. I remember when you first met Nikki,' my dad said, 'She always comes back. Hold on.'

'I hear you,' I said to my father. 'Look I am going to check my messages and call you back.' I hung up my cell phone as I stood outside of Nikki's building.

I wasn't trying to holler up at her window. Her neighbors would just call the cops on me. Her car wasn't in the lot. I was tempted to have it reported stolen and then declare her missing. But I didn't want any dumb stuff coming down the pipes from filing a false report.

I know I called and must have left a million messages on her answering machine. Nothing. I wanted to buy her a new machine, put as couple of messages on there and mail it to her. That's just how bad I was feeling.

I called her job and kept getting the same damn response, 'I'm sorry sir. She's not in.' I knew that. Somebody needed to tell me something.

Maybe she just went home. Just what I needed her grandmother on her deathbed or some shit and the last words she would say is, 'Don't fuck with Reggie. You know he's no good for you.'

I got tired of that woman calling me the devil. I was desperate. I called her grandmother's house and realized that she must have Caller ID in Pittsburgh and was screening her calls. Something is wrong. I can feel that shit. Something beyond this whole shit with Renee.

I messed up and I knew it big time. I was all set to go

home and spend time with Nikki, but who was sitting up in there. Renee. If I hit women, man, I would have beaten her ass. I met Renee years ago through a friend at the club one night and messed around with her when Nikki wanted to act funny.

Renee is a freak though. The kind of girl that will do everything your main girl won't. So I slept with her a couple of times when I was in the mood or Nikki was acting funny.

I was usually drunk. When Renee came back and told me that shit about her being pregnant, I denied it. I didn't know where she has been or whom she has been with. No baby she claimed was mine is coming out with the milk man's eyes. So I was like fuck it. I told her to handle her business.

When she took me to court, I asked my dad, Mr. Big Shot Lawyer, what to do and my father told me that I couldn't fight it if it turned out to be mine.

I cut him off before he could have started his shit about wrapping it up. Who thinks about shit like that at moments like that? I was horny, she got naked. Damn.

I'll be damned if she wasn't telling the truth thought. Yeah, it is my baby. When it was born, my daughter that is, she looked just like me. I loved my daughter the instant I laid eyes on her.

I'm not stupid. I still had a DNA test to be sure. It backed up what I thought from the beginning, so I handled my business. I took care of my daughter. She deserved that much.

I promised myself I wouldn't be the kind of guy that bitched about child support or shit like that afterwards. I did sleep with her. My buddy Steve, stays bitching about shit like that. How he feels like he only works one job because child support takes the other check, he should have thought about that before he slept with his son's mother.

When it came to naming my daughter, Renee wanted to

name the baby some dumb shit. Haliba. Taliba. Shamiba. What kind of shit is that? If you have to explain it, you shouldn't name your child that bullshit.

Why give a kid some name that they can't spell one day? Let alone she won't have to put that on a resume that will let employers already know she's black. I was like look if she was going to have any name it had to be the name of the person I loved most, Nikki.

'Why Nicole?' Renee had asked.

I didn't know what to say, so I called her bluff. 'Look, if you don't name her Nicole, then I'll be a father in name only. Child support and that's it.' We named her Nicole.

When it came to Nikki, when Nikki said she was pregnant, I felt better. Finally, I knew that now she wouldn't leave me. She couldn't. When our baby was born, I would tell her about Nicole. Offer to marry her and all that good shit we always talked about.

Well, she talked about it. When I looked at Nicole, I knew Nikki had to accept her. She is my daughter. I couldn't deny she's my child. But, then Renee turned up at my place and things are messed up right now. I sat on the curb realizing things had gone from bad to worst. I didn't know what to do.

I considered calling Sista but she wouldn't tell me anything. I didn't see Nikki's car parked outside of there either. I did drive past their other friend's place, the guy Day, hoping she was there. I need to straighten this shit out. I'm getting tired of spending hours outside of Nikki's place with no luck.

I hate to admit it but Sista is my only hope. I don't care if she likes me or not. This isn't about her, I was about to dial the phone but when I picked it up, Sista was already on the line…

Renee

I wasn't planning on meeting my daughter's father's girlfriend. I wasn't planning on going over there to his place. But my mother couldn't watch my daughter. I called his mother and nobody answered the damn phone.

I had things to do so I was going to take her to her father. He said he would be home Friday when I talked to him. So I was going to drop her off and go about my business.

What was I supposed to do when she, Reggie's girlfriend, answered the door? She was the same girl from the club. I was scared at first because here she was telling me to come in. I am nobody's fool.

She wasn't going to beat my ass and in front of my daughter at that. But I went in. I didn't want to cause a scene when my first instinct was to run. But I went in anyway. It was better that we end this shit now. I had to give her points; she cut right to the chase.

'How long have you been sleeping with my man?' Nikki asked when she realized Nicole was asleep.

'Excuse me,' I replied. I soon realized this was not the time to play stupid or catch an attitude. She could still beat my ass. I would have. I would have kicked any woman's ass that showed up at my door looking for my man with a child in tow.

'Let's try this again,' Nikki said looking at me. 'How long have you and Reggie been fucking? Is that better?'

'Reggie and I have been on and off for a minute now. We met in a club; we had sex a few times. I didn't know he was seeing you to be honest?' I replied unsure of how to proceed. I tried not to sound too smart. It was clear that she was hurt. I have been there before and with the same man, no doubt. So I figured I might as well tell her everything.

'So, let me get this straight, this is Reggie's daughter? Reggie has a daughter.' The way she is talking I was trying to figure out who is she is trying to convince herself or me? I didn't know what to say or do. I guess it is true that the other woman is always the last to know.

'Look, I think we better wait until Reggie comes back. Then we can all sit down and talk about this,' I offered and tried to gather up Nicole. Nicole had fallen asleep on the couch. Just then Nikki held her stomach and I knew--she is pregnant. She is pregnant with Reggie's baby.

The fact that she didn't know, my daughter is two, blew my mind. I thought he told the world after he found out for sure. Then I looked around his apartment and realized of all the pictures I had Nicole take, none of them were on display.

If she was shocked by my daughter, I guess we were even when I realized why he chose to name my baby Nicole. I guess I just wanted him to accept her so bad I didn't bother to ask. She looks just like him though. Who couldn't look at my daughter and not know?

Now I am scared. I know his dad is a lawyer. A good one from what I hear. I know he is up to something. He hasn't answered any of my calls and when I went to pick up my daughter from his mother's she told me it was best that I didn't come around for awhile. What was that supposed to mean?

What was he planning on doing, fighting for custody? Oh, my God. Was he planning on taking my daughter away from me? I mean I take good care of my daughter. I can't lie. The money that he provides in child support helps me out a lot. If he takes that away then it's over. I can't let that happen. I would die without my child.

All this time I was worried about him even after how he treats me. Now this. Just then my phone rang. Good, it was just Shirley and not that damn Reggie...

Paul

I walked through my front door, checked my answering machine, and saw that there were again six messages on my answering machine. Every day, I had received no less than six.

It was always either Angela apologizing for not telling me about Vanessa. 'Paul, look we need to talk about this...,' she would say.

Or Vanessa was telling me how much of a fuck up I was for kicking Angela out like I did. 'You are a pussy. Yeah, I got your bitch. You weren't man enough for her. You had her body but I got her heart...,' Vanessa would say. Childish shit that I could have done without.

I wouldn't let Angela get her clothes after I changed the locks. I even got a restraining order against Vanessa and an alarm system. After all, it is my house. A man's home is his castle and I needed to defend it against the evil dragon, Vanessa.

Just walking into the house made me think about that day I came home to find Vanessa's car parked out front. I remembered taking a shower; I figured I would find out what was up with my wife and her best friend. I know what a woman's genitalia smelled like. I know pussy. I wanted to know what it was doing on my wife's lips.

Something in me didn't want to believe that she was getting down with Vanessa. However, now was the time to find out right? I stepped out of the shower, wrapped a towel around my waist, and went down stairs.

Since my wife was already in a robe, I came up behind her and began to kiss her neck. She stiffened up at my touch. I kissed her again and she began shaking.

'You know we haven't gotten it in lately?' I said seductively. You know trying to woo her. I was trying to be all romantic. I wrapped my hands around Angela and kissed her

119

neck.

'Paul, this really ain't the time,' Angela said turning to look at me, trying to beg me off. She quickly tried to think of some excuse as to why she didn't want to have sex. As Angela successfully pulled away from me, she realized there wasn't anything she could say. The look in my eyes said it all. I knew.

'Vanessa though?' I said as I abruptly turned, went back up the steps, got dressed, packed a bag to leave the house. My mind raced with questions of when did the affair, if you could call it that, happened and why. As I came down the steps, Angela was still sitting in the same spot from earlier.

'Don't be here when I get back,' I said as I grabbed my keys up. I called my friend Chris on my cell phone before walking to his house.

On the way I called my mother, told her what happened and waited for shit to hit the fan. I didn't want to call my family at first, because I know the questions would start, especially my grandmother. My mistake was telling my mother. After that, the phone calls started.

'You're not stupid,' my grandmother started in. 'You didn't know she liked women?'

'You want us to beat her ass,' my mother said calmly when she called me back. 'Because I'll call your sisters. I got my knife and we can handle that...'

My older sister, Karen, Miss Holy Roller the Sanctified Christian, added her two cents, 'I knew she was trouble. She needs Jesus. How dare she use your heart and home like a rest stop or a shelter?'

My brother, Bernard, was a lot less tactful. 'Damn, so she was a syke dyke. You know about those kinds of girls. They think it's cute to be gay. Tell you all the good shit you want to hear then 'Syke, I'm a dyke.' You know what I would have just

120

climbed in bed and slept with them both. How does her friend look?' I hung up on him. Bernard was the one that gave her the number to begin with.

By staying with Chris, I know that I wouldn't have to deal with Vanessa's bullshit. I wasn't about to go to jail for beating Vanessa down. The thought of Angela kissing her upset me beyond belief. I know by staying with Chris, there wouldn't be a lot of questions either. I didn't need that I needed time to think. What could I do? What would I do?

I realized I was truly upset, feeling maybe like I didn't have what it took to satisfy Angela. However, when I thought about Angela something in me knew that in my heart maybe Vanessa could.

I thought about calling Sista as I was packing my bags. I left Sista for this shit. I wanted to beg for forgiveness and tell her I was wrong. Maybe we still have a chance, even though I fucked shit up. I'm not above begging for a second chance.

By the time I did go home that Sunday, Angela had left but took only a few of her clothes. The mail was still on the floor from the last couple of days.

As I settled in and leafed through the mail, I found one letter that caught my attention. It was from Temple University Hospital. It was addressed to Angela. I opened it wondering, if in fact, Angela is sick. Instead what it said made me sick. Angela is pregnant.

I sat down and tried to remember the last time we had sex and determined by the due date, it could have very well been my child. Damn, sure couldn't have been Vanessa's. In the end, I realized that had been the plan all along for Angela to have a child that she and Vanessa could raise. Ain't that a bitch...

Sista

When I got home from spending time with AJ, I found a message from Day on my answering machine. Apparently, Reggie had been to his place looking for Nikki. He saw Reggie driving off. Day honestly didn't know what to tell him even if he knew what was going on with Nikki. Something is going on and I am not the type to let things go lightly. I did the only thing I could do I called Reggie.

'Reggie,' I asked started that he was already on the line. I don't even think I heard the phone ring.

'Yeah, who is this?' Reggie asked obviously irritated.

'Sista,' I responded, 'where is Nikki?'

'I could ask you the same question,' Reggie replied. I know he isn't going to get smart. He sounded desperate. 'I haven't heard from her. I don't know where she is. Only place I could think of is her grandmother's new house in Pittsburgh but nobody is answering the phone. If she calls you could you tell her to call me?'

'What are you talking about,' I asked. I was lost.

'You don't know. Nikki never told you,' he asked.

'No, what are you talking about?' I asked confused.

'I'll let Nikki tell you. It isn't my place. Just tell her to call me,' Reggie said and he just hung up the phone.

Something isn't right. I sat back down and it was only in hindsight that I noticed the little changes in Nikki. I know I have to go into my Police Woman-like mode and find out the truth. What did Reggie black ass do now?

If it took Day and me to drive all night to get there, there was only one place we needed to be: wherever Nikki is…

122

Nikki

I got up to stretch and look out at the birds flying nearby. 'This is a nice house,' I thought looking around at the house. The white picket fence and the matching white siding gave it a sense of peace. There is plenty of grass that my children could have run around in.

My grandmother, my Nana, when she retired decided to move out here last year in the suburbs of Pittsburgh to be near Mr. Benny's family. I can see why, it's peaceful out here. I was somewhat upset that it took for all of this for me to come back.

I was making myself at home though. My Nana and her boyfriend, Mr. Benny, had gone out for the day this morning, but both promised to be back in time for dinner. My nana tried to get me to eat but I haven't had much of an appetite lately.

As I sat alone, I was glad. Being alone gave me the time I needed to think. I touched my stomach again and thought again, about what I did. It was too soon to replay the last couple of days all over again, but I did again and again.

I called Sista and Day a couple of times when I knew they wouldn't be home to say that I was okay. They needed to know. I wanted to say something more than I am all right, but I didn't know where to begin. I wanted to call Brian but some how I couldn't find the words to say what I really felt. So I just left brief messages on everyone's phone.

I couldn't go into details, I just assured Day and Sista that I was okay and would be back soon. I felt that they would understand my decision to leave when I did go back and understand why I didn't call. I can't lie.

I am hurting in more ways than one. It took a lot out of me just to make the trip out to see my grandmother, but in truth, I know I didn't have anywhere else to go.

Sometimes, I was even tempted to call Reggie but the

feeling soon passed when I thought about Reggie, Renee and their child and I felt a chill go through me when I stopped to wonder how many others have there been. Women he would only claim didn't matter.

I can be a selfish person about everything else, but I never thought I would have to share my man. I was lying to myself thinking that I had his heart. That he could actually belong to me. I have been a fool. That was my mistake and it hurt to admit it.

I began to cry as I watched the birds fly away. It took weeks to say it but now the truth was clear, I have uterine cancer. When I was diagnosed, I did my homework. I went to the library and searched for anything on the topic.

What hit me the hardest is that it is one of the most common cancers that developed by women. In fact, about 40,000 American women receive a diagnosis of endometrial cancer each year, making it the fourth most common cancer found in women - after breast cancer, lung cancer and colon cancer.

Most uterine cancers arise in the endometrium and are called endometrial cancer or endometrial carcinoma. If left untreated, I learned the cancer can penetrate the uterine wall and invade my bladder or rectum, or it can spread to my vagina, fallopian tubes, ovaries and organs that are more distant.

Fortunately, I learned this type of cancer grows slowly and was detected before spreading very far. Giving me a chance to be one of the 80% of this kind of cancer's victims a chance to survive. You know I didn't want to hear this.

Especially when I found out that with most health issues involving black women, the rate of survival is already less than that of a white woman. For African American women, the survival rate for what I have is around 60%. Then I found out why.

African American women ignore the symptoms of a

problem. Black women treat our bodies like we treat our relationships, we ignore the problems. We tell ourselves we don't want to know. In some cases, we can't afford quality medical care. I can't lie. I never heard of what I have.

From what I read, it is a disease that affected most women after their childbearing age but it can happen at any time. I guess I was lucky they found it in time. At first, I thought my period was coming on because I was spotting at first.

Then it felt like my period came on for real, I broke out my pads and everything. I was scared. How can I have a period, I'm pregnant? That was the first sign. I learned I was lucky because five percent of women with uterine cancer experience no symptoms until the disease spreads to other organs.

As I said, I was lucky. I didn't experience the weight loss, weakness or severe pain in my lower abdomen, back or legs that would have been a sign of something worst.

Some women just would have chalked it up to age or life. I didn't. My fears were a lot deeper. It wasn't until I talked to my grandmother that I had to remember, it was also what my mother died from. That's why she didn't have any more children other than me.

I have to believe my baby saved my life and then lost its life in the process. Since it was caught early, and given my family history, my only choice was a hysterectomy. The sooner the better. I took a deep breath and sat back on the porch's top step. The silence was so intense.

I opened my eyes in time to watch as a baby bird fly away with its mother. Suddenly, I realized I would never be able to bear a child again. I rubbed my stomach again and I realized the loneliness felt awkward. One minute, I was looking forward to being somebody's mother and the next...

I have been here for days and it still hurt, physically, mentally and emotionally. Suddenly after days of trying to piece it all together, it finally all made sense. I made a mistake trusting and believing in Reggie and his lies.

Suddenly, it all made sense why Reggie would disappear at times and all the times he lied to me. Suddenly, I realized that Reggie was seeing another female; only this one was his daughter the child that I would never be able to give him...

Day

I thought she was going to beat my ass when she came busting up into my apartment. I had been sitting on the couch of my apartment watching a movie with two of my friends when I heard the pounding on the door. I hit pause on the VCR and looked at Kevin and Mark.

'Who the hell is that?' Mark asked.

'Day, open this damn door,' Sista roared from the other side. 'Day, I know you are there. I can hear you.'

I opened the door and gave Sista a look of 'What is going on? What's wrong?'

'Where is she? What is going on?' Sista asked in a huff. However, before I could answer, Sista put up her finger in a gesture to say, 'wait a minute.'

She looked at Kevin and Mark and said 'Hi, how are y'all doing?' She didn't bother to wait for an answer, because she turned back to me to finish her conversation.

'Who?' I asked. I was confused.

'Nikki. That's who. Why have we been so blind to what was going on with Nikki?' Sista said out of breathe.

'I don't know what you are talking about.' I said, still in shock that Sista busted up in my apartment, out of breath and was now creating a stir. 'What is going on?'

'Don't play with me, Day. You haven't checked your answering machine, what kind of friend are you? I ought to break your neck but right now, I need you. I tried to call you. Where have you been?'

'I haven't been home,' I looked at Kevin and Mark for back up, they were no help. 'We just came in thirty minutes

127

ago.'

'Something is up, Day. Now all of a sudden, Nikki disappears. Day, I love you dearly as I love my own brothers but I will snap your pretty neck if you don't stop tripping. We are going to find Nikki. We are going to Pittsburgh.'

Kevin and Mark sat in complete silence. Maybe out of fear or shock. I ushered Sista into the hallway. I didn't want to cause a bigger scene than I already have.

'What do you mean by we? Pittsburgh?' I asked in disbelief. My mother told me to never ask stupid questions. Before I knew it, Sista and I were driving to Pittsburgh. All it took was one call to Nikki's grandmother and we found Nikki.

Nikki has been there all along but not answering the phone. Sista called AJ and her mother and explained the situation and that we were on our way to see Nikki. We pulled up in Nikki's grandmother's driveway Sunday morning. We had driven all night long...

Nikki

I don't know why, but the last thing I expected to see was Day's car pull up in my grandmother's driveway. I spent days looking out the window praying it wouldn't be Reggie's jeep. I felt the tears begin to fall as I watched Sista and Day walk up the steps to my grandmother's house. I reached out to embrace Sista, then Day.

Sista began to cry sensing the pain in me. I wanted to say thank you but I couldn't. Day looked tired ass hell. When my grandmother came to the door, I asked her to show Day to my room so he could lie down.

I waited until Sista came back out of the house from saying her hellos before we settled into the front porch. I didn't know where to start, but I guess Sista did.

'What happened?' Sista asked searching my face for a sign. My face must have betrayed me.

'I went to Reggie's place, waiting for him to come back from his trip and this woman shows up with this little girl. I didn't want to believe it was his child, but you could see it in that child's eyes,' I said meeting Sista's gaze for the first time.

I pulled the scarf that was wrapped around my head off and ran my fingers through my hair. I stood to stretch and looked at the other houses in the neighborhood.

'I don't want to be the kind of person to say I told you so, Nikki,' Sista said.

'Then don't. That's why I didn't tell anybody. You think I needed to hear a conversation like this one over and over again?' I said not even bothering to look at Sista. 'The last thing I need is for you to tell me that I was wrong. My grandmother didn't give it to me, so don't do it either.'

'But, you and I both know that shit was going on. Not to

this extent, but you knew and were living in denial. We keep giving too much of ourselves as women and in the end all that is left is pain and regret.'

'I take the blame for trying to stay in that relationship and trying to make things work,' I countered, 'I wanted to believe him. I needed to believe him. This my second chance at having a family. A family of my own.'

Sista got a strange look on her face and I looked at her and looked away before starting again, 'Don't sit there and look dumb, Sista, I was pregnant by Reggie. Okay.'

'Pregnant? So what about the baby,' Sista ventured. I couldn't even say it. I tried but the words wouldn't come out and when they did, it was barely above a whisper. I didn't even bother to turn around this time.

'There is no baby,' I replied.

'What?' Sista said taken aback.

'I had an abortion,' I said as my voice gave way. 'I had to. It doesn't matter. I think I wanted this baby too much. Just like the last one.'

'What last one?' Sista asked. 'When were you ever pregnant? I don't miss shit like that.'

'You missed this one,' I said turning to look at Sista and folding my arms in a defiant way. 'I had a miscarriage a couple of years back. Reggie never knew and I didn't bother to tell him or you.'

'Why didn't you say anything? I am your best friend,' Sista asked. 'You are like my sister.'

'What so you could feel sorry for me? Sista, I love you dearly but we all have our secrets. You have yours. Some things you just don't want to tell nobody but God. I just couldn't take you feeling sorry for me.'

'I wouldn't,' Sista said in almost a whisper.

'Maybe, if I told you,' I said looking away suddenly ashamed of myself, 'Maybe I was too busy feeling sorry for myself. I felt that shit all of my life. I always felt that feeling of loss, that need to have something or somebody to hold onto. I didn't want your pity. I hear that shit every time somebody hears that both of my parents are dead. The 'I'm sorry,' I started to cry more.

'You know when people say that it only makes things worst when people are in pain. Then they stand there and don't have shit else to say. They don't know what you are feeling. They can't understand your pain,' I said looking away.

Sista stood up and moved towards me. 'I can't say I know what it's like to lose not one but two children, but I know what it's like to lose someone you love. Somebody you care about.'

Sista wrapped her arms around me as I began to cry. She helped me to the porch chair and laid my head on her shoulders. All I could do was cry.

'What is really going on?' Sista asked.

'Sista,' I said in a voice barely above a whisper, 'I am sick. I found out when they were running test about the baby that I have a form of uterine cancer and it may have spread. Don't be mad at me but I had to have a hysterectomy and I didn't want anybody to know. They did what they could.'

Sista sat in silence listening to me and the words began to slowly sink in. I felt myself shaking. I hadn't cried at all since I have been here and now it all came out. Sista just held me close as I began to cry more.

'I couldn't bring a baby in this world not knowing if I'll

131

be here tomorrow...' my voice trailed off, until there was only silence.

Not once did Sista, or me, mention the fact that my mother died of cancer when I was younger. We knew. We just didn't need to say it. Sista and I sat on the porch in silence listening to the birds in the distance.

That night after saying goodbye to Nana and Mr. Benny, Sista drove back to Philly, playing her Luther Vandross tape to keep her company.

Day had fallen asleep on the passenger side and I was in the back seat. Laying there in the dark, I realized that in this brief instance reality had set in for all of us.

This whole ordeal reminded us how short life is and that it is times like this that we need to face things for what they are. Reality is what people needed, but fantasy and believing in things that don't exist or never will is what people wanted.

Sista, Day and I retired from the fantasy. As I listened to Luther singing, I realized there was still some unfinished business to deal with--Reggie...

Loretta

I don't know why I even try with her sometimes. I begrudging agreed to meet my sister for lunch. Sista is into this new family shit. I don't usually play that shit but at least I could get Sista to pay for a meal or two.

I blew my paycheck and Cliff's allowance on a nice Coach bag I had been looking at for weeks. Cliff has complained about the money I spent and took away my credit cards, but I don't give a fuck. I needed to look good.

Growing up, it has always been Sista this and Sista that. They didn't realize that I am the real star of the show. That is the only reason why I married Cliff to get out from under my Mama. My Mama was all in my business. I turned 18 and I still had a curfew. Shit, I was grown.

Since my father died, I felt bad about my mother being alone in that big house, but I quickly shot down Cliff's suggestion to have Lucy move in. Lucy Belle and me under the same roof would be like the Hatfields and The McCoys. I could see myself not two minutes off my mother's ass. Payback would be a bitch then.

My mother had a thing for smothering Sista's big ass. Eric, I can understand. Eric is the baby. But my sister, I would never understand that mess. I can't stand her any way.

Since my father died, Old Lucy didn't let up one bit. It was sickening how the old bird hovered around Sista like her ass is made of gold. Sista this and Sista that. I heard that bullshit all of my life.

What Sista ass needed to do is to lose some of that weight around her heart before she got so big she would have to go through the door sideways. She needed to see what Oprah could for her.

I shuddered at the thought of ever getting that big. I

didn't care if I had to run five miles a day, work out four times a week or smoke crack to keep from being that big. Sista just don't give a fuck. I thought about how she ate at dinner. I hate it when people suggest we look alike.

I hated family dinners. I found every excuse not to go even if it meant spending Sunday with Cliff's senile old mother. I hated Mama Pearl as I called her. She smelled like Ben Gay and cigarettes. But anything is better than faking the smiles and the laughs at my mother's.

My mother doted on Sista. Sista is fake as shit too. Her and her flaky ass friend Day. I opened my compact and looked at myself again thinking that Day is a waste. I don't even want to know if he is a wide receiver or a quarterback. He damn sure wasn't playing for my team with his faggot ass. I used to like his fruity ass too. Oh, well.

Only thing that made dinner even tolerable is when Nikki came by. Nikki is cool as shit and as a child I wished Nikki had been my sister.

Nikki is the kind of person I needed around. One of those thorough bitches like me. My kind of people. Nikki is just the shit. Nikki isn't like the corny bitches that I was used to faking being friends with and being around to pass the time.

I had already waited more than thirty minutes when my cell phone rang and I learned that Sista wasn't coming. Typical. Fuck her, I thought.

Her fat ass needs to miss a few meals anyway. Sista need to go on one of them Oprah diets. But her ass wouldn't be pulling in a wagon of meat. She would probably eat it and gain all that shit back.

I knew Brian was tied up and Nikki would have been with Sista though she has not been to dinner in a minute. Something must have happened with those two. Who cares? Looking around the crowded restaurant, I did not feel like being here looking lonely so I ordered something to go.

I didn't bother to call my husband. Getting through dinner with his boring ass stories about his job was thankless enough. Shit, I had to have sex with him once in a while too.

Brief conversations are about all I could stand of that player. But he did pay the bills. I waited after I ordered a salad to go. As I paid and headed out the door, I was nearly knocked over by a guy on his way in.

'Watch where the fuck you are going! Dumb ass,' I yelled loud enough that everyone in the store heard. I spit out the words. I momentarily stopped myself as I looked at the guy.

A thug in the making, I thought. He was about 22 and he wore a jersey and some baggy jeans and a pair of Timberland boots. I was all set to curse him the fuck out when he stopped to pick up my bag that had fallen.

As I took the bag from him, he smiled. I realized my phone book had fallen out, which he scooped up off the floor and handed that to me. At least he had some manners.

'Is my number in there?' he asked. When he licked his lips, I handed him the book back and a pen...

Day

'Where on earth have you been?' I heard Melvin say as I picked up the phone. I had just gotten home from Pittsburgh with Nikki and Sista that day and I felt a sense of relief knowing that Nikki is okay. She is sick but with prayer and the right doctors she would be fine.

In the time that I have known both Nikki and Sista, I felt a sense of family. More than sitting here listening to my real cousin. He got on my nerves most of the time based on the things he said out of his mouth. He took being gay too far.

'I was in Pittsburgh, if you must know,' I said to my cousin. Yes, it was that Melvin, my gay cousin. Melvin irked me though because he is that effeminate type. Very flamboyant with his style and at time I wanted to say shut the fuck up, but he is my family. Even if it was from a distance.

'Pittsburgh?' I heard him say. 'Oh, Lord. What were you doing there? There isn't anything in Pittsburgh.'

'Hiding from you,' I said. 'I had to go get a friend. She is sick and Sista and I went to go get her.'

'You are so good to people,' Melvin said now suddenly serious.

'I try to be,' I said as I flipped though my mail.

I made sure the door was locked as I remembered having to explain to my friends why Sista busted up into my apartment and went on like a mad woman the way she did. They weren't upset even after I put them out.

Not that I needed to explain who Sista was, but it just seemed strange to them. I sat back down on the couch. Melvin had been going on about something, so I tried to listen.

'You know my Mother is like MCI,' he was saying. 'But

all I know is that your mother left your father yesterday. We don't know where she went or even why?'

'Wait,' I said now sitting up. 'Start from the beginning.'

'We were all in church and suddenly your mother jumped up, screamed something at your father and left. That being my aunt, my mother and I followed her out and she said she didn't want to talk about. Didn't even want us to drive her home. Made me miss my solo in the choir. I have been dating that choir director six months to get that solo.'

'As long as my mother is okay, I don't know what I can do,' I said. 'She never calls or writes me. But about the choir director, do you think that's cool? That's a small town. Don't go starting shit Melvin. Isn't he married? You know you are going to hell.'

'So? Listen; look at what he's doing putting on that front. There is no future in fronting,' Melvin started in, about to get on his soap box. I could hear it.

'Every Sunday somewhere in America there is a preacher denouncing the sins of homosexuality. The problem is they needed to look at their own choir director, Bruce or Gary.'

"If the choir director or lead soloist wasn't gay,' Melvin went on. 'I would give my left testicle to find out why not. Not once does he blink when the preacher condemned him to hell in the sermon. He simply gets up with the next request and led the choir in song. He'll burn in hell later.'

'You still aren't right,' I replied. 'He has a wife and kids. How can you call yourself a Christian doing stuff like that?'

'Day, be realistic. I was not alone. So what would it be better if he wasn't the choir director,' Melvin continued, 'You know choirs bring members and members bring tithes. The more money you bring in the better the church does. So I figured that it must be okay if the choir brought in members and the group went on to win competitions. It just so happens some of the gayest men in America happen to sing in choirs.'

'If you want to know the truth,' Melvin started again. I groaned into the phone because I knew he was about to say something off the wall. 'I don't put anything past the ministers themselves. I always wondered if the choir directors got so many privileges or seemed to fly under the minister's radar because they were offering up something else to the good reverend on the side. A lick, a suck or a fuck.'

'You know you are nasty right,' I said trying to irritate Melvin on purpose. He was irritating me. 'And wrong. Then you call yourself a Christian man. First a choir director, who is going to be next?'

'I was going through a drought,' Melvin said laughing. 'Even the good girls are trying to hold on to their man by turning into freaks behind closed doors. Better that than losing their man to the streets.'

'Have you tried a personal ad? Somebody has to be out there for you,' I suggested. 'Somebody that will keep you from getting hurt.'

'I don't have time for that nonsense,' Melvin replied suddenly serious. 'Each website taunted the possibility of meeting somebody. On one, some of the guys even posted their picture but claimed to be 'not out. Like who isn't going to see him and recognize him?'

I had to laugh at that one. I laughed because if a guy found the website to post his picture all over so could his sister, aunt, cousin, next door neighbor or gay co-worker who was the world's biggest faggot. Somebody is going to tell on you.

Not to mention the ones who will lie because either you rejected them or they get a bad case of wishful thinking that you were gay so they can get with you. Some people have no shame.

'As usual, you have a point,' I said as I went to lie back down on the couch. "But what you are doing still isn't right.'

'It isn't being sacrilegious to think like that,' Melvin said, sounding dead serious, 'It is called being real. I see you are still in denial. Look what is going on in the Catholic church. If a priest could live his life on the DL, or so called down low, why not the good pastor with a wife and kid?'

I groaned when I heard this. I hated when Melvin talked like that. I wanted to end the conversation as quickly as possible.

'Like I said before,' Melvin said as if he sensed this conversation had taken a bad turn, 'If I hear anything else about your mother, I will let you know. Your daddy was pissed though. I have to run. I will let you know. Nothing happens in this town that gets past my mother.'

'Bye,' I said. I held the phone long after Melvin hung up the phone. I was glad he still down south and could let me know what was going on with my mother and father from time to time.

Although Melvin and his mother went to the same church as my mother and father, I knew my parents barely spoke to them because of Melvin. As I sat here replaying his story in my head, I was shocked. My mother left my father. Why? What did he do now that she jumped up in the middle of church?

I wanted to call the house, but I knew it was useless to do that. I didn't want to get in the middle of it. I sat back and looked at the clock wondering what I was going to do for the night. I got up when I realized I hadn't even checked my answering machine.

There were two calls, one from Sista saying thank you and another from Mark telling him about a party at the club. I wasn't up for going to the club watching a bunch of fake ass people parade around like they owned the club. If I wanted to meet somebody I could go out just to go out. I didn't need that tonight.

Instinctively I called Brian. I needed to let him know what was going on. After two rings, Brian picked up.

'Nikki is back,' I said.

'That's good. Where has she been?' Brian asked.

'Her grandmother's, your sister and I drove out there.'

'Why didn't y'all call me? I would have gone too.'

'Ask your sister,' I said and then heard how Brian got quiet. 'You know don't you?'

'Know what?' Brian asked. Brian is an Aries. His mind races a mile a minute. When he gets quiet, something wrong and he was quiet. He knew.

'That Nikki is sick. She has cancer.'

Brian breathed deep. 'I knew for a minute, but I didn't want to say anything. That's her business. I figured when she is ready to talk she would tell us something.'

'You are right,' I said, 'We just got to be there

'True' Brian said. 'I'm going to call her right now.'

'I'll call you tomorrow for lunch,' I said.

'Cool, talk to you tomorrow,' Brian said and hung up.

I put the phone down. First Nikki, then what Melvin said. I realized I need to get some sleep. As I laid in the dark staring at the ceiling, I realized I wasn't really tired. I looked at the card on the nightstand that had yet to be addressed.

Yet another card to go unopened. I wondered to myself should I even mail this card this time, a Mother's day card and save myself the heartache of having it returned...

Reggie

I slammed the phone down and got up and went out the house. No jacket, no coat, I just didn't care. I am going crazy. Suddenly, Nikki moved and disconnected her phone. She quit her job and was nowhere to be found. Trust me, I looked. She was gone.

It has been a while since I saw her and I'm upset. I got nowhere by calling her grandmother or Sista. Both maintained that Nikki was fine but didn't want to deal with me. It was tearing me up inside. I couldn't eat, couldn't sleep and when it came to other women, I didn't even want to think about them.

What made it worst is even though I was spending time with my daughter; Renee started to call me up with dumb shit. Here I'm trying to do the right thing and she's making it hard on me. I gave her more money and she make up dumb excuses to call saying that Nicole wanted to say good night. Renee knew what she was doing when she came by that day to see me. I told her when I was going to be home.

I played a daily game of what if. Maybe if I had been there to meet Nikki. Maybe if she never opened the door. I should have told her to come get me. But I needed to make a stop at my office first.

If I wasn't stuck in traffic, things might be different now. Anything would ease my heartache except answering the question of why did I fuck with Renee from the beginning?

From what I guessed, Renee kicked that shit to Nikki about being lonely and that I had taken Renee's kindness for weakness. I didn't ask. I didn't want to know. I'm still kicking myself for even knowing her. I was drunk, what could I do? Maybe, just maybe, I should have stopped drinking. Leave that shit alone.

One thing I know is that I wouldn't slight my child to get back at Renee. My Mom loved my daughter and my Dad spoiled

Nicole to the highest degree. Nicole is just so beautiful too. She looks just like me. I got to think about my child with Nikki too.

I thought about what our baby would look like. I hoped it was a boy. Yeah, a son, I thought. Nikki would love that. I never really thought to ask her. I was just so excited when we found out she was pregnant.

I really don't know what she wants as far as a boy or a girl. Whenever she wants to talk about the baby, something in me shut down. She stops talking, so I stop talking. We never really talked about it because I felt uncomfortable.

I hated for the last two years of lying about having a child. I wanted to break down when my Mother brought me my first father's day gift and I couldn't put it out on display for the world to see.

I honestly and truly loved Nikki and wanted to marry her. I wanted to love her forever. I wished I had a clue. I asked my dad, who couldn't help. Like he was ever any help.

I spent the better part of my time with Nicole trying not to be the distant dad that my father has always been. I listened to her when she talked. I played games with her, took her places, even with her mother tagging along. What is good for my daughter is good for me.

I wasn't trying to be the 'here's money because that solves everything' type of father. The 'here is money because I have no time to be a real dad' father like my own dad is. Even my father's advice left me in the dark. Even my friends were clueless.

I asked myself, time and time again how did I get to this point? Suddenly, nothing mattered without Nikki. I thought about all the other girls I messed with and suddenly, they weren't worth it. I fucked up and the more I thought about it, the more I decided that there is only way to correct it. Or die trying…

Nikki

Damn, I am tired. It has been months since I chose to have the abortion and the feelings stayed with me. I found myself at times stopping on the street to watch the children at play constantly wondering what might have been and each time I thought about Reggie.

Sometimes the anger got to be so bad and so great that I felt like screaming. Especially now that I know, I would never have children. I could always adopt but I can't be alone in that one. I'm not strong enough. At least, not yet.

I had my hysterectomy in Pittsburgh and chemotherapy came next ensuring the doctors got everything, the cancer that is. The doctors said the cancer had not spread as the doctors originally believed.

At one point, though they suspected it would be reoccurring. Like I could take on this kind of thing every couple of years, but given my family history, it was possible. I'm barely holding on now.

Chemotherapy scared me. I had only vague memories of what my mother went through. I had started chemotherapy treatments to give myself a little more time, because when they suggested the cancer might be recurring, I thought it would only be a matter of time before it did spread.

If the cancer had spread, I knew the inevitable would take me. I spent many of my days alone in the library, reading about my type of cancer and when I was too weak to get out of bed, I simply stayed in and watched television or slept.

Sista would come in from work and tell me all about her day or Brian or Day would drop by and play cards with me. It took awhile, but both Sista and I breathed a sigh of relief when it was discovered that my cancer didn't spread like it did in my mother. I had to shake my head because I didn't want to think about the hell I went through. I wouldn't wish that on anyone.

It seemed like years since I came back from Pittsburgh. It had only been a few months when I remember sitting in the middle of the floor with Sista one night going through one of my boxes in the middle of the floor. Going through stuff I haven't seen in years.

'You remember this?' I asked as I pulled the locket from the box. I held it up to the light.

'Yes,' Sista smiled. 'I gave you that when we were like 16. It took me a month to get the money to buy that thing.'

I paused and I looked at Sista, 'Girl, sometimes I wish we could go back to the days when it seems like my life was so much simpler.' Sista just hugged me and we didn't say much after that, we just sat there. I wasn't ready for any of this.

My grandmother flew out to see me a few times, but lately, I told her to save her money. I knew it only hurt her more to see me in my condition. I didn't want to see her upset.

It was during this time that I learned one valuable lesson that all women should remember, no woman should ever be embarrassed to talk about their bodies to a doctor and be specific. I say tell the doctor everything, about every ache, every pain and every hurt or drip. It's your life after all.

We can go on for days telling people about the size we wear, the clothes we buy and what we want sexually. But for some women to have to go into a doctor's office and say that you have a discharge or a pain scares the shit out of them, especially black women.

Now when I go to the doctor, you would think I was going to a confession. Ladies, you are the ones who know how you feel, and when something isn't right, say so. If you don't like the answers the doctor gives you, ask for another opinion. Ask until you get an answer you are comfortable with.

Look at me. I have never gone through anything like this

before. When my doctor said I needed to go to surgery, I did it. If it gave me a chance to live, I would do whatever I had to. I just wasn't prepared to deal with all the bullshit that came afterwards.

You know I'm shallow at times. You should have seen me when my hair started to fall out, I definitely wasn't prepared for that. I mean I tried my hats, my scarves and my wigs nothing made me feel any better.

I couldn't stand seeing it come out in clumps, so I had my head shaved. I had never worn short hair in my life, so I knew cutting it short first wouldn't help. It didn't help when I was bald either.

With all you're going through, it was scary, but to be bald, I wanted to die! I hated feeling nauseous all the damn time. A period doesn't have shit on this. I'd take cramps any day over the nausea. God gave me strength, I can't lie. As time went on, I knew I was strong to put up with the six rounds of chemotherapy. I, Nicole Love, did it.

With chemotherapy, for every one cell of cancer that the chemotherapy tries to kill, 763 healthy cells are killed, which accounted for my weight loss and my loss of hair. However, I am a fighter. I'm going to beat this.

Ms. Lucy's house became a Sunday mainstay again. I needed this. Ms. Lucy piled my plate high. With each spoonful, when I did have an appetite, I hoped I would get back to where I was before, but still that feeling eluded me. How the mighty have fallen.

As December of 1998 became January of 1999, I felt better. I had celebrated Christmas at Miss Lucy's like I did every year. My grandmother even flew in. I was feeling better. It was then that I finally looked in the mirror and saw that I was finally beginning to regain some of what I lost.

Day, Brian and Sista treated me to a day at a spa around

March when my doctor finally gave me a clean bill of health. My cancer is in remission. For now, thank you, Jesus. They said it could come back but I will cross that bridge when and if I get to it. Right now, I chose to live my life and not let life live me.

Gone were the days when I went to sleep crying. Or woke up to Sista sitting next to my pullout bed, She had heard me whimpering or crying, she came to comfort me through my tears. Everything is going to be fine. Sista even had a new man in her life.

I couldn't help but to think it is funny how the tables had turned. There was a time when it was Reggie and me and Sista was on the outside looking in. Now, it was me. I wished I had somebody, anybody wouldn't do though. They had to understand my situation.

People get involved in relationship for a variety of reasons, financial, sexual, or even loneliness. People rarely get involved because they care about you and genuinely take interest in you and the things about you. It is always something about you that they like and they just put up with the other stuff.

I was happy for Sista though, from what I could see AJ wasn't just good for her, he is good to her. If I didn't know any better, I would have thought she is falling in love again. Good.

Then, there is Brian. Let's not even talk about Brian. I realized in this man, sometimes the things we want most are right under our noses. Brian is attentive and caring.

Brian listened even when he didn't always understand what is going on. He was there to take me to the doctor's and brought me fresh fruit and vitamins to give me energy when I felt down. He took care of me. Where has he been all this time? I knew, right here. But, I was with Reggie.

Brian to celebrate my recovery took me to dinner one night and encouraged me to eat. I think it is then that I looked at Brian with new eyes. It was like I saw him for the first time. He was so nice and was so attentive. But he wasn't mine.

I quickly put the thought out of my mind that he even looked at me as more than his sister's friend. I secretly wondered if I was wrong to have given up on Brian so easily when we were younger. I wondered what life would be like right now if I had not. We would probably be married by now with a couple of kids.

My mistake was telling Day. It wasn't a problem that he knew, because for the first time in my life, I was talking to somebody other than God and it felt good. My problem is with Day being Day, he laughed at the thought of Brian and me when I said something about it one day.

'What are you saying? I asked. 'You think Brian wouldn't make a good husband?'

Day laughed dealing the latest hand. 'He might but not for you. He is the perennial bachelor. In addition, Brian can't get past two weeks in a relationship. Nikki, you would have a better chance of marrying Bobby Brown.'

'But this is me, Day,' I said. I was surprised Day wasn't taking me seriously. Why should he? This whole thing did come out of the blue?

'He never likes anybody past two weeks. He has ADHD when it comes to dating,' Day countered before winning the hand. I decided not to press the issue. However, my feelings remained. God has a sense of wicked sense of humor and damn good timing. He has to. Guess what happened?

Brian, who called earlier to say he was on his way over, was outside and rang the bell. Day ran down to let Brian in. I thought about what I said to Day and I was dying to ask Sista's opinion. I figured Sista would just laugh at me too. Still, I waited to see Brian come up the steps.

I heard Brian and Day talking and continued to look at

the door waiting for the two to come up the steps. I guess I was still lost in thought that I was startled when I heard more than two sets of footsteps. As Brian emerged from the hall, Brian hugged me. I looked over his shoulder to see who he was with. You know I wasn't expecting to see her. Don't ask me her name. It wasn't important.

Here she was, she had on this tight ass black dress that looked spray painted on, too much makeup and her breast look like they were about to jump out at you any moment and yell surprise. I didn't know Brian liked brown skinned whores with curly weaves.

Maybe she just followed him up the steps like a stray dog. Day looked at me and I looked away. I sat back down and pretended to shuffle the cards. I felt Brian staring at me. I didn't like it one bit. What was I supposed to do? Welcome this nappy headed heifer with open arms? She was taking my man. Wait, did I just think that? I'm jealous of this girl?

'My bad, Tanya, this is Nikki. Nikki is like my sister,' Brian said wrapping his arms around Tanya's waist. 'Tanya is the new lady in my life.'

'His sister?' I thought to myself. 'His sister? His sister is at AJ's.' You know I wanted to beat his ass.

Day looked at me and I knew he realized the true meaning of our conversation earlier. Day realized that there was more to the conversation than what if.

Now Brian is introducing me to yet another girl. Somebody who wasn't me. If anyone listened closely, they would have heard the sound of my heart shattering into a million pieces...

Nikki and Leonard

I'm through with men and their games. I decided that after meeting Brian's new Miss Thing last night. Here he is all affectionate and sweet to me and the whole time he was treating me like a sister. I am a sister but not his. I'm done. Do you hear me? Through. Finished.

I had enough of the men that were taken already, men that wanted to lie and cheat and dealing with men like Reggie who came with more issues and complications than the law should allow.

They can keep their insecurities, especially Reggie. I still thought about Reggie from time to time and every time I was tempted to call, I remembered that it was Reggie that taught me what a lie is to begin with. God, I need help.

When Sista heard about a grief support group for people who were dealing with all sorts of problems from the loss of a loved one to life threatening illnesses and I decided to go. Sista offered to go with me, but I declined. I needed somebody that had walked a mile in my shoes to talk to.

It would have felt good to have Sista there; I needed to do this alone. I was the one grieving the lost of my child, my relationship, my parents even and then almost losing my life. I needed to do this, but like I said I needed to do this alone.

I adjusted my scarf on my head as I looked in the mirror and got ready to leave. I momentarily paused and touched my head as I looked in the hall mirror.

Where once there flowed a long mane of honey brown hair, I now sport a short hairdo as my hair began to grow back in from when the chemotherapy ended. 'It was going to be okay,' I told myself. I grabbed my pocketbook and left the apartment.

When I arrived at the meeting, which took place in a little building in South Philly, I hoped to sit in the back of the room hoping no one would ask me to talk, but found that the seats were formatted in a circle.

Just then, a tall, light-skinned man with hazel brown eyes entered the room and motioned for people, who were standing around to talking, to take a seat. He momentarily stopped and looked at me.

He smiled and something in his brown eyes made me feel at home. As people moved to sit down, I felt the weight of the man's stare again. He cleared his voice and began. I felt like he was talking to me directly. Maybe he was.

'It is good to see so many of you back. I see a lot of new faces,' he said making eye contact with me. 'I am Leonard.' He paused and looked at me again. I blushed and looked down. He smiled and began looking at the other people and started again.

Over the course of the next two hours, I learned that I wasn't alone. I heard the horror stories of losing loved ones to cancer and other disease like AIDS and still others told by the people that those that lost their lives to these plights left behind.

More than once I found myself in tears knowing for the first time in my life, I didn't want to die. It sure makes you appreciate the life you have when you realize that other people are dealing with a lot worst than anything you could encounter.

Leonard had gotten up to get me some tissue. Each time, I felt a hand on my arm from another member of the group and a word of comfort. When the session ended, I found myself wishing it had not. That is until Leonard came up to me in the parking lot.

'Are you okay?' he asked me exuding a genuine sincerity that I have very rarely encountered. His brown eyes also exuded concern.

'Yes, I am fine. By the way, my name is Nikki and I just wanted to say thank you. My friend told me about your group.'

'No, thank you for coming out. Maybe next week we will even get you to speak. By the way, I am Leonard. But you already know that.' He shook my extended hand. 'I just thought I would ask how you were because back there you seemed like ...'

'No, I just know what it feels like to wonder,' my voice drifted of. I looked at Leonard again and began again. 'What it is like to lose something or somebody.'

'I see,' he said still staring into my eyes.

'I lost my parents when I was younger. My mother passed away from cancer, my father was killed in a car accident, and I just listened to some of the stories. It just got to me. I don't know why,' I shook my head. 'But, back there I think I learned something about life and I think, about myself. I just wanted to say thank you'

'That is good to hear,' Leonard said as he leaned up against my car. 'And you are most welcomed.'

I smiled again and began wondering why I haven't met somebody like Leonard before. I felt like I could talk to him. 'And,' I continued this time connecting with Leonard's gaze. 'I figured out that I have been making a mistake. I was so caught up in me, me, me that I never stopped to think about the people around me. The people that I love. I guess I was being selfish. I never thought about them.'

'Your husband? That's who you are referring to,' Leonard asked.

'No, I am not married.'

'Somebody as lovely as you and you are not married.'

'There is somebody. Well, there was somebody, but that is long over,' I looked away hoping to change the subject.

Leonard paused and looked around the now empty

parking lot. 'Look, if you are not doing anything right now, would you like to have coffee with me? I know this place on South Street.' He paused and waited for my answer and sensing my hesitation, he smiled. 'I know I just met you, but look, I'll even let you buy.'

I smiled for the umpteenth time since meeting Leonard. I took my car, Leonard took his, and we drove to the little café. We talked for the next couple of hours. I told him about growing up with her grandmother and Sista and her new boyfriend AJ, Day, and even Reggie. I didn't want to talk about Brian. Not yet, any way.

Leonard told me about how he lost his wife and started the group to give others an outlet to grieve and in the process, himself. He is a teacher by day and a certified grief counselor by night. When the night ended, he walked me to my car and gave me a kiss on the cheek.

'So this is goodbye?' Leonard asked.

'Why would you ask that?' I replied coyly.

'You told me everything about you? What is next?' Leonard asked leaning on his car.

'Dinner?' I said taking Leonard's hand and squeezing it. Leonard took me into his arms and hugged me. It felt good. Real good.

'I would like that,' he replied and handed me his card. 'After our session next week? Or even before? Call me if you just want to talk.'

'It is a date,' I said as I wrote down my number and handed it to Leonard. I got back into my car and drove off. Leonard watched me go, I saw him in the rearview mirror and I waved back. I breathed deeply still smelling the scent of Leonard's cologne and smiled.

I wondered if it is time to move on. I thought about how he touched his wedding band as he looked at me. Is he trying to tell me something or himself? I knew only time would tell and if it would be with somebody like Leonard.

As I pulled up in front of Sista's building, I saw a familiar jeep parked out front. I reached in my purse for my keys and immediately headed for the door. That is when Reggie jumped out of the jeep and ran towards me.

I didn't feel up for a fight. I was tired. When Reggie grabbed me, my whole body was racked with fear. It has been months since I saw him and being around him is the last thing I needed. I didn't want any drama.

'Are you crazy,' I screamed. I realized that Reggie wasn't listening and nobody heard or they would have come to my rescue. I realized I would have to fight.

I attempted to pull away but in my weakened state I was in no position to try to get away. When Reggie realized what he did, he let my wrist go and I rubbed my wrist to ease the pain. Reggie hurt me and I felt it. I backed away from Reggie unsure of what his next move would be.

I watched as Reggie went back into his jeep and pulled out something. Then, he did something I didn't suspect he would. My heart dropped. It was at that moment that I realized my life would never be the same. 'Reggie, no, don't do this,' I screamed...

AJ

I was stacking a shelf with a new Jeffrey Archer novel and was surprised to see Sista come in so early with Day. Day shook my hand and headed over to the magazines. It was only 11 o'clock so the lunch crowds weren't coming into the bookstore to do their daily reading yet. I stopped to give Sista a hug. Sista was early.

'What is up?' I asked.

'Nothing, we were going to lunch and I was wondering if you might want to come along.' Sista smiled at me. I smiled backed feeling good to see her. Really happy, things were going good between us.

'I can't,' I said, looking into her eyes and stroking her cheek. 'But can I take a rain check?'

'Yes,' she said playfully, she kissed me. Day seeing and probably hearing the exchange came back over and he waved as they went out the door. I waved back and smiled.

I have grown to like Day. He is a good person. Day is one of my girlfriend's best friends and I honestly didn't feel any jealousy towards him. I know what you are thinking. I didn't know that he was gay either when I met him.

It didn't cross my mind. I won't lie; it helped me feel better having him around my girl all the time. I guess because I knew Day would never try to sleep with my girl. Plus, when she needed it, Day would give her the support she needed when I couldn't.

With all the stuff going on with her best friend, I knew she needed somebody to talk to. I tried to be it, but work kicked my ass at times. I wished I could have eaten lunch with them but with the regular manager out on sick leave, I ate at the store most days. Some days, like today I had to remember to take a break.

I went back to stocking the shelves and turned over again in my mind the question that had been on my mind all morning. I was wondering if I should take Sista to meet my family. I wasn't sure, because I knew they could be about some ignorant asses.

I met her family, but she still had not met mine and it's been months. I guess she figured because I don't talk about them, she shouldn't either. My mother, Diane, would be okay for Sista to meet. My father had left when I was two to go get a pack of cigarettes and never came back until 20 years later and I was out of school.

I remember my mother took one look at my father and asked him 'What did you do buy a farm and grow the cigarettes yourself?' They never talked since then. It turns out he had been in Philly all this time and never came around to see us or even make sure we were okay.

After my dad left, my mother did what every single mother would do trying to raise me and my brother Kevin and that was to get on welfare. Suddenly, we moved from a nice house to the housing projects of Richard Allen. Richard Allen was okay then, but then it changed.

A little after I moved out to my own place, my mother got onto another program and moved into another house. I wasn't surprised when Kevin went into the Navy to get away from all of this. I didn't blame him.

That is when my cousin Earl, my aunt Bunny, her old man Craig moved in. Earl is on drugs and if the television is missing, nine times out of ten he sold it and smoked the profits. A dumb ass thirty-two year old man who still thought juice came in red and blue.

My Aunt Bunny is my mother's older sister; she could tell you what contestant won what on the *Price Is Right* or who slept with whom on *All My Children* and when her and her man's social security checks came, faster than she could tell you what day of the week it is.

My 'uncle' is another story; I cringed when I thought about my aunt's boyfriend's fat ass sitting around all day.

I hated my frequent trips to my mother's because the house always smelled like the can of grease she kept on the stove and then there is my aunt with her ashy ankles, walking around in her housecoat and some pink rollers telling me to give her some sugar. A cigarette is always dangling from her lip. The problem is she thinks she is cute. She's not.

'Why don't you just put them out?' I asked my mother one day on the rare occasion the house was empty.

My mother just looked at me like she was lost in thought for a minute and smiled. 'They make the house feel full and homely since my boys moved out.'

I wanted to say none of their asses had anywhere else to go. I knew my mother was barely there anyway because she had found a new man named Mr. Dave years ago, who seemed like a decent guy. As the years went by, he became the father my brother always wanted and the man I wanted to be.

Coming up, it had always been my brother, my mother and me. I can't lie; I was upset at times that my father let things get like that. I was moving a display of the book, *Rich Dad, Poor Dad*, when I thought about my father. My father's name is Charles. Charlie. Chuck. But never Dad.

Or should I say my pop because when I see him I am not always glad to see him but I am glad 'he came.' He lives with a lady in the Abbotsford Homes housing project. I definitely wasn't taking Sista to meet him.

I hated visiting him myself. The lady that my father called his girlfriend would give me the eye because she knew I looked exactly like my father only twenty years younger. At first, though I had to admit she looked kind of creepy. She was short, thick and dark skinned with a curly wig every time I saw her. Then it was always that stare.

Then I found out the truth. When I say she was giving me the eye, she was literally giving me the eye. She only had one. The other one was made of glass. I didn't know until one day I was there and my dad was looking around and she was sitting in the corner holding her face like he hit her as he opened the door for me.

'Watch your step,' he said. 'We were arguing and her eye popped out.'

I wanted to laugh so bad that I had to bite my cheek. Now when I came through, it's like she knew I was coming. Image somebody's older and unattractive mother coming to the door in a nightgown and housecoat trying to look sexy and then, there is that eye.

Now I know how Eddie Murphy felt in *Boomerang* when Eartha Kitt was attracted to him. It was the same shit every time, she gave me the once over. I would ask about my daddy and be led in by Bessie, that's her name. She always smelled like she washed her body in a knock off of CK One with a slight dash of funky ass.

My dad said she used to be a dancer but now she worked in security for a mall. I wondered who would hire somebody like her. Granted everybody needed a job, but maybe her looks alone made the robber think twice. Made my skin crawl to think about all of the times I heard her mumble about how fine I am and what she would do if she were 10 year younger. I know what she would do, keep wishing.

When I was there, nine times out of ten, my dad would be sitting in his underwear watching television and scratching his ass. The visits never lasted long, and when they ended, I would slip my father a couple of dollars and go home to my apartment not far away in North Philly.

When I looked at the clock on the wall of the store, I was surprised that it was already three o'clock in the afternoon, I knew I would work to about seven or eight and go home and take a hot shower and go to bed.

As I turned to restock the magazine shelf, I found myself being watched. When I looked up I saw the last person I expected to see my ex-girlfriend--Monica. What is she doing here? Wait, my mother.

I guess my mother figured she was helping me out by telling Monica where to find me. This whole thing was crazy. I didn't matter now. Monica was here now and in the flesh. The worst part is that since I didn't count on seeing her, I don't know what I could do to get rid of her. I'm not the type to stay cool with the girls I have dealt with.

What is she doing at my job? I was hoping she wasn't planning on causing some kind of scene. I got to work here. This didn't feel like an accidental meeting. I just looked at her long and hard, unsure of even what to say.

Damn it, why did she have to be wearing my favorite dress too? In the right light you could see right through it. She knew the effect it used to have on me. Damn what was a man supposed to do? I mean we could just talk right.

It was at that moment that I did the one thing I shouldn't have; I took a break and left the store with Monica. Maybe I was thinking with the wrong head. Maybe she has changed. Maybe.

As she walked slightly ahead of me I had to tell myself, 'Down boy.' It was too late, I was already hard. I know what you are thinking, what about Sista. I mean she only wanted to talk right, what harm could that do? At, least if she planned to cause trouble she'd be as far away from here as possible...

Nikki

I wasn't expecting to see Reggie last night. When he started crying, I was in shock. What for? He should have cried when he did it. Then I saw the ring. He was actually going to ask me to marry him. 'Reggie, no, please, do not do this,' I screamed.

I remembered how he dropped down on his knees and asked me to marry him. I immediately felt flushed with embarrassment and quickly tried to get him to get up, but he kept going on and on about how he loved me and how he needed me back in his life. Bullshit.

A year ago, he would have had me in the palm of his hand. At that moment, it seemed so phony and unreal. I quickly recovered and for the first time I wanted Reggie to look at me. I wanted to see what had become of me. People can look at you and never truly see what's there.

I am not the same person as when I first met him, nor am I the same person as the last time I saw him. I took a deep breath and took off my scarf. Reggie stood up, took a few steps, and fell backwards towards his jeep.

'Damn,' he said unable to control his initial reaction. Reggie regained his composure and asked now noticing the weight loss. 'What happened to you?'

'I have uterine cancer. Well, I had. They managed to get what they could and in the mean time, I also had chemotherapy, which is why I lost my hair and a lot of weight.'

'Baby, all that doesn't mean anything,' he said. Reggie held up the ring box that he still had clutching in his hand and began advancing towards me. 'I want you to be my wife.'

I held up my hand to stop him from coming any closer, 'It is a lot more than that Reggie. You fucked somebody else and you had a baby by this woman. You fucked my head up and you

159

fucked us up.'

'You know there were other women when we weren't together.' Reggie said like I said something wrong. 'You probably had somebody else too. Those other girls, like Renee, don't matter. I love you.'

'No, I was too busy being your fool. At one point I thought that they could have your time and you would come back to me, but now I was wrong. That was my mistake. Better yet, you were a mistake.'

Reggie licked his lips and smiled, 'But, baby, I love you and I want this thing to work out for us. If you were sick you could have called me.'

'No, I couldn't have. I tried to tell you that day in your apartment. But we never got a chance, Renee showed up. Just like you couldn't tell me about your daughter. Reggie, she is two years old. When were you going to tell me?' I stopped myself realizing the truth, 'After our baby was born...'

'I was going to tell you, but I couldn't. I didn't know how.'

'You're lying,' I countered.

'I...' he stopped. He turned around and rested his hands on the car. 'What about my baby? Where is my baby at? Or wasn't you going to tell me?' he asked not turning around.

'Our baby is dead, you selfish bastard' I said fighting back tears. 'I had an abortion because there was no way that I could carry the baby to term and fight this too. The way the tumor was spreading, it could have killed the baby any way.'

'Don't you get it Reggie?' I stared at him in disbelief. 'I have cancer. The same thing my mother died from. The same thing that kills thousands of women every year. Cancer. You didn't ask if I was okay. How am I doing? Do I need anything?

160

Just what about your baby.'

'And you didn't even tell me. Did you stop to think about how I would feel if you had an abortion?' Reggie said clearly upset. 'You are selfish Nikki, it's always about you. I hope you spend the rest of your life wondering what our child would have been like. I don't get you Nikki.'

Reggie wiped his face with his hands. 'I don't. You are saying I was a mistake, you were a mistake. I busted my ass to keep you happy and you go and do some shit like this, Nikki. You could have told me the truth.'

'But nah, you killed my child,' Reggie spat out the words. 'I don't know if it was a little boy or a little girl. That was my baby too. What you want me to do apologize? Well, I'm sorry. There are you satisfied. But you owe me one too.'

'I guess you didn't hear me,' I said moving towards him. I was angry. Mad. Pissed. Whatever you want to call it. 'You already have a baby. I had cancer. I could have died. Then where would you be?'

Reggie turned to look at me and saw I was in tears, 'I'm sorry, baby. Look we can have more if that's what you want. We can get married. We can do whatever you want, all that stuff we talked about. Just don't do this. Don't act like everything we had doesn't mean anything to you. I'm sorry for what I said. Let's just go back to my place.'

'No--WE can't,' I said through my tears. I was heated. 'Wait, all the things we talked about? You mean all the things I talked about. You have a child. Go home to her. Live out the dreams I planned for us. I was a fool for you Reggie. I loved you when I think you didn't even love yourself. You were everything to me. I gave up my life to suit yours and that was my mistake. One that I will never make again.'

I looked at Reggie and felt like I was seeing him for the first time, 'Here I was loving a man like you, when I barely

161

loved myself. It's funny because my last name is Love and because I gave all of myself to you, I didn't have anything for myself.'

My voice cracked. 'I loved you so much. I was so blinded by love for you that I couldn't see past the lies and the dumb shit and the drama. It almost cost me my life. Everybody said you were wrong for me and here I was being a fool. You hurt me, Reggie. You hurt me. If I never see you again, it will be too soon.'

Reggie reached out to comfort me, but I moved away. Reggie looked at me. 'What do you want me to do? I am sorry. Please forgive me. I love you. But to sit here and think about you having cancer is a lot for me to take. It makes me feel like I might lose you. Then all this stuff about the baby, Nikki. I don't know what more I can do or say. I can't--'

'Don't you think you did enough Reggie? You fucked somebody else. You already lost me. Look at me, I don't even know if you were ever mine to begin with,' I interjected. 'There is so much more that you simply don't know... I don't want to love you any more,' I said in barely a whisper. 'I don't know how. Don't you get that?'

'Baby,' Reggie said, trying to recapture the last bit of his manhood and save face. 'Don't you know you are the best thing that ever happened to me? I'm sorry.'

I started to walk away and turned to look at Reggie one last time. 'That is funny because everybody keeps telling me you are the worst thing that ever happened to me.' I laughed half amused. 'Go home, Reggie. Go. To think, I used to feel sorry for myself. Now I feel sorry for you.'

'But, I love you baby.' Reggie shouted as he watched me fumble for my keys. 'You love me too. Can't you find it in your heart to forgive me?' I didn't answer I merely opened the door and went inside and locked the door. I heard him calling but I just locked the door.

As I leaned back on the door, I whispered to myself, 'I am sorry, Reggie. I don't think I ever did love you.'

***

It was a little after four in the afternoon two days later when I picked up the phone, I felt a sense of relief creep through me when I heard Leonard's voice say 'hello.' As I listened to Leonard's voice, I felt at ease. We talked every day since we met. I never told Sista about Reggie and what he did and said. I didn't have to.

Things are over for Reggie and me. I found closure in my relationship with Reggie. I put an end to the years of hurt and pain and questions. I was ready to explore the world, one that included Leonard. With Leonard, Brian became a distant thought in my mind. For now. Leonard felt right when he hugged me.

'How was your day?' I asked.

'Better now that I am talking to you,' Leonard said and I could tell he was smiling. 'Are you free for dinner tonight? I didn't want to wait until Saturday to see you.'

'When and where?' I asked. It was then that I realized that things would be alright. The question is would Leonard feel the same…

Sista

It was getting late and I still hadn't heard from AJ. I went to bed early that night when Nikki told me she was going out. I resolved to go to bed without another thought about him. I thought of the cryptic message on my answering machine, when he told me that something came up. I wondered what that was.

In the morning, when I arrived at work, I was surprised to find Day waiting for me. When does he ever sleep? Day worked late and was always there early.

According to Day, he heard yesterday about a new arrival in the office. Before, he left; he mentioned something about how I was going to be surprised at who she is. When Walter walked in the office, he had an attractive, young woman on his arm. That's when I knew it was his daughter.

I immediately recognized the girl from the pictures sitting on Walter's desk. It was Walter's daughter, Monica or Monique. It was something like that. Walt made the introduction and announced that his daughter would be joining the company's accounting department.

I smiled and tried to be as friendly as possible. I won't lie, I could have cared less. Walt is a great guy but I didn't want to hear about his daughter no more than one of my friends calling me up to tell me all about what little Shay Shay did today. I had only heard about Walt's kids, took their messages, but this is the first time I met one.

At lunch, Day told me that Walt's daughter was all over him from day one. He had been asked to show her around and in their conversation, she mentioned more than once that she didn't like to wear panties. She was down right trifling.

I laughed and for a minute, I felt embarrassed that Walt has a freak for a daughter. It took me a second but I had to remind myself that Walt has been married three times and this daughter is Walt's daughter from his first wife. She might get it

164

from her father.

'She is like a vampire,' Day said feigning shock and surprise. 'She tried to fuck me.' I laughed as Day continued. 'She just met me. She has no shame. I am not that type of guy.'

What kind of guy are you?' I asked.

'Even if I was straight, I'd like to think I can do better than her. You would have gotten it first,' Day said smiling. I tossed the wadded up wrapper at Day, who barely missed getting hit.

'So what are you going to do?' I asked trying to get serious again. I knew Monica wouldn't let up. Women like that never do.

'She looks like a trick,' Day said. 'I am going to tell her I am not interested. She will get the hint. But she still is a vampire.'

'Now Day, she is my boss's daughter,' I replied smiling.

'So, just because she is Walt's daughter doesn't make her a hoe?' Day laughed. 'She looks like the nasty type. Kind of girl that lures guys with her nasty skills. She told me how she would suck my dick so good; I would be pulling the sheets out my ass.'

I laughed so hard that my soda flew out my mouth. 'Please stop, Day. I can't believe she told you that.'

'Yes, she did,' Day said laughing. 'Misplaced love.'

'Give her the benefit of the doubt,' I said. 'I never really talked to her other than messages for her father. She was always a bitch then but who knows. You might end up liking her as a friend. She might be trying to feel you out. See what you are about. Look at us, look at you and Nikki. She might really need a friend. You should be nice.'

'You, Nikki and I are different. This girl was looking to feel me up,' Day said as he gathered his tray up. Day looked at his watch. 'It is time to go. I want to get that report out by two.'

'You know you work too hard,' I said gathering up my stuff.

'Find me a relationship and I will stop,' Day said holding the door open for me. I smiled and Day had to know what I was thinking: go after Monica. Day must have read my mind. He poked me with his finger as I walked out the door.

As Day and I walked back to Medco, I couldn't believe my eyes. It couldn't be. I shook my head and looked again. Day, who was looking in a store window on Walnut Street, looked at me. He followed my eye sight and saw what I was looking at.

AJ standing on the corner being kissed by Walt's daughter. Day looked at me and realized that the woman from AJ's past and Walt's daughter were one and the same. Monica.

Day grabbed me and escorted me down the block, past them on the other side of the street as they continued to talk oblivious of whoever was around them. If he didn't Day knew he would be getting up bail money after I kicked both AJ and Monica's ass...

Nikki

When I got Day's phone call I was upset. Maybe it was because it was like having a flashback to Reggie and I couldn't bear to think of Sista hurt now. I was so glad I didn't owe a gun, somebody would have gotten shot. We'd start with AJ and use Reggie to finish off the round of bullets.

Anyway, from what I gathered from Day is this little bitch, Monica, Monique, some shit, is still fucking Sista's man and turned out to be Sista's supervisor's daughter and just got a job at the company. Now isn't that some shit?

I got on the phone and called Sista. Sista asked me to meet her at a bar and while I didn't drink any more because of my medication, I wanted to be there for Sista now. I found Sista in the back of the bar. She looked bad, but I didn't want to say it.

'Hey, girl,' I said as I sat down and grabbed Sista's hand.

'I messed up again,' Sista said, not wanting to meet my gaze. 'I think I need to just be by myself. I was comfortable being alone.'

'No, you didn't and no, you weren't. You thought you had a good man, we all did and now--' I paused realizing what I said. I decided to change my tactics. I started again. 'We just got lead down the road of promises, but you and I both know that the good intentions of a man don't pay the bills and it don't ensure a happy heart.'

Sista smiled. I ordered a soda as the waitress passed us.

'Sista, did you call him,' I asked. 'At least, hear what he has to say? This might not be another Paul'

'No. What for? To hear more lies, I've been through that shit enough. Did you call Reggie and hear him out.'

167

'He said what he had to say and I let that shit go. But this is about AJ, not Reggie. It isn't like AJ had a baby by this girl. Right?'

'I am not you, Nikki, you dealt with that shit better than me. Would you take Reggie back knowing he slept with Renee?'

'No, Sista, I don't think I could. Maybe if Renee went down in a horrific plane crash, I'd be there for Reggie's daughter. Not for Reggie though,' I said half amused with myself. 'We are talking about AJ. You love this man. Sista, it isn't like he got a baby by her. What are you going to do, quit your job because he used to mess with her? She is Walter's daughter.'

'No. I happen to like my job. I just think it is about time that I learned to be by myself. I'm through with love. Whatever the hell love is. It shouldn't feel like this. If people can't explain what love is, why do they keep using that word?'

'Girl, stop. Good men are out there. Look at Leonard. If you had told me that I would have him in my life now, I would tell you to stop lying. They are out there. Look at your brother. Brian. Good men exist, they just make fucked up decisions some times.'

'Who are you kidding?' Sista said looking at me. 'Weren't you the one that told me to talk to Paul and look how that shit turned out? It isn't like they sell good men at the market. If they did I would have had my fair share of them by now. I would have brought them in packs of six a week.'

'But there are seven days in a week,' I said looking at Sista questioning.

'Even God rested on the seventh day,' Sista laughed. I laughed too. That was a good sign.

'Well, what are you going to do, start a lonely hearts club with Day? Sit around bemoaning your life.'

'Maybe it would be easier to be a lesbian,' Sista looked at me out of the corner of her eye. I grimaced.

'Girl, please, you know we're not any better. Shit I wouldn't even touch my own body on some days,' I said dismissing Sista's remark. 'I heard this guy say today the dumbest shit. He said some shit about never trusting anything that bleeds for three days but don't die. But, I don't trust a man if he don't fall asleep after sex.'

Sista smiled again and I knew I was getting through to her. I didn't like to see Sista upset and with everything I know that we've been through, I know I needed to be there. I made a mental note to call Day when we got home to tell him that we were okay.

'Why is it,' Sista asked while stirring her drink. 'that these men seem to think that we are always the ones fucking up when it is them?'

I looked at her and rolled my eyes. 'Who are you asking? Then, some of them run out and try to get a white girl hoping that a white woman will not give them problems. Take that back, it isn't always a white girl, just some other girl. Somebody that ain't you.'

'That is because most brothers know that a black woman will not take shit from him. We expect more of our men.' Sista laughed at what she just said.

'More than the 'get some pussy free' card that we get. Let me stop playing, we know that shit isn't true about all black men,' I said drinking the last of the Sprite. 'On the other hand, that's not always true about any man. It is just that some things just don't work out. Some things just aren't meant to be.'

I paused, 'Look at Reggie and me. I thought that that was a forever kind of love. But sometimes, that's what happens. We can't go on being bitter. Sometimes girl, you have to let go and let God handle it.'

'Right. But, I keep dreaming Nikki that I am going to get that shit right one day. Some day. Some how. I am hurt because even if he didn't do anything with her that he should have said something. Nikki, he told me everything about her and I didn't put it all together. What kind of shit is that?'

I looked at Sista and reached across the table to squeeze Sista's hand. 'Who knew she would come to work at your job? Or that she was Walter's daughter. Shit happens. This is the time that you move on. If it is truly meant to be God will show you.'

'Sometimes,' I said as if I was almost talking to myself, 'you have do what your mother always say and ask God to show you where you are going wrong. If it's a relationship that is wrong for you, you just have to prepare to get your heart broken. You can't get flowers without rain.'

'You are right,' Sista said. She smiled. I patted her hand and then I motioned for the waitress to pay our tab. The last place we needed to be is sitting in a bar. I wanted to get Sista home. I noticed Sista barely touched her drink. I know in my heart Sista didn't want to get drunk, she needed to talk.

Out of curiosity, I took a sip from Sista's glass. It was soda. As I turned to leave a toothless guy smiled at me and walked over to the table, blocking my path. Sista was out the door and already waiting by the car. I looked at the man again, irritated at being held up.

'You look good darling,' he smiled and blew his breath in my face. 'What is your name?'

I realized I wasn't up for the drama looked him dead in his eyes and said, 'Herpes.'

The man looked at me and smiled like he was thinking about it, 'That is pretty.'

I just shook my head and walked out the door.

170

Paul

I pulled up to the house Angela now shared with Vanessa and watched Vanessa come out of the door. She looked at me with disgust and then turned to go back in the house and called for Angela. I felt like I should be the one upset, she messed up my marriage. Vanessa got in her car and left. Angela came to the door and then moved aside to let me in.

I have been here before but never got as far as the porch. Angela looked sickly and lacking the glow most women had. Angela called me because she said we needed to talk. Angela settled into a seat across from me as I sat down. She would go in any day now.

'How are you?' Angela asked.

'I am fine?' I said realizing that Angela wouldn't look me in the eyes still.

'Paul, look,' Angela said. 'I want this to work for our child. I want us to come to some kind of agreement. '

'What makes you think I don't?' I said looking at her. Angela met my gaze briefly. 'All of this hostility between you and Vanessa has got to stop. I talked to her and now I am talking to you.'

'You were my life and she fucked that up.'

'No, Paul, I ran from a relationship with her. I thought we could make a life together. But I was wrong. I made a mistake.'

'So our child is a mistake?' I said recoiling like somebody had slapped me.

'No, he, it is a boy, is the best thing that could have come out of this. Paul, I love you just not that way.' Angela reached out to touch my hand. I pulled away from her.

171

'I gave up on a good woman for you. But you didn't make a mistake, Angela. No, I did. You weren't worth it. If you did make a mistake, it was getting caught.'

I looked at her, 'In the back of my mind, I wanted to believe that we could work things out and you and I could get back some of what we had but I was mistaken. I feel sorry for you. You wanted her, you can have her. But next time, I will not be so much of a sucker for you to come crawling back to.'

'You are wrong Paul; Vanessa loves me and this baby'

'My baby,' Paul raged at Angela.

'Our baby,' Angela countered.

'Look, I am going to leave it to you one day to explain why he has two Mommies and a Daddy'

'I don't want to fight you, Paul. I think you don't have a problem with the fact that I left you for a woman. I think you have a problem that I am with somebody and it's not you. So maybe it is best that you go before one of us says something stupid. I am not trying to argue with you.'

I got up went to the door. I paused and turned around and said, 'We already did--I do. Remember that Angela, in sickness and health, for richer or for poorer, not until your wife's girlfriend comes back. I had a good woman and I gave her up for you. You know what this conversation isn't even worth continuing. Do you.'

For years, I had heard the rumors about my aunt. My cousin, her daughter, had said a couple of things that kind of confirmed it. Each time, I looked at her, it wasn't possible.

My aunt would always proclaim when the conversation came up that she didn't want any woman's breast on her. But my mother wasn't the type to lie and she quickly put to rest the rumors over dinner. I didn't want to believe it then about my aunt just as I didn't want to believe it now about my wife.

'Mom, did you know Aunt Carol is moving in with Miss Mary to help her out,' I remembered the conversation.

'Boy,' my mother said looking at me and laughing. 'I thought you knew? Boy, you are still in denial. Here I thought I raised you better than that.'

'Know what?' I stopped eating. 'What are you saying, Mom? Tell me you aren't saying--'

'That your aunt is gay, a lesbian. I never gave a damn, I thought you knew though.' I stared at my mother in disbelief. My mother chewed the last of the food in her mouth and continued, 'Listen, if a person goes on a rant about how they don't like something, there is a thin line between love and hate.

'I remember how,' my mother continued, 'she said she didn't like another woman's breast on her? How would she know if she never had it? All she ever talks about is gay people like somebody cares. She isn't moving in with that woman to help that lady out. Child, she is going with that lady...'

First my aunt, now my wife, I looked back at the house one last time. Angela was in the window. I lost her. Now what was he supposed to do? Just then I thought about Sista. Maybe, we still have a chance...

Day

I was on my way home and I knew it was already late. As I walked to the parking lot near my job, I saw a familiar face waiting for the bus nearby. The person called out. I waved back. AJ walked towards me and shook my hand.

'What is up?' I asked.

'Nothing, how about you.' AJ smiled happy to see me. 'I was scared for a minute to even say something. Seeing how...' AJ's voice trailed off.

'You never treated me wrong,' I replied.

'How is she?'

'Sista is Sista. She's going to be fine.' I motioned towards the parking lot. 'If you like I can give you a ride.'

'What are you doing now?' AJ said. 'Can I talk to you for a minute? I need your help.' I hesitated for a minute, not knowing if I should get involved in the situation with Sista and AJ. I know what I saw. He was kissing that girl. But me being me, I agreed to listen.

We both walked back towards Chestnut Street to a small Chinese restaurant. As we settled in, we ordered something to eat and I looked at AJ.

'How is she really?' AJ asked.

I exhaled and looked at AJ, 'She is hurt. I have known Sista for a while, she is like the sister I never had and to be upfront with you, that shit is fucked up.'

'I know Day. But, Monica, it has been over with her for like a while and then she show up and I am with Sista.'

'Did you sleep with her? AJ, look man, I know what I

174

saw.'

'No, I swear. I won't lie, I thought about it. She's been coming to my job and we went out to lunch that day. Then I went to give her a hug and she kissed me. But, I can't tell Sista that, not after that stuff with the other guy. She will not believe me. Monica popped up on me. She kissed me. I saw the two of you walking away.'

'AJ, you don't know, I did you and Monica a favor that day. Sista was ready to kill you both. Listen, did you even call Sista, AJ? I think you should be telling her this. Not me.'

'And have her hang up on me again. Day, I tried. I miss her and I love her and I don't know how to tell her. It has been a minute since I talked to her. Yes, I was with Monica but no, I didn't sleep with her. I have no reason to lie.'

'Just go see Sista then. Sista is one of those upfront kinds of girls. She is evil as shit at times, but she has a heart. One that gets broken like you or me. She hurting, but if you let her go it is only going to cause her to hurt more. Tell her what was up with Monica.' AJ looked at me. I stuck out my hand. 'And I'll see what I can do on my end.'

AJ reached across the table and shook my hand as our food was being served. 'Deal.' By the time I got home from talking to AJ, I was too tired to do anything else but lay down. My talk with AJ had gone well though.

AJ is a really nice guy and I wanted the best for Sista and if AJ is it then by all means, they should be together. I'm going to try to help. We ate and talked. AJ was a cool guy. I dropped AJ off and I went home.

Walking in, I checked the mail; it has been four days after my parent's anniversary. I sat on the couch flicking through the mail looking for the card I recently sent. As I looked at the various bills, I was surprised because it wasn't there.

175

I wanted to believe that it probably got lost in the mail. But, that was only wishful thinking on my part since I knew that eventually every card I ever sent came back. It had also been awhile since I picked up the phone and called my folks and just listen to make sure they were okay.

It has been a long time since I have been home. Melvin hasn't called me in a minute with any news. He only left a message about visiting. That's the last thing I needed, Melvin in Philly.

I won't lie, I missed my folks. I missed sitting around the table at dinner talking to my parents about their day. My mother, Violet, is a good cook. I could almost smell her greens. It was almost 11 as I settled in to watch the news when the knock on my door came.

I wondered why whoever it was didn't call. I hoped that nothing has happened. If it was Sista, I was ready to give her my car keys, call Brian and they can go get whoever, on their own. I knew that the door to my building is broke so if it is her, she wouldn't have a problem getting in. Knowing Sista, nothing would stop her.

I looked through the peephole and realized nobody was there. I went into my bedroom and grabbed my robe. When no other knock came, I opened the door. It was too late for a kid to be playing on my door. In an apartment building, they would have to live there.

As I opened the door half expecting somebody to be there. I moved out into the hall just in time to see a woman going down the stairs with a suitcase in hand. I felt my breath catch in my chest when I realized exactly who she was. I pulled the door closed and ran after her. As I got to the stairwell, I called out, 'Mama.'

My mother turned around and looked up to see me standing there and tears welled in her eyes. I ran down the steps, grabbed my mother up into my arms, and cried.

176

'What are you doing here?' I asked releasing my grip. 'Daddy? Is daddy okay?'

I searched my mother's face for an answer. My mother just shook her head yes. I hugged her again and then grabbed her bag to take her upstairs.

Not much was said because I realized my mother has been traveling all day. I ran my mother a warm bath and waited patiently smoking a cigarette until she came out. I was on my second one when she came out because I was just that stressed. I only smoked when I was stressed and this was one of those times.

My mother looked at my place when she came out and I guess she felt immediately at home. She started to speak, but I ushered her into my room and put her to bed with a kiss on her cheek. We'd talk in the morning. I stayed up for hours afterwards unable to sleep.

I thought about my card and realized for the first time, maybe my mother gave in and wanted to see me. But why not just write me back?

I knew something more was brewing. Something not even I could begin to understand. I know in time I would have to. It didn't matter. My mother is here and she traveled for hours to make it to see me, I know it is something big though. But what...

Sista

I got a call from Day about noon on Friday and when he told me that his mother was in town, I cried. I was happy for him. It seems that his mother had left his father. She couldn't be with a man, claim she loved the Lord and deny the child that God gave her. Apparently for years, Day's father hid his cards and letters. Ms. Violet never knew if her son had lived or died.

'What are you going to do?' I asked.

'I don't know. I missed so much time. I don't know where to begin. All these years,' Day said. "I don't know.'

'Well, enjoy you time with your mother. Make sure you show her the city, the Art Museum, the Parkway, Independence Hall, the Gallery, do it up real big. I'm going to be mad at you if she doesn't see Reading Terminal, Penn's Landing or South Street. Maybe you can bring her over to meet my Mom. She could use the company.' I could tell Day was smiling on the other end.

'All that though? I'm trying to keep her here for a minute; we have time to do all that. Your Mom's house is a definite destination. I've got to introduce her to my family. She would like that. Thanks,' Day said before hanging up.

I realized that we'd have to have lunch another time, giving him a chance to spend time with his mother and catch up. I needed something else to do. But what? I picked up the phone to call my own mother to see how she is doing. But before I got a chance to, Paul was already on the line…

Sista and Paul

When Paul showed up at my door that next night, I didn't know what to think. Nikki was at a meeting and maybe I let that slip to Paul when I spoke to him. Maybe that was the encouragement that I gave for him to stop by.

One thing is for certain, two things for sure, he definitely isn't going to get some. At that moment, I would have felt more content being with Day and his mother finding out about how her tour of Philadelphia went.

I spoke to Day again earlier and heard Day laugh like I never heard him laugh before. Miss Violet loved Philly and Day loved having her there. It was better talking to Day than seeing this married man. He is married. Damn.

As Paul stood at the door, he motioned with his head, as if to ask could he come in. I stepped aside and smelled his cologne as he walked in. Shit, why me, Lord, I thought. That isn't good. Sure wasn't.

I instantly felt a sensation come over me remembering our past relationship. He took a seat on the couch and buried his face in his hands. I wanted to feel sorry for him, but in the back of my mind I know that he dumped me. We could have talked all he wanted over breakfast after he married me. He didn't even try.

'I needed somebody to talk to. Somebody who'd understand me,' he began. I thought to myself, what about one of your boys? Your half ass friends that used to laugh at me. Knowing damn well, I was too much woman for them.

Instead, I responded, 'So you chose me?' I sat next to him on the couch, making a point to keep my robe closed and hide from him the gown I was wearing. I am not giving this man some, I thought. His leg briefly touched mine and I moved away scared I might have to touch him back.

'She, Angela, decided to keep the baby and raise it with Vanessa. I want to be a father to my child, but I can't if Angela is with Vanessa.' I wanted to say no; you're still fucked up feeling like you weren't man enough to hold on to your woman.

Instead, I grabbed his hand and said, 'It isn't your fault what that woman did. Look, you need to give it time and see what happens.' Paul then looked at me and was overcome with a sense of regret. I was being nice and he treated me bad.

'Paul,' I began again, 'You know you are not to blame for that woman's actions. She did what she did. She chose to be with another woman,' I looked at Paul and thought I sensed remorse for what he had done to me. Good, I thought. He deserves to suffer for what he did.

Paul reached out and hugged me, catching me off guard. I was surprised that I would let him hug me and more surprised about how good it felt. My mind was screaming that he is married, but at that point my body was urging me on. My body won the argument.

Paul pulled back and looked at me. It has been a while for him and he knew what he wanted—me. Paul kissed me and to his surprise, I kissed him back. My body gave way under his touch. Suddenly, I felt hot like I was playing with fire. I promised to ask God for forgiveness later on. Shit, I remember what he did that night with those boxes of Lemonheads. Made me change the way I looked at candy.

Yes, Lemonheads, as in the candy, damn it. He popped two in his mouth and swirled them around on his tongue as he sucked on my breast. Shit. I was still thinking about it when Paul kissed me more intensely. I began to wonder what a future would be like with Paul, now. Then I thought about his wife and child. Did I really want to be somebody's stepmother?

Paul is the only man that ever brought me to multiple orgasms and knew that my mouth got dry and cool when I came. That's how he knew I came and never stopped until I was begging for a glass of water. Sitting here, feeling his lips and his hands, I realized Paul had made a mistake dealing with Angela.

No man is perfect. He definitely isn't a lima bean like some men. A lima bean is a man that expected a woman to do everything for him, fucks him, suck him and don't expect him to be shit. Maybe Paul has changed and this is not a rebound thing.

Still, I wanted more. The question is could Paul give it to me? Once I loved him but could I love him once more. Just then I thought to myself that I wasn't thinking about Paul, but about AJ. I didn't even given him a chance to explain what happened.

I was sitting here about to have sex with Paul as a way of easing my pain about AJ. Like my having sex with Paul would make AJ pay. AJ was going on with his life. The phone calls and messages had stopped. I should just let it go right. I know I still wanted AJ in my heart. He deserved a chance to explain.

According to Day, nothing happened between Monica and AJ. Now I was getting with Paul because I didn't feel strong enough to deal with AJ. Nikki's words echoed in my mind, 'At least AJ didn't have a baby by her.'

I couldn't accuse AJ of something other than a kiss that I didn't see myself. Though I genuinely have love in my heart for Paul, I know that we could never been again. I pulled away much to Paul's surprise. He looked at me with this dumb look.

'Did I do something wrong?' Paul asked quietly as I walked to the door and opened it, drawing my robe around my body.

'Yes, you did, Paul, you got married to another woman. I can be a booty call for you, but I think I want more for myself.' With that Paul left without as much as a backward glance. I sat on my couch and picked up a picture that I recently took with AJ and finally exhaled. I closed my eyes as I wrapped my arms around the picture. 'I know, God, I have to get him back...'

181

Brian

I arrived at my mother's house for dinner and was happy to see everybody there. I had a lot on my mind. Maybe since there is a full house, I would have something to take my mind off of things. That is until Nikki popped her head out of the kitchen and then came over to hug me.

Nikki was helping my mother and Ms. Violet cook Sunday dinner? I hope not, I never seen her cook in all the years I knew her. I wanted to live. I didn't need my stomach pumped tonight. I had enough to deal with.

Day and Cliff were watching something on television, so I sat in. As I took a seat and Day immediately recognized the look on my face. Day asked if I was okay but I said we'd talk and dropped the conversation.

This didn't go unnoticed by Sista. I felt an arm go around my neck and smelled Nikki's perfume. Since Nikki had gotten sick, we've gotten closer than ever before. I liked that. Nikki's confidence came back full blast and she looked good.

'Hi, Boo Boo Bear,' Nikki said.

'You know you haven't called me that since we were younger,' I said with a smile.

'Some things never change,' Nikki laughed. 'So where is your new little girlfriend?'

'I could ask you the same thing,' I countered. 'Who is this guy I am hearing about?'

'Are you jealous?' Nikki asked.

'No, but to answer your question about Tanya, she came and went,' I laughed.

'You are nasty,' Nikki said hitting my arm playfully.

'You better not let your mother hear you talking like that.'

'I am grown. But to answer your question, I might be,' I said feigning indignation. 'Who is he?'

'A friend,' Nikki said. She smiled, kissed me and walked away.

I saw my mother come out of the kitchen with a ham, I immediately got up and took the tray to put on the dining room table and kissed my mother's cheek afterward. I ducked my head in the kitchen, said hello to Ms. Violet, and stole a piece of cornbread. Ms. Violet promptly put me out of the kitchen.

Day's mom has been in Philly for months now. She is a very nice lady and it became obvious where Day got his personality from. I liked her the minute I met her. She reminded me a lot of my Mom. It even felt good when Day introduced me as his best friend.

Most of the time, I am too busy working to have real friends except Day and Shawn, my buddy from high school. It's hard to find people that are cool with you for the sake of friendship and not what they can get out of you.

Shawn rarely made it to dinner, but Day was usually there. But, when I met Day, the guy was just cool as can be. My parents raised me well. Who cares about him being gay? I wasn't and as long as he respected me and how I felt, we were cool.

Sista looked out from the kitchen to see me talking to Day. Day noticed her stare first and looked up. I looked at Sista and smiled. Sista knew.

I sensed that she knew what is going on. She had to. Nikki busted in on Day and my conversation when Day was pulled aside by his mother to help set the table for dinner. Nikki looked at me.

'You still curious about Leonard,' Nikki asked.

'I might be,' I said as I saw Sista now staring at me and Nikki.

'He is a friend,' Nikki said. 'Besides every time I turn around you have somebody new, some new heifer.'

'Stop. Those girls don't mean anything to me,' I said. 'But look at you. You really look good. I like it. You look good.'

Nikki couldn't ignore the serious note in my voice. She quickly tried to change the subject out of fear of saying the wrong thing. 'So are you seeing anybody yet?'

'Other than, 'I laughed, 'my lunch dates with you. No, I am not seeing anybody. Don't have the time. Still waiting on you.'

'Stop playing boy,' Nikki said with a grin.

'What if I wasn't playing?' I said, just then Miss Violet called everyone to eat and Nikki walked away. I watched her move into the dining room and soon followed. Day caught my eye and I shrugged. Just then the phone rang as Sista stepped into the living room the telephone rang. It was Eric.

'Hello,' Sista said.

'What is up Sista, What y'all doing?' Eric said trying to sound upbeat. Sista could hear the struggle.

'I just took Mommy's stuffing out the oven and we are about to sit down and eat.' Sista looked up to see me looking at her and she mouthed the word 'Eric.' 'And how are you doing?' Sista asked.

'I just finished up my carpentry program and before I get out next year I am going to work on my thing to study plumbing.' I heard him say as I picked up the receiver in the kitchen.

Sista fought back the tears as she heard Eric's voice crack. 'Well, I'll be up to see you on Saturday and we can talk about what you are going to do when you come home next year.'

Eric's voice finally gave way and Sista could tell that he was crying, 'So are y'all all right? Everything cool? Is Mommy okay?'

'She's better. We'll be all right when you come home?' Sista was crying too. My Mom went over to her and hugged her. Cliff gave Sista some tissue as Loretta, Nikki and Ms. Violet went into the dining room. My mother went over again, hugged Sista, and kissed her. Loretta gave her an evil look.

'We are going to be just fine.' My mother whispered in Sista's ear. As the family gathered for dinner, Sista said a prayer for the people that couldn't join them. In that moment, we all felt my father was with us and smiled. I returned to the family to eat.

I paused and looked long and hard at Nikki and then at Day. I bowed my head as the family started prayer. When I looked up I saw Sista's eyes on me. What was that about…

Nikki and Reggie Who?

I agreed to meet Leonard for dinner and I was dressed to impress. I was still feeling good after spending time with Sista and the family Sunday. I wanted my outfit to reflect that. I also know that Day had spoken to AJ.

AJ is not Reggie. I was rooting for him despite what I told Sista when things happened to move on. If he didn't sleep with that girl then I wanted to believe him. I needed to believe him. He's not Reggie or Paul.

Despite my best efforts, I couldn't get Brian's questions about Leonard out of my head. Since I have been spending time with Leonard, I found myself more relaxed. With Leonard, I didn't feel any pressure to give more than I was ready to. He respected me and I needed that. Things between the two of us started slow.

After our dinner date, I spoke to him several times on the phone each day. I continued to go to each of the grief support meetings where Leonard had even gotten me to open up to the others about my feelings. His logic was that just the same way that they opened up to me, I should do the same. I tried but there were some things I wasn't comfortable telling anyone but God right now.

I knew that Leonard likes me and I like him and not once did he press for anything more serious than the few dates that we went on and a few kisses. My body regained some of its former glory and my hair I kept cut short in a Toni Braxton styled hairdo. I looked good and I felt it.

Leonard had only lost his wife two years ago and I wasn't ready for anything serious. I have to admit he is a breath of fresh air from Reggie. Still I thought about Brian and wondered if he was serious about what he said at dinner.

'Damn it, Brian,' I said aloud. Every time I was sure what I felt for Brian was through, those feelings returned. Sure

Brian can stay out of Sista's relationship problems but was on my ass like a dirty diaper when he thought somebody new was trying to get with me. He needed to step up to the plate then.

I can handle whatever Brian had to offer. It was different with Brian than when I thought about Reggie. I no longer felt hatred towards Reggie, but instead, I felt sorry for him.

Somebody told me that Renee had planned to move to Baltimore with her daughter and Reggie was trying to do everything he could to stop her short of murder. I shouldn't care but I was thinking about little Nicole. She deserved to be happy.

Nicole didn't ask to be born into their mess. My life with Reggie was over and hers is just beginning. Once I thought I had seen Reggie in his jeep but when I saw the driver I felt at last it was over and I was ready to move on with my life.

I had even been offered a job to work at Medco in Day's department. That way I would get to see Day and Sista on a daily basis. The only problem is that I know that I would be seeing a lot of Miss Monica. She needed to get a grip. It's never that serious when it comes to any relationship.

Monica was nasty towards everyone. Maybe because, according to Day, she spent the better part of every day leaving messages on AJ's machine that went unanswered. At least from what Day could see. Miss Monica was miserable.

With the job at Medco, I felt like I would be able to offer Sista a chance to move into a bigger place, just the two of us and we'd split the rent instead of me just contributing to it. I needed a change of pace and I know that working with Sista and Day would make things even better.

I went to the doctor's the day before and was relieved to be told that I would be fine. I smiled at myself in the mirror and I know that I've been given a second chance. I heard Leonard's car horn and picked up my purse to leave. Maybe things would be all right...

Day

When Nikki decided to return to work, I suggested she come work with Sista and me at Medco. Since the job is in my department, I was there to welcome her with open arms. It was only right. Unfortunately, the job put her in a close working relationship with Monica, who was beginning to get on my last nerves.

'She was like a rabid dog now,' I told Sista over lunch. 'She has issues. Serious issues.'

'You should just fuck her,' Sista replied sounding like Nikki. 'She likes you. Can't you tell?'

I laughed but when Sista didn't laugh I thought she was serious. Monica turned into a real bitch with everybody, especially when she visited her father. Sista apparently never let on that she was the woman that was seeing AJ. Sista's job meant more to her than that.

Once Nikki was working there, the relationship between Nikki, Sista and me became apparent. More than once, I heard Monica mumble bitch under her breath as Nikki and I walked by. But, Nikki wasn't bothered by it. She was used to it.

When Sista came to visit our department on our breaks, Monica went into a fit especially whenever she tried to join in on the conversation; the three of us stopped talking.

It wasn't like Monica didn't have friends at the job. She hung out with Keisha Nunyuh and Bette Bette Jones, two cackling hens in the company that talked about everything and everybody. It never failed.

When one of the secretaries got a new hairdo, they would tell her that her hair looked sharp and how it brought out her face. Behind the same woman's back, they would offered to take up collections to get the rest of it fixed.

It didn't help that they encouraged Monica to go after AJ, never knowing that she didn't have a chance. It was funny how they gave out advice about men when Bette Bette didn't have a man and Keisha, while she had one; he isn't a good one.

Keisha's man, as she proclaimed him to be, has been locked up for murder for 10 years. According to Keisha, she was almost single because her man is on death row.

'Girl, you better go on and get your man,' Bette Bette said loud as ever. 'Throw some good pussy on him. Make him say damn. Some good sex will fix him up just right.'

'Then what,' Monica asked. 'He's still hung up on some girl. I want him. I need to find out who she is and go handle that.'

'Men are going to be men. Why fight the other girl? He did it. No, you need to listen to her, girl,' Keisha interjected. 'Bette would know. Bette has got like ten kids.' I immediately tuned them out.

I thought about Brian as I started in on my work and wondered if in fact, he told Sista about what was going on. But, from what Brian said, I know that Brian wouldn't even begin to know how. Just then, the phone rang.

'Day, Day, Day,' Brian jumped in.

'You are going to live long,' I laughed. 'But, shouldn't you be calling Nikki?'

'Funny. You are really funny. You better not say anything. I don't want you saying anything to my sister or Nikki,' Brian told me.

'Who am I going to tell?' I asked. 'Your sister and then get my ass to beat? Or Nikki and get my ass beat when Sista find out her brother was trying to hook up with her best friend and she was the last to know.'

'Cool,' Brian said laughing.

I stopped realizing there was something missing from the conversation, 'What happened to that other girl you were messing with? Leslie. The girl from Darby? Or is it Chester.'

'You don't want to know,' Brian laughed.

'What is so funny?' I asked.

'She stank,' Brian replied.

'Her breath?' I asked now curious.

'No, her ass,' Brian replied.

'Tell me you didn't sleep with her,' I replied.

'No, Day,' Brian laughed, 'You met her, she is that cutesy type. Always acting like she shopped at this store and that store. She had this and that. That was cool, I guess. A bit high strung but cool. I thought she was the one. Then I saw her house. If a strong wind hit it, it would have been knocked over. She didn't even have a set of matching plates.'

'You are lying,' I laughed.

'I kid you not,' Brian continued. 'I took two steps and went from the front door to the back door. It was so small. So we are sitting there and she smells like what the fuck. If there is one thing I can't stand, it is a female that stank. That is a hell no.'

'So what did you do?' I asked seriously.

'Let me finish,' Brian laughed. 'She was dressed nice, skirt, hair done, the whole nine,' Brian continued. 'So I was rubbing on her and I smelled it. I was like no the fuck she didn't. I mean here I was overlooking that her breast had low self-esteem. Her breasts were damn near her waist when she took the bra off. So I told her to sit on my lap.'

'Day, she thought I was trying to be sexy. But I had a plan. When she sat down I inched my hand up her skirt and put my hands in her panties.'

'She let you and she smelled like that?' I asked. 'Some women do have bad days.'

'Don't defend her,' Brian laughed. 'She stank, she stank. So listen, I leaned in and whispered in her ear. 'I want to tear you up girl.' She giggled, 'You do.' I was like 'Yeah, I am going to do what I never did before.' She knew I hated oral sex but the thought of me doing her, she was hot. Her juices were flowing'

'Should I be listening to this?' I asked.

'You asked,' Brian went on. 'So I said, 'But first I want you to do something for me.' She asked, 'What?' 'You aren't going to do it,' I said. 'How you know?' she said. I had her. So I kept messing with her. 'You not going to do it,' I said. 'Yes, I will,' she said as I kept rubbing harder. 'What you want me to do?''

Brian started laughing so hard that he dropped the phone.

'My bad,' Brian continued. Brian knew I was waiting on pins and needles for the rest.

'So I pulled my hands out of her underwear and said 'Smell that shit.' Why did I do that? Day, she got up cursing and swinging like it was me that came over smelling like that. Then she called me a couple of days later while she was in the tub and I had to ask her, 'Shouldn't you be washing?'

'Did she call you back?' I asked out of curiosity.

'No,' Brian laughed. 'Would you? My track record with women is bad. Remember Tanya, the girl I introduced you and Nikki to that day, she was the worst.'

'What did she do?' I asked as I looked around wondering who had been listening to my conversation.

'She told me that she was a freak and just wanted to do it to me one time,' Brian said seriously. 'But would you sleep with a girl that told you she had four abortions and a miscarriage?'

'She's trifling,' I replied as I watched Monica, Bette, and Keisha as they came back to their desks. 'Why would anybody tell you something like that? That's just dumb.'

'Look I got to run, remember what I said. Don't say anything. Please Day,' Brian said.

'Okay,' I agreed and hung up. I put the thought out of my mind, who would I tell? I looked at my watch. I wanted to call my mother to see how she is doing. My mother hadn't made any plans of going home any time soon and I was glad she hadn't even mentioned leaving.

My mother has been here for a while and I welcomed the change of pace she brought. The holidays were coming, the first I would have spent with her in years and I wanted her here.

I picked up the phone receiver and was about to dial the phone, when Nikki popped her head into my cubicle and asked if I talked to Brian. When I said we just talked, Nikki told me that we needed to talk…

Sista

I didn't plan on visiting Brian. Well, I did but not that time of night. It wasn't like I had been invited over. But my curiosity got the best of me. So when I busted up into Brian's apartment and noted the look of surprise on his face that I was even there, I damn sure didn't apologize for doing it. I just took a seat.

I looked at my brother, who was wearing only sweat pants and a t-shirt and said hello. Dressed like that, I know he wasn't going anywhere. He would rather be caught dead than wear sweat pants outside.

I looked around in the apartment expecting someone else to be there. But, Brian was alone and he sat back on the couch and resumed flicking through the channels.

Brian pressed the play button on the VCR again and the 'Color Purple' came to life on the screen. I settled in and picked up the bowl of popcorn on the table. It has been days since the dinner at my mother and I wanted to find out what was going on.

'What is up, Sis?' Brian said sounding bored.

'You,' I said in my most cutesy voice. Brian had to know what was on my mind. We are brother and sister and I know what is going on. It is my friend after all.

'What do you mean by that?' he asked stopping the tape. 'You are trying to tell me something?'

'I saw y'all, Brian. You and Day, you two are up to something and I want to know what it was.'

'Why?' Brian said questioningly. 'Did Nikki say something to you about what was going on?'

'Like what, 'I asked. Brian jumped up. 'What was she supposed to say?'

193

'Nothing.' I wasn't convinced and looked at Brian more intensely. It was almost if I stared hard enough he would start talking.

'What?' Brian said looking at me for the first time since I asked what was going on. 'You act like I did something.'

'I don't know, did you?' I asked again.

'Remind me to kick Day's ass.'

'Kick Day's ass for what?'

'Did he tell you what was going on?' Brian watched my jaw drop. I quickly covered.

'Shut up,' I said out loud.

'What are you talking about?' Brian said turning the television off.

'You...' I ventured.

'And Nikki,' Brian said trying not to meet my eyes.

I looked at Brian again, 'Nikki?'

'I tried to tell her how I felt but the other day wasn't right. To her, I am always going to be like a brother. Nikki is like serious high maintenance.'

I looked at Brian and threw a pillow off the couch at him as he stood up to go to the kitchen. 'What would you rather be, low maintenance? Some starter kit chick that you can feel good about changing her life with a few shots, getting her teeth fixed and keeping her out of bargain basement stores. You don't know that. Nikki needs a good man. A reformed heathen like you might fit the bill.'

'What about Leonard?' Brian asked as he laughed at me. It was then that Brian took his first glance at me.

194

'What about him? From what I understand, he is just a friend. He is cool, but he isn't her man and he isn't you.' Brian breathed deeply at what I just said. 'Handle that. Go get her. I rather her be with you than anybody else. You know and can appreciate her.'

'So what you are saying is that I have your blessing.' Brian looked at me and waited on my response. I smiled at my brother and kissed him on the cheek.

'You are my brother and Nikki is my best friend. You and Nikki are a match made in heaven.'

Brian looked at me and smiled, 'Maybe this time I will get it right. Like maybe she will be the one to love me as much as you do.' I hugged my brother. Only problem for Brian to solve is when is the right time to tell Nikki? I say the sooner the better...

Brian

I was dressed to impress. New suit. Fresh haircut. I displayed a killer smile. When I stepped of the elevator of Nikki's floor, everyone stopped and stared at me. I stopped past the receptionist desk and signed in as I did many times before. I passed Sista's office and waved at her as I was going by.

Sista followed me around to the other side of the office. I almost bumped into a tall, brown-skinned girl and stopped to help her pick up the book she dropped. Her coffee mug said 'Monica.' I smiled and she went on her way. Monica rolled her eyes as she saw Sista following me.

When Monica saw me walk down the aisle to Nikki's desk, she watched as I stopped her conversation with Day and Monica moved on. Monica mumbled bitch as she headed to the elevator. Nikki had been on the phone and Day was flipping through a book on her desk when I walked up. Sista wasn't far behind.

Day didn't even realize at first who I was. I pulled the bouquet of red roses from behind my back and Nikki was shocked. Day smiled and Sista came over and took Day's hand. I looked at Nikki and gave her a hug as she stood up.

'Every since I was little boy, I have loved you. I have wanted you and I never had the chance,' I said almost crying. 'I never had loved a woman the way that I love you and don't intend to love another woman like I love you.' Nikki, crying, tried to speak and I put a finger to her lips to silence her.

Nikki watched everyone mill around as I held on to her a little tighter. Nikki looked over her shoulder, saw Day and Sista, and realized that they already knew. Nikki smiled and kissed me again. Then I woke up, still in my bed and all alone.

'Shit,' I thought realizing it was all a dream and that I had awakened in a cold sweat. 'It is never going to be that simple…'

Day

When I got home from work, my mother told me that Brian had called. Brian, Sista and Nikki and I had lunch together today. I know Brian would be calling to fill me in on what happened after lunch.

I know I was also wearing Sista down about AJ and kind of hoped that she wasn't being suckered back in by her feelings for Paul who called. Everyone wanted to be loved, I guessed. It was just that I didn't want to see Sista hurt by him again. That reminded me that I needed to call Troy.

I still haven't told my mother about Troy or our relationship. I met Troy through a friend and we hit it off nicely. Things were good. We had even gone out for drinks at a bar, but nothing more came of it. Troy seemed to genuinely like me, but I wasn't sure if that is what I wanted.

Troy just seemed rough around the edge and I wasn't sure if I felt even comfortable enough introducing Troy to my mother yet. She might go into a fit like Aunt Esther on 'Sanford and Son.' I laughed to myself.

Looks could be deceiving I know. Troy might turn out to be a warm and sensitive guy after all. Outside of his work clothes, he might be okay. But every time I saw him, he looked like he just climbed from underneath a car. Well, he is a mechanic. I didn't know that Troy was the one. I still have my misgivings. But, I could tell that Troy was trying.

Troy had even introduced me to his daughter, Nisa. Nisa is four. Nisa is the product of a three-year relationship that Troy had with this girl from North Philly. That is until Troy decided that messing with women wasn't what he wanted. Troy didn't also feel like lying about who he was sleeping with either. He liked guys.

Troy like me had tried that live-in thing with another guy, but that didn't work that's why I moved back to Philly.

197

Clubs weren't either of our style, so we both were reduced to meeting people through other people. Eventually, Tracy, one of my friends introduced us.

It was hard though to maintain our relationship since my mother was always there. I didn't want to disrespect her. I did that once and I didn't see her again for like ten years.

In the months that she has been there, it gave me a chance to show my mother that I wasn't some pervert. I am human and by all means, her son first. After I changed my clothes, I took a seat next to my mother on the couch.

'I get a kick out of that *Springer*. I still love my *Oprah*, but you tell me how those men don't know they are dealing with cheating women. Look at them. Thank you for teaching me how to tape these shows,' my mother said then got up to go to the kitchen.

I immediately got up. 'I can get my own food, Mom. Sit down and finish your show,' I said as I watched her walk back to the couch. With my mother around, there was always a hot meal ready. I ate dinner as my mother caught up on the news.

After I ate, I took a seat next to my mother again on the couch and notice the two airplane tickets on the table. My mother looked at me, patted my hand and smiled as I looked at the tickets on the table.

'It is time to go see your daddy,' was all she said…

Violet

It wasn't until we boarded the plane that my reservations about this trip kicked in. It suddenly dawned on me that I planned all along to bring Day home. I just didn't know how or when. While I was now comfortable and understood that he was different from the child I raised, it was my intentions that his father now sees this for himself.

It has been years since he saw his father and now suddenly, it is up to me to clear the air. I started this mess, I will finish it. I looked at Day, saw that he was deep in thought, and know that it took a lot for him just to get on this plane. Not to mention what was going to happen once we reached home.

I know just like Day did that it is time to face Carl and bring an end to this foolishness. I have come to accept the life that my son has chosen to live, just as a mother accepts what he chooses to do for a career.

As the plane left Philly, I knew that my son would have to come home eventually. I didn't want it to be for his father or my funeral and things would be left unresolved. This was a place that I knew my son once felt was home and where he was loved.

I looked at my son, who sat with his eyes closed and instead of the boy I once told to clean his room, was replaced by the man who has his own place to worry about.

I saw the teenager that I had to tell to be home at a decent hour no longer existed. Instead, I saw my son who came home every day at the same time like clockwork.

Day is gay. A homosexual if you must. I am through being a full time mother and could now learn to be a friend. I closed my eyes as the plane took off. He is still my son.

My Christian beliefs told me that it is wrong for Day to love another man that way. But, I am a mother first and I have already missed out on over ten long years of my son's life by allowing my husband's stubbornness to dictate how I was going to live. No mother, who said she walked on the right side of the Lord, could turn her back on her son. Not a child she carried for nine months.

It was a hard choice to just up and walk out on my husband. I did it once before when he upset me when I made a comment in church about Day. I went home then the same night, now it has been months.

I wondered if he even ate these days because I walked out right before I usually cooked dinner. I just packed my bags, reserved my flight and walked out on the man that I promised to love, honor and cherish until death do I part. But, this same man wanted me to forget my only child.

I let my mind wander back to the day I discovered my son in bed with that man and how I simply left the room without another word.

Looking back, I felt obligated to tell my husband about what I saw and what was going on, he had a right to know, I guessed. That was my first mistake. What was going on with my son was between him and the Lord.

For the first few months after Day left home, my husband would quietly profess his hatred on his 'sissy' son. A faggot. It has been years now. I came to realize that I wasn't the only one missing him, my husband did too. He is our only son.

I saw Carl, sitting in Day's room, looking at a picture of my son and him when Day was about 12 years old. I have been in Philadelphia for months now and as much as I loved Day, I know that it was time to go home. I couldn't stay in Philadelphia forever.

It has been a long time since Day has been home. When I first arrived at his place, I told myself it was because I really wanted to see how my son was doing. Meet his friends. Tell him that I loved. Then, when the time was right, I know I had to convince him to go home with me. Day agreed to go but not without a fight.

I soon learned even after all of these years, Day is still hurting from all of the things that his father called him. Inside, I know my son is still a little boy that wanted his father's love. He needed it. This was my way of trying to give it back to him. It was the least I could do after everything that happened.

I smiled knowing that I raised a fine young man. My first thoughts when I arrived in Philly that my son would reject me. I had even turned to leave, fearing he thought that I felt the same way as his daddy. He fooled me because he welcomed me with open arms.

He was glad to have me there and I was glad to be there. On that first week, we talked, we laughed, and we even cried. I explained how I found the last card before his daddy marked it return to sender. That is how I knew where to find him.

'What made you leave,' Day asked one day.

'Couldn't say, it just wasn't right,' I saying not wanting to meet Day's gaze. 'Wasn't fair to you or me. I spent too much time wondering where you were and what you were doing.'

'You could have asked Melvin,' Day said. 'He always knew.'

'I treated Melvin just as bad over the years. I didn't know where to start. Right now, I wouldn't be upset if you hated me.'

'I don't. I just don't know why didn't you leave years ago?' Day asked me. I breathed deeply then looked at Day. I reached across the table and took his hand.

'I didn't have anywhere else to go. For a long time I didn't know where you were and when I found out, I thought you hated me. You are my son and I love you deeply. I realized years ago, I couldn't turn my back on you and still call myself a mother. Your daddy, what he did was rotten and I am sorry. But-,' my words seemed to get caught in my throat. 'I love you. You have to believe that.'

Day reached across the table and took my hand in his hand. 'Thank you. I never said I was sorry for what I did.'

'No, need baby,' I said. 'It is your life and I should have respected that. You are still my son.' Day was about to speak but stopped. Enough has been said already. We sat there for a few minutes quiet before I got up.

After I met Sista and I met Nikki, Brian and Loretta, Day's friends Lance, Mark, Kevin, Gary and Tracy, I knew Day was in good hands. Of all the people I met, Lucy Belle, who I talked to almost every day, is my favorite. Lucy and I became instant friends.

Over coffee one day, I asked Lucy what Lucy would do if her son came home and told her he was gay. Lucy simply said 'Love them. Children never asked to come here. Seeing all the people in the world that can't have children, children are a blessing just to be here. Your son loves you, love him back the same way he loves you: unconditionally.'

I instantly know why Day bonded so well with Lucy Belle, she reminded me a lot of myself, but she did the one thing that I only learned to do. Lucy loved Day for who and what he is.

When God closes a door, he always opens a window. God has a funny way of sending the right people in your life when you needed them most. It isn't my fault or my husband's that Day is gay. It is how God intended for him to be.

I opened my eyes and looked at Day. He squeezed my hand a little tighter. He was nervous as a child going off to school for the first time. I closed my eyes again as I thought about what I planned to do next when I arrived home to face my husband...

Day

I pulled the car up to the front of the house. It is true what they say that the house doesn't get smaller, you just get bigger. I stepped out of the car and saw my father sitting on the front porch. Seeing me, my father immediately went inside and slammed the door after him.

My mother moved to my side of the car and grabbed my arm. I patted my mother's arm and kissed her cheek. My mother braced the hood of the car for support as I made the walk across the grass to the house. Once at the front door I took a deep breathe and then went inside.

'Get out,' my father growled. 'Before I--'

'Before you do what? I am not leaving,' I countered holding my ground. 'Not until I say what I came to say.'

'I don't want to hear anything you have to say.' My father said jumping up from his chair. 'What more can you say or do? You shamed me and your mother.'

'By being who and what I am?'

'By living your life as a queer. We didn't raise you like that.'

'Queer, daddy? Faggot? Gay? Sissy? Homo? Fruit? Cupcake? I heard it all before. Worst part of it, is that I heard it from you. What does how I live my life have to do with you? I didn't stop being a man the day I started loving one.'

'People talk.'

'People? I am your son, who are you concerned about people or me? I am your son. Look at me.'

'I raised you to be a man. It isn't natural.' My father almost spat the words out. My father sat back on the sofa and grabbed the remote for the television. 'I hope you didn't expect to walk in that door and expect me to welcome you back with open arms. You messed up my life with the way you were living as a sissy. Me and your mother's.'

'It is the way I am,' I said clicking off the television set. 'When I left this house it was out of respect for you and my mother.'

'Respect?' My father said indignantly looking at me, 'How can you even fix your face to say that you are respecting me and your mother prancing around with those fairies?'

'How do you know who I am around? Do you know anybody that is gay besides me and Melvin?'

'I watch Jerry Springer,' my father growled. 'All that finger popping and things. Faggots are like vampires. Boy, it ain't right.'

'What do they do suck your penis and get you hooked,' I said laughing. 'I am not like that. I am the same man that you know and raised me to be. If you take a minute to see past your delusions and lies, you will see that.'

'What about the diseases? AIDS, what about that? Faggot disease. Sissies need to die for acting like that.'

'I know about AIDS and HIV. I get checked out every three months, daddy. I am negative. I practice safe sex and am selective about my sex partners. AIDS is more than a gay man's disease. You can get it from being exposed to another person's bodily fluids. Even a woman's.'

'I don't want to have this conversation. It ain't right. It ain't natural to talk sissy talk with your son.'

'When then? How?' I said following my father into the kitchen. 'When? After your dead? Tomorrow isn't promised to anyone and you can't even deal with me today. If the fact that I am gay hurts you so bad then I will leave and you don't have to ever look at me again, you don't have to see me, but you will still be my father and I will still be your son.'

'It ain't right,' my father mumbled. Just at that moment the screen slammed on the front door and my mother entered the living room walked across it into the kitchen drawing our attention.

'For who, Carl?' My mother asked in almost a whisper. My father tried to speak and my mother raised her hand to silence him.

'For years, I didn't know where my child was. My flesh and my blood, the child I raised all because of you. I watched you pretend and go on like he was nowhere to be found. Like he didn't care, well he cares.'

'I am his mother and you are his father and I'll leave you here and the life you wanted to know him again. He is a good man, Carl. I have seen the kind of people he is around. His friends. His family. They are good people and your stupidity has kept me away from him for all these years.'

My mother wrapped her arms around herself to keep from shaking. "Regular good, clean decent people. They aren't like Melvin. God knows you always hated my nephew. Out of respect for you, I rarely talked to him. The bible said it wasn't right. You said it wasn't right. But I was wrong.'

'Violet,' my father attempted.

'Shut up,' my mother screamed. I watched in silence, partly in shock and partly in awe. 'Shut up, you know where he was, you knew about the cards and the letter, the pictures and you didn't care.'

I saw the hatred building in her, my mother was shaking. 'You never cared. All you cared about is your pride. People are going to talk. Who cares? Who cares? He is my child and you kept him from me. I will forgive you, Carl, but I'll be damned if I will forget it. If you can't accept him then you can't accept me. I will file for divorce in the morning.'

My mother stormed out the house without another word. I turned to look at my father one last time. My father sat down in the kitchen chair and buried his face in his hands. 'I am sorry, Daddy,' I said and followed my mother out to the car. It has only been ten minutes since we pulled up.

'I am sorry,' my mother said to me.

'No need, Mama,' I said. 'It was time. It was time.'

'Yes,' my mother said clasping her hands to keep from shaking. 'Yes, it was.'

As I drove back to the airport, I thought about what just happened and wondered if my coming home had been a mistake. My mother had not said a word since we left.

We waited in silence until we were ready to board the plane back home. I thought we might have been here for a few days, I never knew we would be leaving so soon. My mother was so angry she refused to eat. I didn't have an appetite.

As the plane took off back to Philadelphia, I squeezed my mother's hands and watched her cry for the first time since the day she came to see me. What am I going to do? Whatever it was I would do it with my mother by my side...

Nikki and Brian

'Damn, girl,' Brian said lugging in the last of my boxes into Sista and my new apartment. 'What do you have in here?'

'My stuff. If I knew you would be so weak, I would have asked Day to help me.' I said taking the box from Brian.

Brian went into the refrigerator and pulled out a bottle of water. 'Why didn't you ask your friend, Leonard? The one you dragged to my mother's house.'

'Leonard and I aren't dating. We are friends. Why, Mr. Robinson if I didn't know any better I would say you were jealous. I thought I told you he is a friend.'

Brian grimaced. 'Why would I be jealous? If I wanted to talk to you I would have?'

'Then why haven't you,' I said sitting on the couch next to Brian.

'You were hung all up on that Reggie cat and that is cool for as long as I can remember.'

'You could have made me change my mind,' I said with a smile. 'Or aren't you man enough?'

'Yeah, right. Now maybe,' Brian said and then took another sip of his water. 'Guys like me don't stand a chance with females like you. Y'all have too much stuff with y'all.'

'How do you figure that?' I asked curiously.

'Females like you end up with a brother that isn't right and by the time somebody like me comes along then you dismiss us. Not to mention all the emotional baggage y'all come with after a break up. No, not baggage, let me correct that, luggage.'

'I know Brian that you are not talking. I have watched

207

you dog females out all my life. You are the consummate player.'

'Really?'

'Really!' I said indignantly.

'I wouldn't dog you out. I have loved you all of my life and the only reason I never said anything was out of fear you wouldn't love me back.' Brian looked at me intently now. 'So where do we go from here?'

Brian looked at me and then leaned in and kissed me.

'Brian, I can't offer you a family, kids, or anything.' I said as I forgot he's been in my life for over 20 years.

Brian pulled back from me and looked at me again. Brian licked his lips and began again, 'What if all I want is you? You are enough.'

I looked long and hard at Brian. 'Brian, you can't be serious? Don't do this if you aren't.'

'What if I am?' Brian said standing up. 'What if I love you and now I have the heart to say it. So what you can't have children. I know this. I want you. We'll adopt. I just don't want to waste another minute thinking about you and not being with you.'

'Brian,' I began but Brian sat back down and put a finger to my lips. 'How do you know? How can you say you truly love me?'

'I don't know what to say,' Brian said closing his eyes trying to fight back the tears. 'I don't know what to say.'

I reached out, grabbed Brian's hands and squeezed them. Brian looked at me. I leaned forward and whispered in Brian's ear, 'Try. Do it for me. Tell me what is in your heart.'

Brian pulled back and looked at me again. Brian let out a breath and began again. 'I know. I know. I think I have loved you all my life. When you were going through your cancer treatments, I never loved you more. When I prayed for you, I think I was praying more than I ever prayed ever for myself. I just didn't realize at that moment that I wasn't praying for your health but a chance that God would make you strong enough to love me like I do you. Can't you see I have always loved you?'

'But,' I tried to speak realizing I was crying. Brian put his fingers to my lips and then he leaned in and kissed me.

'I love you,' Brian said barely above a whisper but loud enough for me to hear, 'I know in your heart you love me. I know you. I want to be with you and I can't explain it. Give me a chance. Let me show you just how much.'

'Brian, the last time somebody told me that they loved me, they lied...' my voice trailed off. I tried to look away before I started to cry more remembering my relationship with Reggie.

Brian gently grabbed my chin and turned my face towards him. 'Don't make me apologize for his mistakes. Love wouldn't do what he did to you. I love you, always have and always will. But if this is going to work, I don't want half of you. No more talking about Reggie. How can I become your next man if you are still lingering on your ex-man?'

'Brian, it isn't that simple,' I started in. 'He hurt me, he cheated and he lied. I don't think I can deal with that again. And he, he--'

'And he isn't me,' Brian said cutting me off. 'Again, don't make me apologize for his mistakes. I am here. I am here, I love you, and you need to let him go to allow me to get in. Can you do that for me? Don't make me apologize for his mistakes.'

'Yes, I will.' I said wiping away my tears. 'I love you too. I promise I will show you how much.'

I looked at Brian and then allowed him to hug me. Brian pulled back and kissed me again. Brian stood up and grabbed his water.

'Look my sister will be back soon. I know I threw a lot at you and I am going to leave and let you think about it. I will call you. Tell the hurricane I call my sister to call me.'

Without another word, Brian was out the door and down the steps. I watched from the window as Brian walked to his car, got in and finally drove off.

I stood at the window long after Brian left. I wrapped my arms around my body and cried some more. I realized I have always loved Brian. He is what I needed in a man and finally, I got him...

Nikki and Leonard

I picked Nikki up outside her house and as we usually did, we went jogging up Valley Green, a vast stretch of trails and paths along the Wissahickon Creek. As we ran, I realized that something was on Nikki's mind but waited until we slowed down to talk to her.

'What?' Nikki asked returning my stare.

'You seem like you have something on your mind and I would like to know what it is. You know, see if I can help.'

'Well, you know Brian and I are kind of dating.'

I stopped walking and looked at Nikki. Nikki turned back realizing that I stopped. She just looked at me.

'Did I say something wrong?' Nikki asked.

'No, it is just a surprise you admitted it.'

'Wait, Leonard,' Nikki said looking at me questioning. 'What do you mean 'admit it?' Leonard, this is new to me.'

'When I met you Nikki I know we were going to be friends, just that. You are a great lady, but I come with too much baggage right now. But then when you invited me over to meet your family. I didn't see the same things with Brian, things were different. You two were more tender and loving.'

'I.' Leonard took a deep breathe, 'I saw the relationship between you and Brian. It was so tender, more loving. The way you looked at him and the way he looked at you. I knew. Remember when I met you and you said there was somebody, were you talking about Reggie or Brian?'

Nikki looked at me in disbelief, 'You saw that?'

'I did. I could see it when you couldn't. Nikki, I have

learned that the best things happen when you aren't looking at them and for you, you couldn't see what is right in front of you all along.'

Nikki stepped up and hugged me, 'Thank you Leonard for being a really good friend to me. I needed this and I needed you.'

'No, thank you, Nikki,' I said. 'You got me out here running again. I haven't felt this good in years. I needed this.'

Nikki smiled, 'That is what friends are for. Okay enough of the rest break. I will race you back to the car.' Nikki dashed off with me in pursuit.

As we neared where we parked the car, I think Nikki suddenly felt a pang of guilt for what she just did to me. She just looked at me briefly and looked away. She was letting me go.

While I said I understood her reason, who really understands rejection. On the ride home, I looked at Nikki several times because I knew it would come to this. I know Nikki is at last happy. She deserved to be happy. Even if it wasn't with me.

In my heart, I know Brian is the reason why. I just had to learn to let go. What bothered me is why it took so long for me to see it? Maybe I always did know the truth and was afraid to say it. All I know is that in an instant, I lost Nikki and maybe it was for the best. Maybe Brian could make her happy. I tried...

Sista

I settled into work and turned on the radio. I was jamming to Teena Marie's 'Square Biz' and began to sing to the music and move to the beat. I didn't even realize that Monica was standing there.

When I looked up, I was momentarily startled. It has been a while since I saw AJ and Monica. I couldn't tell you how long it's been. Still the image wouldn't leave me. Her attitude around the office didn't help things.

Day and Nikki have been trying hard to get me to just pick up the phone and say something, anything, but I wasn't feeling it or him every time I saw Monica. I have been here before. Can you say Paul?

AJ called and we even shared a few brief awkward conversations but that is it. I wanted more but stopped myself from going any further when I found out from Day and Nikki that Monica have been quite clear and very loud when she announced that her boyfriend had proposed.

I saw the picture of AJ she had on her desk. I don't know when it was taken, but it was him. So I just accepted that he had pulled a Paul and planned to marry his ex-girlfriend.

Apparently, they had gotten back together and he popped the question. Monica was supporting a new diamond ring and knowing that Monica was once the girl AJ was going to marry, I just accepted it as the truth.

It took a minute but Monica had somehow discovered I had been seeing AJ and had turned into a bigger bitch towards Day, Nikki and me.

Though it was clear that Monica also hated me for ever laying hands or eyes on AJ, she hated Nikki from the moment she walked in the door. She also hated Day because she couldn't fuck him.

Until Monica found out that Day was actually gay, she thought that Nikki and Day was an item. It didn't help when she tried to give her number to Brian, but soon discovered that he isn't only my brother, but Nikki and Brian were close. Monica wasn't having a good day that day.

'I am sorry, if I startled you,' Monica said like she could care less. 'That is my song. At least the way Teena was singing it.' I looked at Monica and turned the radio down.

'Oh,' I said fighting to control my temper.

'Well, let's not even play nice. My father isn't around. I know you really don't like me. What is it that they call you-- Sista? I know you heard I am getting married. I think it's time.'

'What do you want?' I said through clenched teeth. 'Like you said, your father isn't here, why are you here? I have work to do. Don't you?'

'To clear the air. I think you believe I am responsible for your break up with AJ. I'm not. He always loved me and always will.'

'My break up with AJ is none of your business,' I glared at Monica. She just couldn't take the hint. Bitch.

'You do know Ted,' Monica said sitting down uninvited. 'That is AJ's best friend and apparently you stopped talking to AJ after you saw the two of us. Now you had that boy crying, for what I will never know.'

'Your point, Monica. I thought you were keeping him happy.'

'I am here to say you can have him.'

'Oh, really?' I said throwing down my pen.

'Really, I mean I've already had him. If you like

214

leftovers then by all means he is yours. I am done. What AJ and I had was so college. I am through. I mean yes, he and I shared some good times, but that was years ago. I am a grown woman now and I think I deserve a real man. Oh, I see you staring at my ring.'

Monica held up her hand and acted like she was admiring the diamond. 'I am getting married but not to AJ. AJ can't afford a ring like this on what he makes. So look, you can have him. I am through. I'm grown and AJ is a little boy.'

I glared at her, 'If you are grown then why don't you act like it. It seems obvious that you have something to prove or you wouldn't be here. A few weeks ago you felt a need to proclaim your happiness. I saw the ring. Again, why should I care?'

'Actually, diamonds are a girl's best friend. Like I said 'I am through with AJ, he is yours.'' Monica said getting up, 'I am doing you a favor. All I have to do is snap my fingers and he will come running back. You are no competition. Look at you. You got a cute face but you really need to lose 50 pounds then you'd be the shit too. Wait, you will never be me. Never mind.'

I started clapping. 'That was good. You deserve an Emmy. I feel like giving you fifty, fifty cents, so you can call somebody who actually gives a fuck about what you have to say. So what that I am fat? Who cares?' I said.

'Men must feel sorry for me. That is the only reason why they'd get me. You're wrong Monica, Unlike you, I have nothing to prove. I'm comfortable with me and everything about me. It got me AJ didn't it? I have always been heavy and what you say is the least of my worries. Right now, I would prefer to get back to my job.'

Monica walked to the door and looked back at me, 'That is about all you have left. AJ? Wait, from what I understand you don't even have him.' Monica was temporarily startled to see AJ standing in the doorway.

215

'What do you have?' AJ asked quietly. 'Tell her the rest. Tell Sista the rest. You aren't right Monica. That is why I am not with you. Tell her how you slept with my friend, Dave. Tell her that I didn't sleep with you. That I haven't dealt with you in years.'

'AJ,' Monica started to speak. But nothing else came out and Monica looked at me and simply walked out without another word. AJ moved into the office and stood in front of my desk. I got up to put a file away unsure of what I should do next.

'I called you after the last time we talked. You never answer my calls any more,' AJ began. 'Now I see why and I am sorry.'

'How long were you out there?' I asked avoiding AJ's eyes. "Did you hear what she said? Is it true?'

'Long enough. And yes, she lied,' AJ began again. I felt a lump in my throat and looked away. Monica lied. If I looked at AJ, I feared he might see what a fool I have been.

Here I am in love with this man and I allowed myself to believe a lie. Nikki is right, there are some good men in the world and AJ is definitely one of them.

'You don't have to say a word. I don't know what more I can do to get through to you. I tried to do everything I could. Called Day, Nikki. They told me to stay. They said you were stubborn. They said you love me. Probably not more than I love you.'

'I hurt you, I know this. I didn't tell you about Monica and that probably hurt you the most. Day and Nikki said to keep trying and maybe you'll come around to seeing things my way. But, when you didn't answer my calls, I ran out of options.'

AJ laughed, 'Maybe, I should date your answering machine. I could never give up on someone or something that I love and you should know that. I know I have a lot of shit with me. Shit you would never probably understand. The thing with Monica was wrong. I never told her about us, because it is none of her business.'

'Yeah,' AJ went on. 'I should have. But I didn't sleep with her, because I am in love with you. I am in love with you. I feel stupid because I am losing the best thing that ever happened to me. The woman I loved as deeply as a man can love anyone. No man is perfect and without sin.'

AJ took a deep breath and moved towards me. I felt him. 'We make mistakes and I feel obligated to own up to mine and try to make them right. I apologize. I am sorry. If I could make the time we lost disappear, I would but I can't. If you let me, I promise, I'll try to make the rest of my life right with you.'

I felt a tear fall from my eye. I didn't turn around I was afraid that if I did, he would know how much I truly needed him. Every fiber of my being told me to tell AJ, I still needed him and wanted to be with him, but the fact that he didn't tell me about Monica is what hurt the most. Then again, I never thought to ask.

If he had just been upfront, but in truth, I really didn't want to know. I was wrong as he was to let him go. I should have asked. When I mustered the strength to turn around I discovered AJ had left and I wondered if what just happened is my imagination. I got up and went to open the door. I found AJ staring back at me.

'It isn't that simple,' AJ said before leaning into kiss me. 'I'm tired of waiting for you. I'm tired of spending my nights without you. I need you in my life and I won't settle for less. I am not going anywhere. Not now, not ever. So you better get used to me...'

Day/Sista/Nikki

Day drove Sista and me home from work and we talked about Monica and AJ and what happened earlier. Where was her father when she was tripping like that? We couldn't stop laughing at Monica. She really is crazy.

Monica spent the day in a huff about what happened. She didn't even look at Day or me once. When Sista came by after work, Monica got up and left.

Sista had to tell Walter what happened. When she did, Walter told Sista that she should ignore Monica. Walter knew his daughter had been dumped by AJ but like his ex-wife, she didn't know when to let go.

Walter wasn't about to let his daughter drive away the best assistant he ever had. He could handle his business at work because Sista handled her business. We asked Day to come in. I asked Day and Sista why some people can't take a hint.

'She told me,' Sista said settling into the couch, 'that I could have him. He was leftovers.'

'Touched is what that bitch is,' I said laughing and sat next to Sista. 'I have been there before. Can we say Reggie?'

'I thought guys in the club can't take a hint,' Sista said as she closed her eyes. 'Monica is remedial, down right clueless.'

'When is the last time you were in a club,' Day asked looking up from his magazine. He was trying to be smart, I knew it. He knew Nikki left me that night in the club.

'That night your friend left me in the club with that brother in the gators. It has been over a year, two years?'

'Damn,' I said looking at Sista. 'It is been that long? How did you get home?'

'I took the bus,' Sista replied. 'Thank you very much. I wasn't going home with Mr. Gators. He was cross eyed.'

'Don't knock a brother with a disability,' I smiled. 'They get a check and they get all the best parking spots. Better than half the guys you meet in a club.'

'What do you mean guys in the clubs though?' Day asked. 'That's just stereotypical male bashing.'

I looked at Day, 'Where have you been, Day? Guys come up with some of the corniest lines to get into your panties in the club. Like where have you been all my life?'

'Hiding from you,' Sista chimed in.

'No wait, what about the classic one?' I sat up.

'Haven't I seen you somewhere before?' Sista said. 'That is when you go, 'yeah, that is why I don't go there any more. Some people just can't take a hint. Damn.'

Day laughed at the two, 'You both are not right.'

'But it is real,' I said. 'What would you do if somebody came up to you and said 'How do you like your eggs in the morning?''

'Unfertilized,' Sista said laughing. Sista gave me a high five. Day should his head.

'I am not going to sit here with all of that male bashing you two are doing,' Day said laughing.

"It isn't male bashing, it telling the truth. If people don't want to be talked about, then don't do it,' Sista said with a frown on her face. 'Wait until somebody comes up to you and ask if you are a parking ticket?'

'Now that sounds dumb,' Day said, 'I don't even want to hear it.' Day stuck his fingers into his ears.

'Now that is new.' I said suddenly concerned. I looked at Sista and then Day and held up a finger. Day pulled his fingers out of his ear.

'Girl,' Sista laughed and moved her head back like she was shocked I hadn't heard the latest pick up line. 'A guy will ask if you are a parking ticket and when you ask 'why,' he'll say something dumb like 'because you got 'fine' written all over you.'

'What would you do,' Sista asked seriously, 'if a guy told you there is a party in your mouth and could he cum?' Sista paused and looked at Day who looked up and raised his eyebrow and smiled. Sista laughed. 'Never mind you nasty freak.'

I threw a pillow at Day that he blocked. 'Then you know how people are Day?' I started again. 'It might be different for you.' I said teasingly. 'But some guys fuck things up by speaking. Sometimes, they need to just sit there and look good.'

I gave Sista another high five. We all laughed. 'It might not be that different for you, Day, but for a woman, a good man is hard to find.' Sista said kicking off her shoes. 'Especially in Philly. Philly is a one horse town that shuts down at six o'clock.'

I leaned towards Day like I was about to tell him a safely guarded secret. 'Philly brothers are their own breed; a bad cross between the South and a wannabe New Yorker. Then they are so quick to get mad when you tell them about themselves.'

'Well, if the shoe fits,' Sista laughed. 'Most guys aren't about shit. Just like most females. Day, if you should would have seen what I saw that night in the club. Desperation was all around.'

'You ain't never lied,' I said. 'Day, have you ever been to a Philly club? I mean we are not trying to hook you up, we can just go out and have some fun. But be warned, they are going to be all over you if you go, sisters lose all their inhibitions in the club.'

'I'm cool with it,' Day commented putting down his magazine and getting ready to leave. 'Clubs were filled with people that out of loneliness or desperation would offer somebody, anybody, a trip around the world. But what would be left after you came?'

'He's right,' Sista said agreeing with Day. 'It seemed though that the more people wanted that next hook up, the harder that some people were trying to hold on to what they have. If a good man is hard to come by, it is even more so today.'

'Don't get us wrong, there are some good people out there,' I offered. 'But people like your friend Monica, they come a dime a dozen.'

'Well, I have had enough of Ms. Monica. I feel like going out and having some fun. Doing something. So are we going out and this time, when we go together we all need to leave together,' Sista said looking at me.

'That's the idea,' I agreed. 'We are going out. We can go hang out, dance and have fun. Brian and AJ should come too. I feel like celebrating.'

Day looked at me and I just shrugged. It was a date. Little did Sista know the can of worms she was opening up by even suggesting the whole evening...

Loretta

I was dressed down, you hear me. Looking like a million buck in large bills. I decided I needed a night out and a night away from my boring ass husband. I was supposed to meet Kareem, the guy I've been seeing. Kareem have just got out of a halfway house and we were going out to celebrate.

I know from the first time that we met that he had been locked up for drug possession and was locked back up a little after we met. He spent the last six months in a halfway house. I didn't have the heart to pry any further.

I didn't want to know. I didn't care. He wasn't going to hurt me. Kareem still looked familiar and that bothered me since I first met him in the restaurant that day I was supposed to meet my sister.

Kareem and I met off and on since then. I even gave him some money to get by on. Cliff didn't question me once or the shit I did. I wished I could start some shit at that moment though. A fight, an argument or something would help get me out of the house faster.

Instead when Cliff came into the room and saw me dressed up he said I looked nice and went down stairs. Motherfucker. He always has to be this goody goody. What I need is a good argument to allow me to stay out all night.

'You are staying in tonight?' I asked Cliff as I came down the steps.

'Yes, I want to finish up some work. Your brother did invite us out to a club,' Cliff said not looking up from his work. 'Why didn't you tell me? I might have liked to go.'

'I figured you didn't want to go,' I said putting my other earring in. 'He asked me earlier. I had to tell him I had other plans.'

'You always do lately,' Cliff said coolly. 'Something you want to tell me. For example, where are you going and who are you going with? Anything could happen.'

I turned and looked at Cliff when I realized that Cliff was now staring at me. 'Don't start your shit Cliff. We are not are not at my mother's and I don't have to be polite. I told you that Bernice is having a girl's night out. So just because my brother wants to go out, I am supposed to drop everything. You must be crazy.'

'I bet Sista put him up to this bullshit,' I said. She never did reschedule our lunch. The fat bitch was planning this shit. 'You want to go out with him, go. I am not holding you back. You are grown. I have some place to be. Bernice is my best friend. I will not stand her up.'

Cliff threw down his pen and looked at me. Cliff gathered up his work and moved to the couch. 'Have fun,' was all he could muster. Fuck him. If his money wasn't right, I would have left him a long time ago.

I looked at Cliff for a minute then turned back to the mirror. I continued to watch Cliff through the mirror's reflection. 'Damn fool,' I thought. After Kareem and I went to the club, I planned on giving Kareem some.

We had sex before and when we did it. I felt I was on some natural high. It was that good shit. I just hated the fact that that first couple of times his monitoring device kept scratching my damn leg.

I couldn't tell if it was love yet. I grabbed the keys to my car and kissed Cliff goodbye on his cheek. I pretended to call my best friend Bernice, but instead called the weather hotline.

'Yes, I am on my way, Bernie.' What I heard was at there was a chance of rain. I looked at Cliff who didn't bother to look up from his work. I then walked out the door...

Cliff

Loretta didn't bother to look or come back. If she had, she would have seen me press the redial button. I listened intently as the phone rang and the automated recording came on.

I clicked the receiver and dialed another number. It was time to do what I had to do. When I was finished with the conversation, I began to pack.

I suspected that Loretta was cheating on me for years, but my upbringing wouldn't allow me to walk away without trying. For years, I watched my mother and father grow distant.

Somehow they stayed together and it was only recently that I realized my parents didn't have anywhere else to go. So they went through the motions of a loveless marriage.

No love, just two people living together with no where else to go. They didn't even sleep in the same bed or the same room. I looked around the house and it was too quiet. After all these years, Loretta still didn't want to have children. Every time the subject came up she had an excuse.

I was smart enough to know when her period came on and it was during those times that Loretta begged off when it came to sex. I didn't want to admit during those times that I made a mistake in marrying Loretta, but it was the truth, I did.

All these years and no kids, only a few friends that we've in common. Most nights I would rather work than to come home to a wife that didn't care. She wasn't like this when I met her. She was something special. Now, Loretta felt like somebody I didn't even know.

Loretta is a stranger in my bed, a stranger in my heart. My heart sank as I realized I wasn't only about to lose my wife, but as an only child, the only family I ever really had. I would lose the dinners at Miss Lucy's and spending time with the family. Things wouldn't be right for me ever again. I hoped Ms.

Lucy can find it in her heart to forgive me.

Loretta had brought me to this point. Loretta just couldn't be trusted. I didn't know how many others there have been but I suspect there were a few. I definitely knew about this one. I saw her sneaking him out on a night I told Loretta I would be late coming home. Little did she know I would do the one thing she never expected, I called her sister to ask. It was wrong but I had to.

'Sista,' I said when I heard Sista pick up on the other end.

'Hey, brother-in-law. How can I help you?' She was always cheerful with me. She always was so sweet.

'I need to ask you something and I need for you to be honest,' I heard her take a deep breath on the other end.

'If I can,' Sista replied.

'Is you sister cheating on me?' I asked. Silence came back. I had my answer.

'Cliff, I love you dearly but that's between you and my sister,' Sista replied. I heard her take a deep breath on the other end.

'Sista, I need to know. I saw a man leaving out of my house. She was sneaking a man out of my house,' I think my desperation was starting to show. "Is my wife cheating on me?'

'Cliff, that's between you, my sister and God. But if I had to weigh in on things, you already know.' That's when I knew. I knew my marriage was over.

I needed to move on and find somebody else as soon as possible. I might even do what my brother-in-law Brian says and just keep to myself and that way I won't be disappointed because I will only have myself to blame.

I was trying to be a good husband. But with Loretta, it's like she has no conscience. I ignored all of the signs of a cheating spouse. How she always answered a call in hushed tones was always a give away.

How she took a shower when she got in from being out all night is another. A shower after work is cool but not after a night you claimed to be hanging out.

It was out but not hanging. Even, smelling like you just showered at two in the morning is another dead giveaway. Women knew, why didn't I? I was so in love I guess.

I am past the point of prayer. Loretta isn't right. Loretta just couldn't compare to what a wife is supposed to be. She simply didn't care. Sometimes I wished I could go back to the days before I met her and not go through with this frustration.

I looked around the house I could never call a home, laid the divorce papers on the couch, and walked out the door...

Loretta

I pulled up at Kareem's mother house and beeped the horn. He came bouncing out the house in a set I brought him for tonight. Kareem got in and kissed me making a show for his boys on the corner.

'Sup, baby girl,' he said and kissed me again. Kareem dug in his pocket and proceeded to roll a blunt as I pulled off.

I looked at Kareem out the corner of my eye. This wasn't the first time that Kareem did that shit. I thought to myself 'fuck no' the first time he did it after sexing me, but after a few tokes I was gone. Sex got better to me after that.

With Cliff, I would lay there wishing that shit was over. It felt like a wet fish slapping against me. With Kareem, he fucked like a man that just got out of jail.

Wait a minute, he did. A lot better than a faithful husband who believed sex should only be done between seven and ten and only in the missionary position. Motherfucker.

Kareem lit the blunt and passed it to me. I took a couple of puffs and handed it back. Kareem looked at me and began to rub my leg. Fuck that, I know I had to give him some.

As we pulled up outside the club, I was ready to party. I looked at my watch and knew Cliff would be taking his tired ass to bed soon. Good. I rubbed Kareem's leg and realized he was already hard. We wouldn't be in the club long. I had other plans for him...

Day

I had given myself enough time to stop and see my mother at Ms. Lucy's where she planned to move soon. My Mom only stayed over my place a few nights out the week because Ms. Lucy welcomed the company.

According to my mother, it was to give me the privacy I deserved. I welcomed the space, even though I wasn't seeing anyone any way. Troy turned out to be trying to reconcile with his daughter's mother. He said some stuff about wanting to marry her. It ended as quickly as it started.

I was all set to meet Nikki, Sista, and Brian at the club when as I stepped out the door I almost ran into a ladder near my door. As I watched some guy climb down the ladder, he quickly offered his apologies.

I recognized the brother as Mike, the building superintendent. I met him briefly, but never got an opportunity to see him close up. He handled his business as the superintendent of the building the minute he started and finally fixed that broke front door.

'You always work so late.' I asked as Mike looked me up and down. I was curious about that one.

'Nah, I just wanted to get a jump on next week and needed to fix that light near your door,' Mike said looking more intently at me.

'I am sorry for knocking into your ladder,' I offered up, suddenly feeling no need to hurry up.

'No, actually it would be my fault if you got hurt, I would be liable.' Mike wiped his hands on a rag that he tucked back into the back pocket of his blue jeans. I looked at Mike and for the first time realized that Mike had to be at least six foot five. That's tall, I am only five nine. He could have changed the light from the floor.

Light skinned with braids, Mike looked more like a drug dealer than somebody with a regular job. For weeks, I would only see him from a distance or briefly in which, Mike would speak and then move on.

'Look at you?' Mike said looking at me more intently I suddenly felt self-conscious. 'You are going to make somebody happy tonight.'

I smiled and said 'I try.'

'Your girl must like it,' Mike ventured as he removed his ladder.

'Girl?' I said taken back momentarily.

'The fine light-skinned girl that stops by or the caramel sister?'

I laughed and Mike looked at me curiously, 'Nah, they are just very good friends. That is Nikki, the light-skinned one and Sista, the caramel sister. Her brother is the guy you probably see, that is my best friend. They are good peoples.'

'Oh,' Mike said. 'My bad.'

'Why did you assume that one of them was my girl?' I asked now curious. 'You like one of them? Sorry but they are both taken.'

'Nah, actually, I don't go around proclaiming it, but I like guys. Actually, I like you.' Mike said almost like he was prepared to run away. At six foot five, he didn't have to. 'But you are not about that. If I disrespected you, I apologize...'

'Oh, you're gay?' I said trying not to laugh. 'That is cool.'

'No labels,' Mike ventured, 'My mother gave birth to a boy and from a boy I became a man.'

'Oh, I see,' I said smiling. 'You are one of those 'I am not gay' guys. That's cool I guess.'

Mike looked at me and said, 'What you mean by that?'

'You know,' I offered 'One of those guys that are gay but call themselves something else. Out of denial, guilt, family and peer pressure. It doesn't matter to me. Do your thing.'

'Wait,' Mike said wondering where the conversation was going, 'It isn't like I fuck around on my girl with a guy. Telling her that shit about me hanging with my buddies and really end up in some club, whirling and twirling. I am a regular guy that happens to like guys, what?'

I could tell that Mike was clearly getting upset. I began to laugh. Mike looked at me again and I laughed. I jingled my car keys and laughed and started to walk away.

'Why are you laughing? Mike asked curiously. I stopped looked at him long and hard before speaking.

'When you were going through all of that, did you realize that I might be one of those kinds of guys too?' I asked before walking away. I waved at Mike as I left the building...

Nikki

When we hit the club, Day, Sista, Brian and I, it was packed with people. I didn't realize that it's been a minute since I was in a club. All of the usual suspects were there though from the old guys to the tricks. The usual people that show up in the club come hell or high water.

AJ had to work late with a new shipment coming in so he missed all of this. I took a seat to hold a table for the four of us. Day and Sista immediately went to the dance floor.

I watched Day and Sista on the dance floor. In all of the years I have known the two, I never saw them dance like that. I laughed because it was so funny.

As the song changed and people left the dance floor, I stopped smiling when I was given a clear shot of the last person I expected to see: Loretta and some obvious little boy all hugged up on her.

It was only then did I get a clear view of the couple that was sitting near by: Reggie and Renee. Even at that distance, the diamond on her finger accompanied by a wedding band showed me that Reggie made a choice.

He married the bitch and she was pregnant too. She was clearly showing. In a club at that point in her pregnancy with all the loud music and smoke, she was just trifling. Some women didn't care but it was clear she didn't trust Reggie. His cheating is how she got him in the first place.

Looking at the ring as she held his face, I suspected it is the same ring that Reggie offered me. Reggie must have felt somebody staring at him and he looked up. He nodded and when Renee saw this she reached over and kissed Reggie.

I suspected that that was a power move to say 'Look bitch, I got your man.' But when Reggie continued to stare at me, I knew he wasn't over me. The best revenge is always looking better than when they saw you last. Reggie continued to stare despite Renee's best efforts. Did Renee know that if he cheated with you, he'll cheat on you? Dumb bitch.

Sista and Day came back at the same time Brian did with the drinks. Brian saw Reggie staring and immediately went in for a kiss with me. I peaked and saw Reggie wouldn't stop staring despite Renee's best effort to stop him. He wouldn't stop looking. I touched the back of Brian's head for effect. Damn, I'm good. Fuck Reggie and Renee. They deserve each other.

As Brian broke away with from the kiss, Renee was storming away. Sista and Day immediately saw what I saw in the first place. When Brian realized what the two was looking at, he put down the soda in his hand down.

Brian got up to go over to Loretta but Day stopped him. We all knew Brian would only make things worst. Sista wanted to go slap the shit out of Loretta as we watched her grab her friend in a very private place.

'What the fuck?' Brian said.

'No, not here,' Sista said grabbing his arm.

'What is she doing?' Brian asked. 'She needs to be slapped for the shit she doing with that guy.'

It was Brian's turn to grab her. By that time, Loretta was out the door...

Loretta

I dropped Kareem off at his mother's place after spending the night in a motel. I planned to tell Cliff that I was so tired that I stayed at Bernie's. It made sense. He wouldn't call there. Shit, if he only knew where I really was.

Kareem sexed me six ways to Sunday. I didn't mind when he said he needed some money to get some new clothes to look nice for me. Kareem was trying to find a job and I was glad I could help. I wanted Kareem to look good.

Kareem is my man after all. What I didn't expect was to walk into my home and find Cliff gone. Brian was sitting there in the dark. He must have been asleep. How long has he been there? I looked at my brother in disbelief.

'Where is my husband?' I asked.

'Gone,' Brian said like it was a matter of fact. He had slept on the couch since arriving at the house and finding the door open. 'Where have you been?'

'I am grown; I don't have to answer to you or anybody else.' I looked around, putting my keys down, as if Cliff would magically appear. He didn't.

Brian looked at me, 'When I got here the door was open. I came here because Sista said somebody should talk to you.'

'What does she have to do with this?' I snapped at Brian, 'Because if her fat ass had anything to do with this. So help me Brian, I will whip her natural black ass.'

Brian looked at me like he was trying to keep from smacking the shit out of me. 'You will not do shit. We saw you. We all saw you last night hugged up on your little friend.'

'Saw who?' I said defensively. 'My little friend has a name. His name is Kareem.'

'Well, call the little bastard because he just fucked up your marriage. I found your divorce papers on the couch.'

'Divorce?' I said picking up the papers and slumping into a chair. I let the papers fall to the floor.

'Yeah, you fucked up. You need to slow your shit up. You got caught.'

'I need to talk to Cliff,' I thought about last night and pressed the redial button and found out that the last number Cliff dialed was to the Holiday Inn. I realized that somehow Cliff knew. But how? I thought I did everything to cover my tracks. Damn it.

'Look Brian,' I began again quietly. 'I need to find my husband. Could you just leave? I don't want to talk about this.'

Brian stopped and picked up the papers off the floor where I let them fall and looked at me, 'Apparently, neither does your husband.' Brian handed them to me and walked out the door...

Sista

I spent the day at my mother's. Not much was said when Loretta or Cliff didn't show. Nikki did her best to calm Brian down. Brian was on a rant on how irresponsible Loretta is.

As Brian's best friend, Day just stood by and watched things unfold. Dinner was quiet, except my mother and Violet talking about their work at the hospital. Day still hadn't heard from his dad, but Miss Violet didn't show an ounce of concern.

Day and his mother helped my mother clean up after dinner and Nikki and Brian had already left when I quietly left the house. I took the bus out to the last place I expected to go. With my father gone, I know what I had to do. I had to talk to Loretta. I know that a lot of bad blood existed between the two of us but I knew I had to try.

I got off the bus a block from Loretta's house. I walked grudgingly to my sister's door not knowing what to expect. Loretta isn't the greatest sister on the planet but as far as I was concerned, Loretta is mine and had to be dealt with accordingly.

I thought about my call from AJ, who called just to see how I was doing. We've just started to get back to where we had been but in the back of my mind I wasn't sure if I was ready. I know I loved him but I didn't know if I was up to the job. I opted to let things take their own course and see where things went with AJ. I had to, there's nothing cute about baggage.

AJ is definitely not Paul. I know I was still attracted to Paul. But I know we could never be friends. Paul called days ago because things weren't going any better with Angela and the sharing custody of the baby. This was definitely a case of making your bed and now having to lay in it. I needed to let him lay in it.

I tried to be that friend to Paul but I had to remind myself that Angela was Paul's excuse to let me go. So that is what I did and asked him to not call me again. I know what I wanted and right now that is AJ. Good, bad or indifferent, AJ is the one. If he isn't Mr. Right, he would be Mr. Right Now. He even invited me to meet his family the next weekend. It was a nice new beginning.

As I rang the bell again to Loretta's house, I looked through the glass of the door hoping Loretta would appear and that Loretta's neighbors wouldn't think I was a Jehovah's Witness. I finally saw movement and breathed a sigh of relief.

Loretta looked like shit. Her hair wasn't done. Loretta must have realized she looked a mess and drew her robe closer to her body. Loretta moved aside and let me in.

I looked around the house and wondered if the news knew a hurricane had hit town, missed everybody else and only hit Loretta's living room. Loretta tried to clean up but I stopped her.

I took the bag from Loretta's hands and emptied the marijuana joints from the ashtray. I then dumped in the empty beer bottles and gathered up the rest of the trash. Loretta buried her head in her hands.

'Don't say shit,' Loretta said looking finally at me, as I took a seat across from her. I just looked at Loretta dumb founded. She is tripping already.

'What am I supposed to say?' I asked evenly.

Loretta went to lie down on the couch. 'I already called Mama and told her that I was fine. What did you come over here for to gloat and say that 'I told you so?' Well save it, the last thing I need to hear is some of your holier than thou shit.'

'Let me cut to the chase,' I said beginning again like I had never spoken, 'I didn't come over here to gloat, I came over here as your sister and you hand me some bullshit about gloating. I came to check on you.'

'You don't even like me,' Loretta said in disbelief.

'I think it is the other way around. You have always hated me for no reason. But I am your sister. Your flesh and blood and you don't give me any respect.'

'Respect? Respect you for what Sista? For always thinking you are better than me.' Loretta asked.

'No,' I said evenly. 'That would be you. You think I am better than you. Don't make me apologize because you fucked up.

'Well,' Loretta continued like she never heard me. 'It is always Sista this, Sista that, is all I have ever heard all my life. I married Cliff thinking that if I got married first, then maybe this family would talk about me. But even then all they wanted to know is if Sista would be in the wedding.'

'That was my day and I had to share even that with you. All my life, I have to had live in your shadow. Pun intended. Then even on the day that was supposed to be mine, about me, you still stole my thunder. Why are you really here? You want to point fingers and make me feel bad? Go ahead.'

'This isn't going anywhere. Why bring all of this up now? You have been married for how long? I came to see about you,' I said gathering up my things to leave. 'I came to check up on you. I do care. Believe it or not. But like I said this isn't going anywhere.'

'What isn't going anywhere? I have been holding all of this in, but now, I don't care. I was telling you the truth.'

'You lost your husband, I didn't. I came here to find out what is going on. Mommy is worried about you. You look like shit and then you spend all of your time ranting and raging about how I am. This isn't about me; this is about you and the shit you do. Why do you always want to turn this into some kind of contest?'

237

'What do you expect me to be the kind and noble sister that you try to be? Don't fake the funk, bitch.' Loretta delivered the word bitch like a slap in the face. 'You do whatever you got to do so you can sleep at night. I am fine. I am going to have my cake and eat it too.'

'Isn't that what got you here?' I asked. 'How much will it take for you to realize that Cliff isn't coming back? Cliff is tired of your shit. You are busted. Your jig is up. We all know. We just never said shit.'

'It isn't over until I say it is over and even then, it is my choice. You, Brian, Mama all of you can say what you want. Let Cliff leave I don't need his black ass any way. I don't need anybody.' Loretta buried her face in her hands. Her tears came easily.

'I can do bad by my damn self. You hear me. Fuck Cliff and his tired ass. He served his purpose fuck him.' Loretta's voice got louder. 'I can do bad all by myself.'

'You always did,' I said in a whisper. I got up, grabbed my bag and walked to the door. I didn't even bother to look back. I just closed the door. Once on the other side I took a deep breathe and fished in my bag for the bus schedule. 'Please help her, God,' I whispered. 'Help her. She needs you.'

Day

I pulled up to my building as I watched Mike sitting on the step. My mother got of the car and started to take the groceries out of the trunk when Mike offered his help.

My mother looked at me and smiled. I told my mother that I would bring the groceries in. My mother went into the apartment. It was one of those rare days that she stayed with me.

'That was smooth,' I said smiling at Mike.

'What is?' Mike asked as he carried the bags up the steps. He looked lost.

'Trying to get to me through my mother.'

'They say the way to a man's heart is through his mother.' Mike smiled as did I. Mike and I put the bags in the apartment and my mother began putting the stuff away. I saw Mike standing in the hall through the still open door and told my mother I would be right back. I walked into the hall closing the door behind me.

'I know you weren't trying to hit on me in front of my Mom. That would just be wrong.'

'No, I wouldn't do that, so I waited right here. Plus I already met your Mom on several occasions.'

'Waiting for what a tip?' I asked fishing in my pocket for money. Mike immediately put his hand up. I stopped and looked at Mike.

'No, just a chance to get to know you. You have been among the missing since that day in the hall and I kind of like to get to know you a little better. Nothing serious.'

'Really?' I asked.

'Really, I am placing myself at your disposal.' Mike said trying his best to look serious. 'What about this weekend?'

'He is free and he'll see you about two,' she said opening my door and poking her head out, 'because I have my Bingo game at one and he has to drop me off.'

My mother then closed the door leaving us both speechless. I then started to laugh; Mike smiled and then started to walk away. He turned back and waved at me.

'I though we were going out?' I asked suddenly serious.

Mike turned back, looked at me, smiled, and said, 'We are at two on Saturday. I wouldn't want to disappoint your mother.'

I smiled and went back into the apartment and my mother was sitting on the couch. When I sat beside her she didn't even look away from the television.

'He seems like a nice young man,' she said and patted my hand. 'But baby, if you want me to not hear what you have to say, close the door. If I heard you sneaking in all of those nights when you were younger, what makes you think I wouldn't hear somebody asking you out right outside the door?'

Brian

I parked the car and watched Nikki get out of the car. Nikki knew it is one of my favorite spots in the city when she suggested we go. It's called the Azalea Gardens and is a park behind the Art Museum where the old Philadelphia Waterworks was. I wanted to show Nikki it.

Nikki and I walked over to the restored gazebo and looked over the waterfalls. Nikki leaned back as we stood against the rails, allowing me to support her weight. I held Nikki and kissed her neck. Nikki turned and kissed me on my lips.

'What are you thinking about?' I asked. 'Me?'

'You are funny,' Nikki said with a smile. 'No, I was thinking it is nice out here. I have lived in Philly all of my life and I never had been here.'

'I come out here to run with Day,' I said between kisses. 'Then one night I came out here at night and it was peaceful. So I come out here to think. To find peace within myself.'

Nikki turned to look at me. 'If somebody would have told me that we'd be here right now like this I would have looked at them and laughed. We've known each other so long and that we could be like this, it just never crossed my mind.'

I smiled. 'I thought about it. But you are a dime and I couldn't just try to talk to you. You are like family and...'

'And,' Nikki said. 'I was with Reggie.'

I looked away and sighed. 'Yeah that too. But you are mine.'

'I love you Brian,' Nikki said hugging me. 'I think I am falling in love with you.'

I let go and walked away. Nikki moved near me and

grabbed my arm gently.

'I am sorry. Did I say something wrong?'

'No, you are saying all the right things. I just don't know if I should.'

'Should what?' Nikki inquired. 'Love me back?'

'Yes,' I said quietly.

'Brian, look me in my eyes and tell me that you don't love me.' Nikki said.

'I don't,' I replied and looked away.

Nikki was hurt. She grabbed my arm and turned me around to look at her. 'Then look me in my eyes and tell me you are not in love with me.'

I looked at Nikki and replied, 'If I told you that I would be lying to you and myself. I am in love with you, Nicole. I always have been and always will be.'

Nikki stared at me long and hard, which seemed like an eternity to me but it was less than a minute. Nikki smiled and hugged me. She kissed me twice and then grabbed my hand and let me back to the car. I was surprised.

'Did I say something wrong?' I asked.

'No,' Nikki said settling in. 'But, I want to go home. But not to Sista's. Your place.'

'Are you sure? I mean are you ready. Physically. I mean, are you okay to do that--' Nikki put her finger to my lips.

That night we made love for the first, second and third time. Damn, you talk about making love. I ran my tongue all over every inch of her body, massaged her body from her scalp to the tips of her toes and when she climaxed, I knew this had been worth the wait. Every single minute. Nikki was mine. Mind, body and soul.

It's something about taking your time with a woman and not going in for that quick climax that made it that much better. Like on cue, it started to rain. I led Nikki to the window and with the thunder rattling the windows and the lightning lighting our way, we started again.

I lifted Nikki up and sat her on the edge of the window sill and placed one of her breast in my mouth as I made love to her again and then again. When she rested her head against my chest, I knew she had enough. There would always be tomorrow. I carried her in my arms to the bed and nestled her against my chest. She was sleep within minutes.

As I lay staring at the ceiling, I couldn't help but to think about all the time I wasted. I promised I would never let Nikki go no matter what. Nikki stirred in her sleep and I stroked her back until she settled back down. No, I would never let her go…

Day

I had been leafing through a magazine for over an hour waiting my mother to finish up in the market when the last person I would have ever thought he see came walking through the door. Troy. At first Troy seemed startled to see me and I just waved. Then, I continued to look through the magazine and suddenly felt Troy's presence upon me.

'How you been?' Troy asked.

'I've been good,' I said extending my hand, which Troy shook. I felt the weakness in what used to be a firm handshake. 'How are you?'

'I've been good.' Troy felt uneasy and then started to walk away. 'Take care.'

'Yeah,' I said, 'How is your family? Your wife?'

'Who?' Troy asked.

'Exactly,' I said putting down the magazine. 'Remember you told me we couldn't be friends because you were getting back with your daughter's mother. You were getting married. You are sick, aren't you?'

'I have cancer,' Troy said as he looked away.

'They always say cancer to make it sound nice. You shouldn't lie about that,' I continued, 'We were friends and you stopped being cool with me because you have HIV. Why lie?'

Troy looked at me and the tears welled up in his eyes but he didn't cry. 'I don't know.'

I breathed deep. I didn't know what to say.

'I couldn't be around you at that point in my life, when I found out,' Troy said, 'I have a lot of things going on.'

I held up my hand, 'No need to explain. It isn't like we slept together. I understand. You used to say treat everybody you deal with like they are positive. In your case it was true and you lied about it. We all do what we got to do. I could have dealt with many things but not you lying. HIV isn't a death sentence.'

'I still have your number. Maybe we can talk, hang out.' Troy tried to sound upbeat.

'I am good.' I said putting the magazine back before going to look for my mother. 'I can deal with anything. I wouldn't have cared if you were sick, but the lies. That I couldn't deal with.'

'You telling me you would have still been around me for me. This isn't something you can go around telling people.'

'How would you know? You never gave me the chance.' I stopped and looked at Troy for a minute then walked away. 'Be honest with yourself. You never tried. So how could I?' I then walked away…

Sista

I did every thing that I could to look perfect for meeting AJ's family. I changed like three times until Nikki pushed me out of the door. Apparently, his brother is coming home from the service and the family is throwing a welcome home party. All of AJ's extended family would be there, including his grandmother Ethel, his other aunt Marie and a few other cousins.

I know AJ's father is supposed to be there. Kevin hasn't seen their father in years. Ms. Diane knew Kevin resented his father for leaving but tried to help bridge the gap between the two by telling AJ to invite him.

I talked to AJ about the real reason. Diane wanted to show Charles that a boy can be raised to be a man with or without a man around, especially if that man isn't a good man. Of all the things that any woman could do though, I always felt though that a boy still needed a father and a father's place should be with a son.

Not to say that having a man around would ensure that child would grow up right, but at least the mother wouldn't have to go at it alone. She didn't lay down by herself, so why should she did she have to bring that child up by herself?

At his mother's request, AJ had invited his father. I knew things would hit the fan because his mother and father would be in the same room for the first time in years.

If AJ's father is smart, he would leave his girlfriend at home. I met her at the mall where she worked one day and she was everything AJ said. I stopped short of asking what is up with her damn eye. At least, I would be there for AJ's sake. As we walked up to the house AJ was kind of nervous.

AJ introduced me to his aunt's boyfriend who was at the grill and then to his mother's man as he came out of the house with food for the grill. Just then, AJ's mother came out of the house too. I waited for the evil looks and the nasty tone. But to my surprise, I didn't get any.

'Hey, baby,' Ms Diane said. She kissed AJ on the cheek and looked at me. 'So you are the lady that has my son all wrapped around his finger. Good, he needs a good woman in his life.'

Diane then leaned in and gave me a hug. 'You two go in the house and see the family.' I felt like maybe things would be all right. That is until I got in the house.

'Somebody done shitted.' A heavyset black woman said coming down the steps. She moved over to the older woman that from AJ's pictures told me that she is AJ's grandmother.

'Mama,' Bunny said shouting at her hard of hearing mother. 'Somebody done shitted and funked up the bathroom and we got company coming. Mama was that you smelling like you want to be alone?'

I cringed waiting for a sharp reply but the older woman just frowned her face, rolled her eyes and looked away. Just then who I assumed from AJ's stories is Little Earl, his cousin, came bouncing from the kitchen with juice in his hand.

'Mom, I thought you were going to fix the juice like I asked. I really wanted you to do it.'

'Fix it your damn self.' Bunny said, much to my amusement. 'Sorry ass,' Bunny mumbled as she eyed me while sucking a piece of food out of her teeth. She smiled at me.

'Look at you,' Bunny said giving me the once over. 'I see AJ done gone and got himself a big girl. Big ole cute thing. Girl looks like me when I was younger. Big boned. You know they all wanted me. And I was married to Big Earl back then. God rest his soul.'

'Is he dead?' I asked.

'He is to me,' Bunny said and laughed. I looked at Bunny not knowing what to say. Bunny went on.

'So many men, only one of me. Yeah, they all wanted me. I have had so many men on me at one point that my little black book looked like the yellow pages.' Then she laughed, not a chuckle but a big laugh like she was amusing herself. 'My pussy should be made of platinum child.'

I watched as Bunny reached into her bra and pulled out a pack of cigarettes. 'Shit, I wasn't like these bitches today. I didn't play that cute shit. See nobody wants you when you don't have somebody. But the minute you get somebody everybody wants you.' Bunny motioned for me to sit down.

I looked at AJ who shrugged and took a seat across from Bunny. 'But you know what I did, I let them have me. One man for breakfast, a brother for lunch, and somebody's husband for dinner. I shared the wealth.'

AJ went into the kitchen and left me alone with Bunny. 'So, what is your name again Sista, right. But what did AJ say your name is Clawja. Like Claw-juh. Now that is different. You are a pretty girl though. I see why my nephew is crazy about you. You hold on to him.' I nodded.

You ever met his daddy, he look just like his no good daddy. That pimp. And who is this thing that man is with. Now that heifer used to live in South Philly. I know she did. Her pussy was like a clown car back in the day with all those kids climbing out.

Bunny paused then went on like for a moment she was lost in thought. 'Welcome to the family child. Now that one over there is AJ's grandmother, Myrtle. She can't hear shit. But I love my Mama, but I need to ruffle the old bird's feathers at times.

Even though the old bird keep the heat on 'lose weight' at her place. That is between hell and got damn. You met my husband, Craig. My sister Diane, the one with the mustache and the jheri curl at the door.'

'My other sister Ethel is bringing her bad ass kids. Wait until her daughter Keisha gets there. Watch her oldest boy; that boy ain't right.' She made a wavering hand gesture.

'It is one in every family that you know been touched by more than God. Make sure you don't eat the potato salad the bitch Aretha made when she brings her tired ass here. She is my Mama's kin and she can't cook worth a dime.'

'That Laura, now that is Aretha's daughter,' Bunny went on without pausing to breathe. 'She is something. Don't know who her baby father is. None of them. Check day bitch. And I hope she don't bring her thrown off brother Aleem.'

Bunny threw her head back, 'That son of a bitch is here every holiday asking if there is pork in the food. He keeps saying he is Muslim. That bastard isn't Muslim. That isn't a kufi he is wearing. It is just a tight ass hat. As-salaam a fuck him.'

Bunny laughed again then got up and looked at me. 'This is our messed up family. But enjoy yourself.'

As quick as Bunny sat down she was gone and I didn't even get to say hello. I sat there for a minute before AJ came bouncing back in the room.

I didn't even want to begin to tell him about the conversation with his aunt. AJ seemed to know and just leaned over and whispered in my ear, 'She is nuts.' I smiled.

Bunny came back into the house with AJ's mother. I could only catch the tale end of the conversation. 'No, we are not going anywhere with Ethel. She can go to a comedy show and turn that shit into tragedy real quick. Bitch got seven kids and ain't none of them twins.'

'When does she breathe?' I thought as Bunny kept on going on without breathing.

'And we not taking Nita either, her stank ass. Calling me an alcoholic, I'm a drunk. Alcoholics go to meetings. Remember we were kids and she used to come along to hold the purses. What do the kids call that nowadays? Cock blocking. Bitch should have worn shoulder pads with the defense she played for us.'

'She's crazy,' I thought. I was scared to move, she might start talking to me again. I didn't want that.

I spent the rest of the afternoon in the same spot. I didn't know if I should move around. When I did it was twice. I moved once to help AJ's mother and yet another when AJ's brother, Kevin, came in.

I would say my goodbyes to the family and allowed AJ to take me home. When we got to my front door, AJ begged off coming up because he had to get an early start tomorrow but instead stayed to talk outside.

'So what did you think?' AJ asked.

'Crazy isn't the word. Your aunt--' I started to say. 'She talks too much, but I like her. She's real. Even if she is nuts.'

'I know. Earl, Craig and then my Mom. My grandma is old. She is hard of hearing and with my aunt around I understand. Still want to be with me? Because I can just go.'

I smiled. 'I am with you, not your crazy ass family. I am disappointed your dad didn't show.'

AJ looked at me and smiled 'Maybe that is a good thing. He would have only got my Mom going and plus Kevin and him aren't that close. Kevin kind of hates him. Growing up without a father. Mr. Dave was there and it was better for Kevin that Mr. Dave was there than my own father.'

'Right,' I agreed with AJ.

'My father is one of those kinds of dads that talk a good game but doesn't back it up,' AJ paused. 'He likes to take credit for things but never offer up help to do it. I remember when I graduated and he showed up. I shook his hand. No hugs, no fanfare.'

'Why?' I asked before I realized what I had done. I wished I could take the moment back. AJ paused and looked at me like he was thinking back to that time. Finally, AJ spoke.

'I did it to thank him, had he not walked away I wouldn't be half the man that I am.' AJ tried to smile.' Charles is many things to many people but he will never be my father. Not now, not ever.'

I could see the hurt in AJ's eyes at the mention of his dad. 'You'll be the better one when it is your turn.'

AJ smiled and looked at his watch. 'You think?'

'I'll call you when I get in,' he said then kissed me before hopping into his new car. I watched him drive off before I ventured into the house. Nikki was asleep on the couch. Nikki looked tired.

I turned off the television and went to go undress and take a shower. After about 15 minutes, AJ called and I called it a night. AJ would be back in the morning to take me to church. Things were back to normal for the most part and I intend to keep it that way. Finally, I am happy but for how long...

Nikki

It started again. The pain that is. I scheduled an emergency appointment with my doctor because something didn't feel right. They told me this might happen, that my cancer could come back. Maybe the medicine wasn't working.

It felt the same way when I found out I had uterine cancer. A pain that until that day I couldn't bear to think about even though it has been almost two years since I first found out that I had cancer.

Until the cancer, I led a fairly normal life. But lately, I didn't feel right. This didn't even feel like the first time that I got sick, but something still felt wrong. That day when my period, at least I thought it was my period, came on. The pain was unbearable at times.

I was spotting along with excruciating cramps. At one point, after a trip to the emergency room that night, I was told that I might have a cyst on my right ovary.

I tried to agree with the doctors but my body was saying this was something bigger than a cyst. So when I went to see the specialist for a follow up.

I finally got my nerve up to ask my doctor to do a laparoscopy like a nurse told me to. At that point, I was going to do anything to get to the bottom of what was going on.

A laparoscopy, to be clear, is an examination of the interior of the abdomen by a laparoscope. I was about as lost as you are. A lapro what? Trying to ease my mind, the doctor suggested that I have an ultrasound first. Hesitantly, I agreed.

I remember being at the doctor's office and I was cleaning up in the rest room after the nurse had given me the exam. While in there, I overheard her on the phone, asking for the doctor himself. I immediately knew something was wrong, so I just sat there, listening.

The nurse, in a voice as low as she could make it, asked the doctor to come into the exam room. I was especially worried since I had been told before the exam that I would have to wait three days for the results.

When I came out of the restroom, I found the doctor standing there with the nurse. He asked me to lie down, and I did, heart pounding and all. He performed the ultrasound himself. He had this look on his face and finally asked me, 'Have you been in pain?' I told him yes, and that while I hated to admit it, I had grown used to the pain.

That is when he informed me that I had a tumor across my uterus, connected to the right side of my pelvic wall. He called my gynecologist on the phone in front of me and told him of the findings. He also told me to see my gynecologist right away considering I was pregnant. It was a chance my baby wouldn't survive.

The gynecologist assured me that there was no way this tumor could be cancer--I was too young. Too young my ass. He said that it was probably an unusually large, but common, teratoma that would have to be surgically removed.

So, one week later I was scheduled for the operation. Then, the doctor came in with a peculiar look on his face. 'Nicole,' he said, 'it is cancer.' I just sat there in shock. The initial diagnosis was advanced ovarian cancer; the prognosis was dismal. But I had already sensed something wasn't right.

That was the day that I called Brian, when I snapped out at the doctor's office. That was also the day before I found out about Renee. It felt like a life time ago.

With my head still spinning, I contacted a comprehensive cancer center and got in right away. After hearing my symptoms, the doctor ordered a uterine biopsy. The results indicated uterine cancer, not ovarian cancer after all.

I asked what was next and quickly found out: I was to

have a radical hysterectomy in one week, just two and one-half weeks after my abortion. I went to Pittsburgh to have my Nana by my side. I love Sista, Day and Brian dearly but I needed my grandmother.

Though I had to lose my child in the process, I was ready. Even though I know I never would be able to bear children after the hysterectomy, I know I needed to have the abortion in order to live. I didn't have any other choice. After the hysterectomy, the surgeon told my grandmother and me that a few things didn't look good.

We would have to wait for test results for a final staging. The final results came in: the cancer didn't spread but chemotherapy would try ensuring it wouldn't return or hadn't progress. Just in case the tests were wrong.

After Sista showed up in Pittsburgh to bring me home, I started my radiation. I was very, very sick. When I say sick, I was a mess. I had no hair, no feelings, and was meaner than hell. It was awful. I completed six rounds. Six rounds will make a nice person change their dispositions.

I shuddered at the thought and was snapped out of my state when I heard my name called. I know if I survived the cancer before I could survive what I would hear in the next couple of minutes from anyone, including my doctor. I thought about Brian. Here I found the love of my life and now have to face this. Yeah, I am going to beat this and I am going to win...

Brian

I stopped past my mother's house after work. As I entered I heard my mother and Miss Violet deep in conversation. Laughter was all around. I hadn't heard this much laughter since my father died. Miss Violet gave me a hug and then excused herself.

I grabbed something to drink from the refrigerator before settling in. My mother gave me that look that told me to not hold back and to spill my guts. Who needed a confessional when my mother is around?

'What brings my oldest to visit me in the middle of the week?' My mother said taking on her serious look. A look she had front and back. I knew like all mothers that my mother has eyes in the back of her head. My mother could be so nice some days. Yet, this is the same woman that threatened to beat me within an inch of my life.

Now she was being all warm and wonderful. It was because of my mother that I learned to pray after hitting her in the supermarket playing racing car with my brother in the cart. I hit my mother in the back of her heel. Claire Huxtable she isn't.

'I needed my Mom.' I said this and for a minute felt embarrassed because I felt like a little boy.

'Or do you miss your daddy? I know about your little talks. Man to man, as he put it. Lord knows there are some days; it feels like he is right here until I call his name…' My mother said as if lost in thought. I extended my hand and my mother took it and squeezed it. 'But talk to me. I'll see what I can do.'

'I think I am going to ask Nikki to marry me,' I said not wanting to meet my mother's gaze. My mother's smile is evident as she squeezed my hand.

'But?' my mother asked, sensing my hesitation. 'That is your favorite word.'

'What will we do about kids?' I smiled at what she said.

'Adoption. I wouldn't love an adopted grandchild any less than I would one of my own. If you thinking about the fact that you and Nikki can't have kids and that being the only thing stopping you, child, then you are crazy. Go get that girl and marry her fast.'

'Mommy,' I stopped realizing I just called my mother that. 'I just don't want to do anything wrong. I love her.'

'Child, listen when things go wrong, don't go with them. You have built something with Nikki that any man would kill for.' My mother paused. 'When you and Sista were growing up you were the two I never had to worry about. Sista, she is a good girl, head strong like her daddy but you, you are ruled by your heart like me.

She went on, 'But I always knew you would turn out okay like Sista. I used to feel like I had to worry about Eric. But out of all my children, you and Sista, I didn't. You two surprised me. Loretta now that is another one all together. I love her but she is blocking her blessings. I see it but I don't say anything.'

'Mom, this is Nikki, I don't want to mess this up?' I jumped in. 'I know Nikki.'

'Brian,' my mother started again. 'When are you going to stop being afraid to love somebody and let somebody love you with out all the pretense and expectations? When you love you need to love unconditionally. The same way you deserve to be loved.'

'But,' I protested.

'No 'buts'. We often make deals with ourselves, sometimes the devil when it should be God. This isn't one of those times, if you love her go get her,' my mother continued, 'When I met your Daddy, I thought he was a fool. He was too quiet. He was just too uppity always in his good shirt and slacks.

All the girls were crazy about him. I used to ask myself who does he think he is? Damn fool.' I laughed with my mother.

My mother continued. 'But as time went on, I realized that his quietness wasn't arrogance. It was just how he was. He was the person I would come to love for over thirty years. When you take vows you promise until death do you part, but he is gone but I still love him.'

'We fear,' She began again almost unsure of what to say next. 'We fear what we want most. The biggest lie we tell ourselves is that when we get what we want most that for some reason we'll be happy. Forget that. Be happy even when you don't. You have something good in that girl. Hold on to it.'

'But Mom, I don't know.'

My mother silenced me. 'That is why I called you Mr. Five Hundred. Your confidence equaled five times of all my other children. Don't you know your Dad used to always say that you were the most self confident of all his kids? Don't doubt yourself now.'

My mother patted my hand, 'Whatever you are willing to put up with is what you will have. Those chicken heads you dealt with before, and none of them can hold a candle to Nikki. None of them. If she is the one, then be with her.'

At that comment, I laughed. My mother smiled and continued, 'Every one of them prepared you for this moment. Every relationship prepares you for the one you are meant to have but don't block your blessing in doubt. Let God handle your doubts.'

I started to say something and instead kissed my mother on the forehead and gave her a hug. My mother's mood seemed to change at that moment. She stood up and I did too. My mother hugged me and I left. I know what I had to do. It was late when I called Day and told him to meet me for lunch tomorrow. We were going shopping for an engagement ring…

Day

I watched Sista styling her hair as I did my usual and read. That's all I did was read. 'I never know it took you this long to get dressed and ready.'

Sista looked at me and smiled, 'This is a big day for me.'

'Is that right,' I said curious enough to put down the issue of Essence and give Sista my undivided attention. Something is up. 'What happened? Don't tell me something happened with AJ.'

Sista breathed deeply then paused, 'My period was late and I found out I was pregnant. I mean I took a home test and then went to see my doctor to confirm it.'

I looked at Sista and then moved over near the mirror, 'I thought you said you used protection?' Sista know my stance on using protection. She heard my speeches on safe sex.

'You know that isn't 100%. You said it yourself. Plus I did ask about his HIV status. I asked about it again after the whole thing with Cliff and Loretta when Cliff told me he got tested to make sure Loretta didn't bring anything home.'

I took another deep breathe, 'AJ is fine.' Sista said looking at me for the first time. Sista took a deep breath, 'Right now, I am pregnant.'

I took a deep breath and looked at Sista. 'Is AJ ready to marry you? I thought you said he was. Is that what you are planning on doing?'

'I am not ready,' Sista said meeting my intense gaze. Sista then realized that I knew what she was thinking about: Nikki. Sista couldn't begin to try to figure out what she would say or do. I instinctively hugged Sista, 'So what do you plan on telling Nikki?'

'I honestly don't know. I didn't even consider it at first. If you can't have kids would you want somebody to call you Mom, even if it is as a Godmother,' Sista asked.

I looked at Sista long and hard, 'She might. She might love this child like it was her own. I know I will. I am not saying she will not take it hard but try her. Nikki has dealt with a lot worst. So have you.'

Sista kissed me on the cheek. 'We'll see.'

I looked at Sista, 'You need me to do anything?'

'Yes,' Sista smiled, 'My baby needs another uncle and a godfather. You have always been a good friend.'

'Thank you,' I smiled. 'I think I can do that.'

'You better,' Sista laughed. 'Or I will give Miss Monica your phone number. Track her ass down wherever she moved to.'

'Funny,' I said and picked up the magazine I was reading again. 'Now, let's go. You are slow as molasses. AJ wants to meet you for lunch not dinner and if you want me to drop you off. Let's go. I am meeting your brother to go shopping.' Sista hit me and we prepared to leave...

Sista

I met AJ as planned and soon was distracted as we ate by a table of women near by. A posse is what they should have been called. The kind of women you would see mostly in clubs and bars. They were getting on my nerve.

It usually three of them, the diva, or the cute one, who never carried a pocketbook because she knows somebody, is going to buy her a drink.

The cool one, yes, she could be a bitch at times, quick to set it off, but over all, she is the one that kept every one straight. Then there is the troll, the ugly one that makes sure everyone goes home together.

If they all came together they would leave the same way. Their conversation got louder and louder. I showed my disgust. AJ sensed it but didn't say anything.

I continued to just pick over my salad having spent the better part of my morning with my head in the toilet before Day showed up. I didn't want to tell Day that is why I had to fix my hair again. AJ sensed something was wrong and reached across the table. I looked at him.

'You sure you are all right?' AJ asked for the third time since he met up with me.

'Yes, just nervous. My brother is coming home.'

'That is good,' AJ said. 'Eric seems like a good guy.'

'He is.' I realized I have to put a better face on or AJ would know. I hated keeping secrets. But this is something I couldn't even tell Nikki. I wasn't sick, I am pregnant. Can't just spit that one out. Day is different, but telling Nikki is going to be hard.

In my heart, I know that even though I didn't want to

marry AJ, I wanted to be with him and I wanted things to be right. I didn't want to marry him just because I was pregnant; I wanted him to marry me for love. A baby is a lot of responsibility. I also didn't want him to feel I was trying to trap him.

I know he loves kids. AJ recently made the decision to return to school this time Drexel to get his Master's Degree in Education. He had started working with kids.

Every day he told me of another one of, as he calls them, his 'kids' and their daily adventures. I know though that he got to send those kids home. I wouldn't have the patience. I would have to beat somebody's ass.

Now that I am pregnant, I know I needed to learn some patience. Sitting here, I still didn't know how or when, but our protection failed. But obviously it did. AJ looked at me again, snapping me out of my day dream.

'When does he come home?' AJ asked again.

I was momentarily shaken out of my daze. 'Huh?'

'Something is wrong. I think I know what it is? When were you going to tell me?'

'Tell you what?' I ventured cautiously.

'That you are pregnant.' AJ said with a smile. 'My Mom dreamed of fish. She can always tell when she dreams of fish that somebody is pregnant. You never heard that, when somebody dreams of fish, somebody is pregnant.'

'Am I that transparent?'

'No, I had a mean craving for some apples and chocolate milk,' AJ smiled. 'To answer your question, no you aren't that transparent.'

I seemed lost for a minute. 'Apples and milk. That is nasty.' I got quiet and then squeezed AJ's hand. He rubbed my hand with his other hand. 'But--'

'But what? I kind of sensed you didn't want to get married. I get that. All the stuff with Monica didn't help. Listen, I can wait a week or two for you to change your mind.'

'Silly,' I smiled. 'Are you prepared for my late night cravings and morning sickness tossing all of that stuff back up?'

'I would even hold your hair back,' AJ smiled.

'You have issues, you know that,' I laughed. I got the strength to eat and tried to eat a little of the chicken.

'I am sympathizing. It is about what you want right now. What you need. I want to make you happy.' AJ laughed. I smiled. 'What do you think it is going to be?'

'You are taking this very well. What do you want?'

'I love you and I am going to love our child.' AJ said touching my hand. 'A healthy baby boy or girl.'

I looked at AJ and realized that maybe it is more than like with him at this point. I think I was truly in love. Not the kind of love I read in a book, but the kind you can hold on to in the middle of the night. The kind of love that my parents shared. I reached for AJ's hand.

'You know I am not ready to get married. I know it is supposed to be the other way around. But when it comes to a baby and getting married, that might be a bit much.'

AJ smiled, 'We are going to do whatever it is you want. I love you. I love you. I do. Let's just take things slow. I know one thing; I don't want to lose you again. That shit hurts.' I smiled. For the rest of the lunch, we talked about the baby and possible names.

AJ shot down Shawn, Tyrone and Michael right away fearing that any child or person with those names would be crazy. Think about the people you know.

Michael especially when Tyson and Jackson came to mind. I was taken back by how well things went. At that moment, I realized I was looking at my child's father. My child.

'Lord,' I said a silent prayer, 'Please don't let me turn into my Mama.' I looked at AJ with new eyes. AJ promised to be there no matter what knowing what.

AJ knew what it is like to grow up without a dad and his child would never know what that is like. As I walked back to work, I realized it isn't over just yet. I still had to tell Nikki.....

Nikki

I got up in the middle of the night and went into the bathroom to splash water on my face. I didn't bother to slip on my robe. Brian was still asleep. I returned to the bed and he was still sleep. I looked at him. He looked so peaceful. It has been months since I began to stay with him.

Most of my stuff is at Sista's but I stayed with Brian most of the time at his request. I never regretted it for a minute. I just wished I could tell Brian what is going on. I promised never to keep any secrets like before, but this one I had to keep to myself. I didn't want to shatter the happiness that I know he felt.

For the first time in my life, I was in love and it felt right. Brian is the only thing I ever asked for. All the things Reggie could never be. It helped that Brian is so predictable.

Brian went to work, he spent time with his family and he hung out with Day and Shawn. There were no other women and those that called once they heard my voice usually hung up never to call again. Except some girl named Sabrina who couldn't get the hint. I wasn't Brian's girlfriend, I am his woman.

I thought about everything I endured just to get to this point. I didn't regret a thing. But it is coming to a point where everyone would know what is going on with me. I fought once but didn't know if I could fight this time.

My cancer came back and things didn't look good this time. Not even aggressive chemotherapy. I want to fight, I have to. Not only for me but for the love I found in Brian.

As Brian lay there peacefully, I closed my eyes knowing the family would be celebrating Eric's release. The family planned a big dinner. I didn't want anything to upset that. Not me or anybody else would. I love Eric too. I closed my eyes and touched my chest. I know what it would come to....

264

Sista/Day/Nikki/Brian/Loretta/Eric

Sista arrived at her mother's earlier than everybody else. AJ drove her. With each turn he reminded her of how she didn't have a chauffer. One of AJ's pet peeves is that Sista had a license and never used it. Since she has been pregnant he was guilty of spoiling her.

When it came to driving he begged to differ. Sista promised she would drive more before the baby came. In case, she had to drive herself to the hospital. Just in case.

Sista was two months and was already making plans. AJ and Sista agreed to move into a bigger place together. Not get married but to consider it. Since Nikki was always at Brian's, Sista felt it wouldn't be long before Brian and Nikki would be together on a regular basis. Nikki practically lived there now.

Today would be the day she would tell every one. Including Nikki. Ms. Violet and her mother were in the kitchen cooking as she walked in the house.

Ms. Lucy hugged AJ instinctively. Sista hated when Lucy called AJ her son-in-law. Nikki, Day and Mike arrived. Ms. Lucy playfully yelled at Day for not talking to her about Mike before. Violet hugged her son and then Mike. But all conversation stopped when Loretta walked in with her new boy toy, Kareem.

Her divorce was already final. Loretta, though, had turned into a bitch. She made Monica look nice. Loretta even ignored the family's advice when she let Kareem move in.

Both Loretta and Kareem smelled like reefer which set Sista off but and Nikki grabbed her. Loretta is on a one way ticket to hell with nobody to stop her.

When Loretta and Kareem first came in and Loretta was introducing everyone, Mike went over and shook Kareem's hand. As Mike and Day stood by watching, Loretta whispered something in Kareem's ear that made Kareem look at the two and laugh. Day already heard the last word--faggots but instead went into the kitchen to help his mother.

Kareem grabbed his dick and blew a kiss at Mike. Mike just ignored him and finished talking to AJ. Sista watched and again Nikki grabbed Sista. The commotion was interrupted when Ms. Lucy heard the phone ring and announced from the kitchen that Eric was on his way up the street. Brian just called and they needed to find a parking spot.

Loretta was too far gone to realize that every time Nikki made a move Kareem's eyes were on her. This didn't go unnoticed by Mike and Day. Sista could see why Loretta never brought Kareem before, he was ignorant as hell. Day to change the pace of things decided to start up a game of Spades. Spades is the national black past time in black colleges and universities.

Sista watched Nikki swerve and sway earlier like Nikki was beyond tired and when asked Nikki said she just needed to eat. Nikki knew she was fatigued and she knew why.

Nikki felt light headed and grabbed a chair. She knew it would come to this. Sista reached out to Nikki almost instinctively.

As the door opened a cheer erupted from everyone. Everyone went to hug Eric and Sista placed her arms around Nikki. Sista fearing that if she let go Nikki will fall. Sista felt how thin Nikki had become. Nikki closed her eyes.

Brian then held up his hand. 'Okay, okay. Now that the family is together. I have an announcement to make, more like a question.' Eric looked at Kareem and the last five years came flooding back to him. 'This mother fucker is in my house, messing with my sister. It's not that simple. I'm going to get that nigga.'

'Hey, look, I was going to wait until dinner but now I can't wait,' Brian said. 'I got to do this now?'

'What?' Eric asked still eyeing Kareem. Just then Brian grabbed a pillow and sat Nikki down in a chair. Nikki held the side feeling weak. Brian got down on one knee and pulled a jewelry box from his pocket. The room grew still and everyone was quiet.

'Nikki, I have love you all of my life. There isn't a woman alive that I could want to love and spend my life with more than you. If you will have me, Nikki,' Brian said through teary eyes. 'Will you marry me? Will you be my wife?'

Nikki took a deep breathe and closed her eyes. When Nikki paused too long Brian know something is wrong. Nikki went to stand as Brian put the ring on her finger. Suddenly, Nikki reached out to a chair and she felt herself collapsing on the ground.

The next few minutes became a blur as Sista cradled Nikki's head in her lap. Brian moved to Nikki's side scooping her up in his arms and taking her to his car and to the hospital.

Eric watched Loretta sitting in the same spot. As he moved out the door, he looked back and saw Kareem pull a blunt out his pocket.

Eric realized things haven't changed in years. Kareem was so high that he didn't realize who Eric was. Eric knew he would deal with them both latter on. Both of them. Kareem and Loretta.

If you asked Brian how he got to the hospital, he wouldn't have been able to tell you. Brian rushed Nikki into the emergency room and stood by as he watched the medics take care of her upon entering the emergency room.

Lucy, Violet, Day, Mike, Sista, AJ and Eric arrived and when they saw Brian alone moved him to the waiting room to hold vigil. It was a wait and see thing.

Day found himself pacing the halls and outside not sure

of his place or what to do. Sista remained inside holding her mother's hand. In Sista's heart, she felt like she was reliving the day her father had his heart attack.

When Brian had gathered enough change, he placed the faithful call to Pittsburgh. He didn't want to leave the hospital to call Nikki's grandmother on his cell phone, knowing you should not use a cell phone in a hospital. But, Brian was afraid that if he left he would miss something.

Nikki's grandmother vowed to be on the next flight out to Philly. Brian reached the hall and found a quiet spot and as he felt the strength of the wall he felt himself sliding down it. As he fell so did the tears. Just then he felt a hand on his shoulder as he sat in the hall and looked up to find Eric next to him.

'I remember when I was a little boy, when I used to get mad and used to want to be by myself, you would sit with me.' Eric said smiling. 'You never said anything, you just sat there.'

Brian laughed for the first time since all this had began, 'You needed a big brother.'

'I got one. I got one.' Eric looked at Brian and gave Brian hugged Eric. 'Nikki is strong, dude. She is going to be okay. You and Nikki will be alright.'

'You think so,' Brian said looking at his brother and hearing the maturity in Eric's voice.

'I know so.'

'Sometimes, E,' Brian's name for his brother. 'I think sometimes God gave me too much. Because the things I truly want, I never get. I have been in love with Nikki and was too afraid to show it.'

'Now,' Brian breathed deeply. 'Something like this happens and I find myself losing out on something. The material things man don't mean anything without somebody you can share all of it with. Somebody you can give it all to and start over as long as she is there.'

Eric looked at his brother. 'I learned God gives you what you need instead of what you want man. Nikki is still here, man. If she has cancer again, give her a new reason to fight. Something to hold on to.'

'You are right,' Brian said. 'But—'

'No buts, Brian. It was the same I felt about y'all after daddy passed away,' Eric said wiping his face in his hands. 'I sat in my cell many nights staring into the dark. Counting the days when I would go back to my family. That was my rock, man. You have to be that for Nikki, be her rock.'

'You got to trust that God is going to see you through. I did, B and I am still here.' Eric looked at his brother for a minute and then he put his arm around his brother and gave his brother a hug.

Day watched the two in the distance before walking away. Day felt it was good Brian was with Eric, they needed that time. Day walked to the other end of the hall. Mike quickly followed. Day turned and Mike extended his arms. Day hugged Mike and Mike felt his shirt get wet as Day cried.

'I am here as long as you need me. I know how you feel about Nikki' Mike said as he held Day. Day continued to cry. Sista stepped in to the hall and went to the emergency room door watching for any sign of the doctor. AJ was close behind her.

Brian with Eric's help got off the floor. Brian told Eric he needed a minute and quietly went to the chapel. As Brian knelt before the altar, he looked at the cross and the tears came again.

'It is me and you again God. It seems like I always end up here. On my knees asking you for your mercy. I know it seems like most people only come to you in their time of need, but I always thanked you for everything that you have done for me. I was one of the lucky ones. I had a mother and a father. A good family with a brother and sisters that any man could be proud of. But then, you opened my eyes and placed one of the most remarkable women in my life and I couldn't have been happier.'

'I have done everything you have ever asked me. I have been a good friend. I have been a good son. I have been a good brother. I have been a good man. I have done all you asked and now I am here on my knees asking of you in return to give her back,' Brian cried.

'I know it isn't my place to question you. I know that you give people what they need instead of what they want, but I need her. I need her...'

Brian

I sat in the chapel for what seemed like an eternity. I lost track of time. It was over an hour when the doctor would return. Sista didn't want him to speak until I got there. Sista had Eric come get me. Sista can be a bully at times when she wants to be. This time it served a good purpose.

After explaining the situation to the family, Dr. Lincoln then looked at me and asked, 'Are you Brian? She is asking to see you.'

I brushed past everyone and went in and sat by Nikki's bedside for what seemed like an eternity until she opened her eyes and realized I was there.

'Boo Boo Bear,' Nikki called me weakly.

Brian smiled, 'You haven't called me that in a minute.'

'You grew up.' Nikki smiled.

'I know.' I said. 'You promised me no more secrets.'

'I wanted to fight this to be strong for you.' Nikki said and then turned away. I gently reached out and grabbed her chin turning her back around to me.

'Hey,' I said as I saw the first tears come. 'You know I hate to see a woman cry. I am not going anywhere. Nowhere, you hear me. I love you. I have always loved you and I will always love you.'

'But not like this,' Nikki said through tears.

'Nikki,' I said smiling. 'In sickness and in health. I was there the first time. I have always been here. I will always be. Just give me the chance. Please Nikki. Please. Don't shut me out. I can't handle that. I don't ever want to be without you.'

'I didn't want you to see me bad again. I didn't want you to see me sick. Not again. I love you too much for that.'

'I saw you at twelve when your hair was all over your head and you stayed at our house. I was there when you used to have that nasty face mask on your face when you and my sister were sixteen. When I went away to school, I used to miss you. But I know when I came home you would be there. You were never bad. Love does that; it blinds a person to everything but you.'

'Brian,' Nikki said hoarsely. 'Why didn't you ever say anything the first time around when I found I was sick.'

'It wasn't my place. I know but I didn't want to think about it. I didn't want to think about what it would be like to live without you....' I said. Nikki put her finger to my lips. I kissed Nikki's hand.

'I love you, Brian.' Nikki said.

'I love you too. Nikki, I never knew I could love a woman as much as I love you. I didn't.' I got up. I still hadn't let go of Nikki's hands. I smiled. I held up the engagement ring and said, 'This is a down payment on forever.' Then I laughed.

'Why are you laughing?'

'Trying to remember where I parked my car. I don't remember driving here.' Nikki laughed a weak laugh. I turned to see Sista standing by and kissed Nikki. Nikki saw Sista and tried to smile. I hugged my sister and went to go see my mother...

Sista

'Damn, girl, all he did was to give you a ring for you to go passing out like that,' I said smiling taking Nikki's hand as I sat down.

'My hair must look a wreck.' Nikki said. 'Girl, you got a comb.'

'No,' I said as I sat next to Nikki's bed. 'But you are wearing the hell out of that gown.'

There was silence again before I chose to speak. Nikki moved and cleared her throat.

'You're sick again.'

'Yeah,' Nikki looked away then looked back at Sista.

'I thought it might have been my Mom's cooking, she has been slipping lately.' I said and Nikki responded by laughing. 'I am sorry, Nikki.'

'Sista, for what?'

'For not paying attention. I promised the last time…' I stopped. 'You deserved better than that.'

'You have your own life. You just got your man back. Be happy. This wasn't your fault we knew the chances that it would.'

'It isn't that, Nikki.'

'Then what?' Nikki asked sitting up weakly.

'I am pregnant and I was going to tell everybody today. When I had my whole family there. You, Day, Eric, Brian. But then, I saw you looked weak. And I felt like I couldn't tell you. I wanted to tell you.'

Nikki smiled, 'Don't block your blessings. Your child will be a blessing in both our lives. I can't bring a life into this world but I will not watch yours from a distance. I am going to love that child like it was my own.'

Nikki reached out her other hand to cover my hand as my hand held her own. 'You are my very best friend and nothing will ever change that. Ever.'

I sat by Nikki's bed and watched as the sedatives the doctor gave Nikki kicked in. I stayed a few minutes before leaving. I returned to the hall and told everybody that Nikki was sleeping peaceful.

I looked around and discovered that Eric was gone. Brian noticing this gave me a look that told me that I should end it there. There wasn't anything more for me to say.

I remember the look he gave Loretta's friend. If Loretta didn't recognize him. I did. Obviously, so did Eric. If she didn't know, she was about to find out soon enough. I only prayed that Eric had enough sense to do it outside and that Loretta didn't try to stop him.

Day looked at Brian and then at me. We all knew where Eric was going. My mother and Violet missed the look. Good. Mike caught it. Day raised his eye brows.

Day and Brian quietly left when my mother and Ms Violet went back into the waiting room. I felt Mike grab my hand and I gave his a squeeze. Trouble was brewing....

Eric

I don't know what came over me. I don't know just seeing Kareem in that house after everything he did upset me. All the years without my family came down to that moment. I ran all the way home.

It wasn't far and considering where we live to the hospital, it didn't take long. It seem like all the hatred I had in me was fueling my run.

My mind was on one thing and one thing alone. I wanted to do as much damage to Kareem that the law allowed. He was in my house, high and with my sister though.

Like I said, it wasn't going down like that. I couldn't. I asked the Lord for forgiveness and I opened the front door. They were just sitting there.

I busted into the house and smelled the air even before I was inside. I grabbed Kareem in one leap and began choking him. I started hitting Kareem, beating him. I shouldn't have but my anger got the best of me.

He was gone, six sheets to the wind and too high to even realize what happened. Not even when I physically threw him out. Tossed his ass onto the sidewalk. He got up and started run away at first confused by what happened.

Then he saw me and left. Loretta, shaken out of her stupor, screamed hysterically as I walked back into the house. She threatened to call the police.

Brian and Day arrive within minutes. Loretta jumped on my back and I grabbed my sister after I shook her off. I held on to Loretta as she fought to free herself from my strong grasp.

'I am your brother. He don't mean shit to you. Call the fucking police,' I boomed as I finally let Loretta go and she began throwing things off the table at me. 'You bring that little pussy up into our mother's house. What the fuck is wrong with you.'

'You don't have any right to tell me what to do,' Loretta screamed at me. 'You aren't my father.'

'Don't you ever,' my voice boomed as I got into Loretta's face. 'Don't ever say shit about my pop again. Ever. You are going to bring up daddy because you fucking with some no account nigga I used to be locked up with. He isn't shit. Did he tell you all the shit he did when I was locked up? That nigga's a snitch.'

Brian looked at Loretta who was more shaken than if I physically hit her. Day began picking up stuff of the floor and Brian grabbed me and I shook Brian off me.

'No,' I said. Brian let me go. 'Don't you know that little nigga ain't shit? He is the nigga I went into that store with. He turned on me to save his ass.' Loretta was stunned.

'Yeah, you are fucking with the nigga that kept me away from my family. You are fucking with the nigga that kept me from my father during the last years of his life. I never got the fucking chance to say goodbye to my dad because I was around that nigga. Now you don't have shit to say.'

'I am sorry,' Loretta said. 'I didn't know.'

'You are sorry. You left Cliff for him. Are you stupid or dumb? You had a good man. Did you know your husband used to send me money? Used to look out for me when I was locked down. Where the fuck was you, huh?'

'Eric,' Loretta tired to speak. "I didn't know.'

'Fuck your sorry,' I laughed with contempt. 'Fuck you didn't know. Then to have my family telling me you fucking with Kareem and out of respect for Mommy, I would have fucked him up when I first walked in.'

'But I know,' I spat the words out. 'I know I would do what I just did. Now you saying you are sorry. Fuck you and you are sorry. We used to be close. You were always my big sister. You were to me what Brian is to Sista. What happened?'

'I don't want to be anything to anybody,' Loretta screamed, crying hysterically. 'That is all I hear about. Sista this and Sista that. Fuck her. What about me? I lost my husband because of her.'

'Sista didn't bring some no good nigga up in our Mother's house. You are smoking weed in Mommy's house. You fucked up your marriage to Cliff. Nobody told you to sleep with that guy. You are fucking up your life. You got that nigga all up in here. You aren't shit.'

'You aren't shit,' Loretta screamed to counter me. 'You let Sista talk to you any old kind of way and you act like she is God's gift. Everything is about her. Everything. When is it my turn.' Loretta screamed. 'When do people start respecting me? Earl Robinson was my father too. I hurt too. I have feelings.'

'You had your turn. You had it all. You want all of us to apologize because you fucked up. Daddy has been gone for a while; don't use him as an excuse for why you can't get your shit together. You did all your shit before Daddy died. When Sista talked about me, she was telling the truth. I fucked up.'

'Do you know what it is like to have to come home to your father's viewing in hand cuffs and shackles? I had people coming out their house to watch me get ushered in by armed guards into a funeral home. I lost years of being with my family for some dumb shit. And you want to talk to me about having your turn. You are still on your dumb shit. '

'We used to be so close, Loretta. But outside of a card and some money, I couldn't even get a visit out of you. Brian is my brother, but not once did he miss a visit. You could have kept your money. You could have kept all that shit you sent me. I wanted my family. You know how many nights I laid in my cell crying my eyes out wishing I could be home with my family.'

I continued, 'Wishing I could sit on that couch and watch Westerns with my father. Wishing I could play Spades with Brian, Nikki and Sista. Pretending that a piece of bread and a cup of noodles was Mommy's cornbread and chicken noodle soup.' I began crying.

'I missed a lot of time. But I will not do it again. It took for me to get locked up to see what good I had in this family. Sista isn't right most days, but when it comes to being a big sister, she can do no wrong.' I continued.

'You need to get your shit together. You already lost a good man and you are about to lose a good family because you have it in your heart to hate your own sister for being her. Who better than somebody that knows you to call you on your shit?'

I looked at Loretta, 'Right now, my sister's best friend is in the hospital and that is where I need to be.' I walked out of the house and Day followed. Brian stopped and stared hard at Loretta. Loretta sat back on the couch and cried...

Sista

I unlocked my door and went in the house. I heard about the events, or should I say hell that broke lose at my mother's earlier. It is funny how the tables turned. All my life, Loretta hated me without cause.

It bothered me to think about it but in the end, it was the truth. I held my stomach and promised myself that I would never let my children go through such drama in their lives. I smiled at my thought my children. AJ made me a cup of tea as I settled in.

Brian had gone back to the hospital after taking my mother and Ms. Violet back to the house. He left the night my father passed away and this time, he wouldn't allow Nikki to be alone. Even though the doctors said she was resting comfortably.

Eric vowed to stay all night if that is what Brian needed. When Brian discovered my condition, he insisted I go home with AJ to get some rest. AJ promised he would take care of me. I know Brian he is going to send everybody home. But he won't go.

'Why are you so quiet?' AJ asked.

'Thinking,' I said between sips of my tea. 'I am afraid for Nikki. She has been through so much in a short time'

'You were right there. Every step of the way,' AJ replied.

I couldn't shake the image of Nikki laying there so sickly. 'I should have paid attention more. I should have seen it. I was too busy dealing with my own issues, my own stuff. I am Nikki's best friend.'

'Trust in that. We didn't know. There are reason's why some people keep things to themselves,' AJ stopped and rested my head on his shoulder.

'I feel like I should have paid attention,' I said. 'I should have been more aware.

'There was no way of telling this would happen,' AJ replied. 'We never know what is going on in a person's heart and mind until we ask. Nikki was trying to protect you. Don't fault her; we all have been there before.'

I sat there quietly. 'Have you talked to your father, AJ?'

'No, but I feel it coming. He and I need to have a serious conversation.'

'Be nice,' I said 'when you do.'

'I will try but no promises. He hurt me bad by not showing up. I used to think I had it bad. Growing up without my Dad. My Mom trying to do the best she could. There were some days where I felt like screaming because it hurt so badly. But I held on. But as long as we can live to tell the tale, we'll be all right.'

I looked up at AJ and yawned. 'You promise?'

'I'll try.' AJ said obviously in deep thought. I knew about what. He had to hand things his way. AJ sat with me until I drifted off to sleep. While I slept I knew he was planning his next move, but would his father be ready for the consequences...

Day

I hugged Mike again once we got inside my apartment. I looked at Mike long and hard before, I decided to ask Mike the question that had been on my mind me since earlier. Mike sensed what I was going to say and sat down as I rested my head on the back of the couch.

'Why did you stay tonight? You didn't have to,' I said quietly. 'I didn't know why, so I decided to ask.'

'You were my ride.' Mike said making me smile. 'No, seriously, you needed me. I know Nikki is like family to you. The siblings you never had and you needed to be there and I wanted to be where you are. Brian is your best friend and you didn't want to see him hurting. But who was going to protect your heart? Nikki is your family too.'

'But you didn't have to,' I said. 'Thank you.'

'I wanted to be there. Like it or not, that is your family and a big part of my getting to know you is getting to know them. The people you love and care about.' Mike realized his choice of words and Mike looked at me again and I smiled. Mike shook my shoulder lightly, 'So, since we never got to eat dinner, I am hungry. Starving. Hungrier than a hostage.'

'Then order something,' I said handing Mike the menus that we collected since we started spending time together.

'I meant to ask you,' Mike said leafing through the menus. 'What ever happened earlier with Sista's other brother?'

'Eric took care of things. Out of all of Sista's family, Eric is the one I don't know very well. He has been locked up. But I respect him all the same because he had to wreck shop tonight.'

Mike leaned forward and put the menus down and hugged me again. 'You are good man. You were there tonight

281

when your family needed you to be, and I promise I will be there when you need it.' Mike moved back as the line connected and Mike placed his order. I nodded that I wanted my usual and Mike ordered.

When Mike got off the phone, he sat back down next to me, 'I am going to be here. How you said it, for as long as you need me and a few weeks after in case you change your mind.' For the first time, I found myself believing that it might be true...

Eric

Against my wishes and at Brian's request, I went home. I was looking forward to my first night in my own bed in my own house. After I spent the last couple of years staring in the dark of my cell, that's what I wanted most.

I felt somebody's presence when I walked into the living room. I turned on the lights, knowing it could only be one person since my mother and Ms. Violet should have been asleep.

'What are you doing?' I asked.

'Minding my business and leaving yours alone. How is my girl doing?' Loretta ventured, I could tell she was now sober.

'Clawja,' I said referring to my sister by her real name, 'Or Nikki.'

'Nikki,' Loretta said without putting up a fight, I turned on more lights. 'Turn that out. Damn, you are trying to be smart.'

'Nikki's cancer was back if you must know. If you weren't fucked up you could have been at the hospital with the rest of us,' I said looking at my sister who looked like hell. I turned on another light.

'You need the light, hope it hurts. Maybe it will help you see yourself for what and who you really are and you can get your shit together,'

'I still don't get what happened to you, Eric. You bust up in here like a mad man earlier. We used to be close. We were like Janet and Mike. Now you come back here with this holier than thou attitude.'

'Maybe, I grew up. You should try it to,' I said still standing looking at Loretta. 'I had a lot of time to think about the shit I had been doing. My father died and I said to myself you know what you can either make him upset with the shit you are doing and make him turn over in his grave some more. Or I can do what I need to do when I got out of here. I am trying for the first time in my life to make my father proud. Proud of me and the things that I do and the things that I say and the man that I am. My question is where you were?'

'I couldn't see you like that all locked up,' Loretta said feeling suddenly ashamed. 'You are my brother.'

'Funny because that is what would have helped me more. Did you know for every time I sat on that phone beefing with Sista and having to hear Daddy holler at me that he came to see me every Tuesday? He would tell Mommy he was going to the center with his friends, but he came to see me. He told me not to say anything because he claimed he didn't want his wife to know he was getting soft.'

I laughed at the thought. 'I have pictures of every visit he made. All I ever wanted is a sense of family, to know my family cared. Somebody to love and care for me at a time when I didn't love or care about myself. I got that from everybody but you.'

Loretta looked at me long and hard. 'I tried to give you that. We were close growing up but then lately you changed too. You started treating Sista like she is made of gold and she use to knock you at every turn. She talked about you like a dog and you just took it.'

'Clawja is my sister. I grew up since Daddy died. I took time out to re-evaluate what I was doing and where I have been in my life. I haven't done shit. Yeah, Sista and I argue but that's what we do. We are brother and sister,' I sat down and wiped my face using two hands then looked at Loretta again.

'She did stay on my case and no, I didn't always like it. Could I blame her though? She was right,' I laughed.

'She was telling the truth. Something I wished you did back then,' I said almost to myself. 'You have some deep issues

284

with her. You are taking sibling rivalry to the next level and back again. She is your sister too. Yeah, she gets on my last nerves but that is what sisters do. I learned to respect her words and wishes just like you need to do. We are all adults now. But you are the only one that don't act like it.'

I breathed deeply and sighed. 'Right now, her best friend and now I see the only sister that she will ever know is in the fight of her life and she doesn't need any drama. Then, Brian, damn. I don't know what to say.'

I looked at Loretta, 'I never loved anybody like that, not the way he loves Nikki. I saw that tonight.' Loretta sat in silence. I grabbed my door keys and moved to the door.

'Where are you going?' Loretta asked.

''My brother might need me...' I said then left.

Brian

I stepped out onto the street after waving to the guard at the front desk. I needed a breath of fresh air now that Nikki had been moved to a private room. Her grandmother is on her way.

I watched Nikki sleep for what felt like hours and while I was tired, I didn't want to leave. I couldn't. As I sat stood outside of the hospital, I saw Eric walking up the block. I don't know why but I began to cry.

'What are you doing back here, I told you to go home,' I said searching Eric's face. I smiled, 'You never did listen to me, did you?'

'You held it down without me for all these years, let me be here for you.' Eric said giving me a hug. 'It's the least I can do.'

'My little brother is a man now,' I said laughing and crying at the same time. 'Wow, if Dad can see you now.'

'He does. He does. Between you and our dad, I had good examples. I just didn't pay attention. So look, I know you haven't eaten so let's see what we can find in one of those machines. I'll eat anything right now. When Nikki gets better, you know I am going to scream at her for messing up my first home cooked meal in a minute.'

'You got money?' I asked.

'Who said I was paying?' Eric said and I shook my brother by the shoulders. I hugged my brother again as we walked back inside. I stopped past the guard's desk and William, somebody that I knew from high school, allowed us to go back into the hospital...

Paul

I had just dropped my son off at his mother's and decided to meet my buddy Chris, at the bar for a drink. It has been a long day and all I wanted to do is unwind. My son, Paul Junior, is getting so big. I loved the way he would yell 'Daddy' at the top of his lungs when he sees me. He tired me out today. I needed a beer to unwind down.

The bar wasn't crowded as I sat down shook Chris hands. I motioned for the bartender and ordered us both a beer. I went over to the jukebox realizing it was too quiet up in here. I had a good day and wanted to celebrate.

I flipped through the selections and was startled when I felt a hand on my shoulder. I turned around to stare into the face of a caramel brown skinned chick with a tight blue dress on. She is drunk as shit.

'You trying to dance,' she said. Yes, she is drunk. I smelled it. This was too easy. It has been a minute for me since I have been with a woman like this. Since the shit with Sista and my so called ex-wife, I stopped caring. A woman was a woman and sex was just sex. A woman can be pouring her heart out to me and all I can think about is when I can fuck her. Who cared as long as I got the nut?

'Nah, not really,' I said trying to place where I saw here face before. She looked familiar. I just wish I knew from where.

'Never mind, then,' she said slinking off. I watched her move over to another guy as a song came on that I never heard. The guy got up and started grinding against her as I tried to remember where I knew her from.

She is drunk and I felt bad that the guy is about to take advantage of her. I can't let that happen. My conscience kicked in. It was bad. I had to do something.

At one point, the guy got rougher with her. The girl tried

to pull away. The guy pulled harder. I decided to step in. I looked over at Chris who was watching the whole scene to see if he had my back. He nodded, so I walked over where the two stood. The guy looked at me like move.

'Damn, girl,' I said as I moved over the female and grabbed her around her waist.

'Stop playing and being mad at me. You didn't have to dance with him to make me jealous.' The guy looked at me again. So did she. She realized what I was up to. He let go and she moved closer to me.

'I think it's time to take you home,' I said. I nodded at Chris and helped her out the door. She seemed to sober up as we got outside.

'I asked her where she lived and when she mentioned not far, I drove the three blocks to her house and then walked her to her front door.

'I'm sorry,' she said, realizing that she had been avoiding my eyes. 'I don't really get drunk like that but I have been having a bad time with my husband and my family and—'

'No need to explain. You didn't deserve what he was trying to do,' I said. She opened the door.

'Oh, what do I deserve? Look, I just didn't want to be alone. You want to come in?' she asked looking at me. I guess it must have been her first time to really see me because she just stared.

'You know you look familiar?' She said almost to herself. She definitely reminded me of someone. I couldn't figure it out.

'I was thinking the same thing about you.'

'I'm Paul,' I responded still looking at her.

'Loretta,' she said as she got this devious look on her face and then she held the door open for me. She was lonely and I figured I'd only stay a minute. Still in the back of my mind I couldn't figure out where I knew her from. I rolled the name around in my mind for a minute, but couldn't place it.

I stepped inside and when I sat down, what she did next, surprised me. She took her clothes off. It's been a minute. That's all I could think as she stepped out of her dress and walked towards me. It wasn't until I was deep up in it with no plans to stop when it clicked in my head that Loretta is Sista's sister...

Nikki and Brian

When I woke up the next morning I was startled to see Brian sitting there next to my bed.

'Did you go home?' I asked weakly.

'No, Eric and I have been here all night.'

I smiled, 'Then your breath must be humming.'

Brian smiled and kissed my forehead. 'Well when we get married, you are going to have to get used to it.'

I smiled. 'I love you. Brian, I am sorry I ruined your proposal. I am so sorry. I didn't mean to.'

'There is no need to apologize. We're going to get through this like the last time. But this time I know what's going on. I want you to know that I am here. I know you have a lot to deal with right now, but I am here. You are not alone. I will not let you do this by yourself.'

I stared at Brian intently, 'That is all I know is how to do things by myself. I am an only child remember.'

Brian looked at me, 'Then remember I am here when you need me. I promise. I'm here for you.'

'So where so we go from here?' I asked half to myself and half to Brian. 'I don't know what you want me to do.'

'You marry me, Nikki,' Brian said.

'Like this?' I whispered.

'For better or for worst and in sickness and in health.' Brian countered and watched the tears fall from my eyes. Brian slipped the ring on my finger as Eric walked into the room. I took a deep breath.

'Hey, does that mean there was going to be a wedding?' Eric leaned over and kissed me on the cheek. 'I got dibs on the second slice of cake. A big piece too.'

'Yes,' I said trying to wipe the tears from my face and laughing at the same time. 'You are still so greedy.'

Brian looked at Eric and smiled, 'Yes. Yes. Yes. And I want you to be my best man.'

'What about Day?' Eric asked looking confused. 'We could both do it. I mean that's your best friend and all.'

Brian shook his head, 'He already told me to ask you…"

AJ

I knocked on the door again and waited. I had knocked already but figured my dad was sleep or in the bathroom and hadn't heard the door. Finally, I heard my dad shuffling around inside, through the door. My father looked at me and smiled a smile like he was happy to see me. Charles opened the door wide and then moved aside to let me in.

'What strong wind blew you over here?' Charles asked adjusting the sound on the television.

'I haven't heard from you since the party and I was curious as to what happened to you.' AJ ventured taking a seat.

'Been busy here and there, you know your dad has a life. Trying to make moves. I was going to call you about the party. Had a lot of stuff to do that day. Wasn't really feeling good. You know how it is.'

I just shook my head. 'No, actually I don't. Well, you know Kevin is home. I thought you might want to see him.'

'Oh, yeah, how's he doing?' my father said sitting back down in his seat. 'He has been in the service a long time. How is school coming along for you? My son goes to Drexel. Drexel."

'I'm good. School is great, Why you don't come see him,' I ventured. 'Be a father for once.'

'I am going to make some time,' my father said still watching whatever was on television. 'You know how it is.'

'When?' I asked firmly. "When will that be?"

'I got to see,' Charles never once looked at me. 'If the Lord allows me. Got a lot on my plate. Tell him to call me sometimes.'

'It is cool,' I said as I got up to leave.

'You are leaving already? Stay awhile.'

'Why?' I said growing angrier by the minute. 'For what. You ever notice our conversations are always brief. You don't have shit to talk about. For years, my mother told me never to hate you. She said I had a right to dislike the things you did but not to hate you.'

'I asked you to come to your son's welcome home party and you couldn't come. What was I thinking? When have you ever done anything we asked of you, Charles?'

'Now look boy, I am your father. You call me dad, pop, father but I don't like it when you call me Charles,' he said indignantly.

'No, actually, you fathered me, but you never had been a father to me. Much less an example of how a man is supposed to be. When you came to my graduation, people complained that I just shook your hand and walked away.'

'Well, it was my way of saying thank you for walking away from my mother the way you did. If you didn't I wouldn't be even half the man you will never be. It gave my mother the incentive to raise me to the kind of person that a man should be. The kind of man you don't know how to be and will never learn.'

'I am your father,' Charles yelled and I laughed.

'Is that right?' I laughed. 'Funny thing is you never acted like one. Did your sister actually tell you I have a baby on the way? A child with a woman I love. My chance to show you what you never could be--a father. A real father. You poke your chest out and is quick to tell people I am your son but you never did anything to live up to that.'

'Now look here, Mister...,' Charles said.

'Look at what. A broke down sorry excuse of a man.

You pretend to be something you are not.'

'You are just like your mother,' Charles said returning to his chair. He stopped and looked at me long and hard.

'Thank you,' I countered. 'That is about the nicest thing you ever said to me. That makes me less like you.'

'You are a bitch. A pussy. She fucked you up,' Charles growled. 'Get out of my house until you learn some respect.

'Now I feel sorry for you, Charles. That's all the things you feel about yourself and you wished them for me. That's why I can't be your son, I don't know how,' I laughed. "Coming here was a mistake.'

Charles looked at me long and hard. 'What do you want me to say? That I am sorry for not being a good father.'

'No,' I countered, 'I wanted you to be a father. Somebody I could be proud of. Notice I never say I love you. I can't love somebody I don't know. The bible says honor thy mother and thy father and thy days will be long. But with you I can't. Like I said about being your son, I don't know how.'

'I know you know better than to stand there and just talk to me any old kind of way. You are my son,' Charles said standing up. 'I know I was wrong, I don't need you to keep harping on it.'

'Charles, the sins of the father don't just rest on the heads of their children. They are taught. You wanted me to respect you, and then you should have been around to teach me. I'm leaving.' I walked to the door. 'I'll be back when my child is born to show you how a father is supposed to be with his child.'

I walked out the door and closed it behind myself. I took a deep breath, realizing it was over. This was years coming. I said what I came to say. I said what needed to be said. Now it is time to go home to my family...

Sista

Pulling up to the house, things felt different. It's been almost three years since my father died, since Nikki got sick. So much has changed and yet, in there own way things felt better. I saw Eric on the front steps as he put out his cigarette and waited for me to get out of the car. I waddled up the steps and Eric moved to help me.

'I see you are a smart man,' I said looking at the cigarette. 'First for putting it out before I got out the car and not smoking around Mommy. Does she even know you smoke?'

'Yeah, she knows,' Eric mumbled. 'I know you would have told if she didn't and you know I would never smoke in the house. All that plastic around. I saw you parking that car where you get your license from Fisher Price'

We both laughed. We went in the house. My mother screamed when she saw me. I am seven months and I showed all seven. But I still possessed a healthy glow that only a mother had.

'My babies,' my mother said as she rubbed my stomach. My mother went on to do her usual baby talk. My mother read that if you talked around the mother before the baby is born the baby would be more inclined to be around you when it is born. She can have that. I feel like I'm carrying triplets instead of one baby.

I looked around the house and watched as Ms. Violet had gathered up the last of the bags after she came over to give me a hug. We were all going to the hospital that morning. Today Nikki and Brian were getting married. I prayed for this day and today, it came true.

Nikki's cancer came back and it came back with a vengeance. What Nikki feared most was happening. During Nikki's frequent hospital visits, Day, Brian or I were by her side. During Nikki's hospitalizations, I made a point to always visit.

Nikki had chosen her treatments to be at my Mom's job to ensure that my Mom could be there or Ms. Violet when nobody else could.

Still Nikki fought for the last five months. She fought hard and for a minute, it seemed like she might win. I hoped so.

But this last bout, Nikki had been sidelined by this round with her cancer. Nikki was growing weaker than ever but Brian kept his promise and was there through thick and thin.

Not once did he flinch. Brian planned to meet everyone at the hospital. He was picking Ms. Mae and Mr. Benny up from the hotel. The wedding would start soon.

When Loretta came into the house, she looked a mess. Nobody spoke to her. To be truthful, nobody has seen her since that day at the house with her little friend. Why was she even here? My mother looked long and hard at her and just shook her head. I tried to move past her and was surprised when I felt Loretta grab my arm.

'Paul,' Loretta said with a devilish smile. 'You know Paul, he told me to tell you hello.'

'How do you know Paul?' I asked pulling away from Loretta's grasp. She wouldn't let go, she just laughed.

'Oh, we know each other very well. He was at that bar next to Max's on Erie Avenue one night. One thing lead to another. Well, you know the rest. Did he ever do that thing to you with the two Lemondheads candy?'

Eric who watched the whole scene when he came from the kitchen, 'Don't do it Loretta.' Eric could tell Loretta was high or drunk and it was still early in the day.

'Don't do what?' Loretta laughed. 'What is done is done? I'm so glad he dumped you. He hasn't had a good woman in a minute. His marriage fell apart. My marriage fell apart. It was you, Sista that started all of this. You told Cliff about Kareem. I know you did. You fucked me over so I feel obligated to fuck your man. Don't worry you can have him back when I am through. Leave the lemonheads. AJ is looking good.'

'No, if you want the truth, Cliff told me he saw you sneaking Kareem out of the house and I told him that was between you, him and God. Why are you doing this?' I asked.

'I don't want Paul; I have somebody in my life. I am pregnant for God sake. Why do you have to be such a bitch? You hate me, fine. I get that, but you need to let it go.'

'Isn't it clear, I don't like you? I never did and I never will—' Loretta didn't finish. My mother hauled off and slapped the shit out of Loretta. Slap. I felt it. Somebody needed to slap Loretta. She should have hit her again.

'You have gone too far,' my mother said quietly. 'Go home.'

'But,' Loretta said holding her face. "Why did you hit me?'

'You are mean and spiteful. Your father always said that. You hate and hate and hate. You messed up your marriage. You brought that boy into this house. You took him to bed. Now to get involved with a man that wasn't good for your sister, that's trifling. Your father and I raised you better than that.'

'Sista was always stronger than you,' My mother said as if she was ready to hit Loretta again, 'Because she never allowed people to dictate how she should live. You never learned how. You always did what you want and couldn't accept responsibility for the things you did. Until you can get yourself together, I don't want you here. Now go home. Get out of this house or so help me I will beat the hell out of you.'

Just then, Day came in the door. Day hugged his mother. Mike was waiting in the car. Day looked at Loretta and then watched as Eric opened the door wider for Loretta who stormed out.

'We need to get a move on it.' Day said unsure of what just happened. 'We need to get the best man to the wedding.' Eric looked at me and smiled. Eric looked at his watch and then walked over and hugged me.

I tried to dismiss what just happened with Loretta. That was crazy. What did she have to gain by all of that? Then Paul, he is crazy. He slept with Loretta?

Eric nudged me to bring me out of my trance. Since coming home, Eric had gotten a maintenance job at the hospital and is doing better. He has changed so much. I am so proud of him. He even took an anger management course that surprised all of us. Sometimes a thug in the family is a good thing though. He did kick Kareem's ass after all the shit he did.

Eric made a point to join a mentoring program for youth offenders that would have made my father proud. I picked up my bag and shook off Loretta's negativity, Paul is the past. AJ and my baby are the future.

As everyone filed out of the house, I watched as Day was sent back for something by his mother. I watched as the older man got out of his car and followed Day into the house.

Ms. Violet hugged my mother and I realized who that man is. They did this. I knew it. I felt it. Here he was. The last person Day would ever expect to see, his father. But what is he doing in Philly…

Day

I was all set to turn to ask my mother what she needed, when I came face to face with my father. He was about the last person I expected to see. You could have knocked me over with a feather. I watched as my mother came back into the living room and watched my father move closer to me. I moved back.

Just then my mother stepped forward. She moved closer to me. What is he doing here? Why? Why is he here? I wanted to say that but the words didn't come out. My eyes searched my mother's face for an answer. She just nodded her head to signify it was okay.

'It is too late for me and your Daddy,' my mother said. 'But not too late for the two of you. I'll take a ride with the rest and you two talk.' My mother placed her house key on the table and she touched my arm and walked out.

'Did Mama set this up on her own or did you?' I asked.

'No, I asked her to,' my father said. 'It gets lonely in that house since your mother left me. Lonelier than when you left.'

'Imagine spending all those years away from my mother. I am 34 years old now, almost 35. It was over 10 years when I saw my mama again. All those years of cards and words and I thought she hated me. But all that time, it was you.'

'I am sorry, son.'

'Son? Do you think you had even a right to call me that after everything you said to me? Even when Mama took me back there to see you. Your hatred was evident. You hated me.'

'I didn't hate you,' my father said. 'I hated what I thought I did. I thought I made you gay. As if the way I raised some how made you like this. I was raised to believe that a man is meant to be with a woman. I thought I did something wrong. Your cousin is gay and that is an embarrassment. People talk.'

'So I was an embarrassment,' I asked quietly. 'I thought I was your son. Who is more important me or people, Daddy?'

'You are my son. I know I don't deserve your forgiveness but I am asking for it. I am begging you to let me back in your life. Son, I am sorry for all the hateful words I said. Can you find it in your heart to forgive me?'

'You called me a faggot. You called me a sissy. You called me a homo. Said I needed to die like all the other faggots in the streets. Daddy, I am not like them. I never had been like that and I never will be---'

'You are my son,' my father's voice echoed through the room as he cut me off. 'You are my son. I need you.'

'What about my being gay?' I said trying not to cry but I did any way. 'Can you love me if I am gay?'

My father put his hat down on the table and stepped forward. I instinctively moved back. My father extended his arms and my father hugged me. For the first time, in a long time, my father hugged me. I'm almost 35 and I felt like a little boy. I couldn't talk, I just cried.

'Yes,' my father said as he started crying. 'I will love my son, no matter what. You are my son. I'm sorry.' He just kept saying it.

'I am sorry,' my father said barely above a whisper. 'I love you son. I know it's not going to be easy. I know I have a lot of time to make up for. But if you are willing to try so am I.'

I couldn't believe it. I was crying so hard that I didn't even hear Mike come in the house. It seemed like an eternity before I finally let go realizing I had to be at the hospital soon. I wiped my face and looked at Mike. I then looked at my father.

'Dad, I want you to meet somebody very special to me.' I said. 'This is Mike.'

Mike shook my father's hand.

'Nice to meet you,' my father said shaking Mike's hand. It was a start. Who knows what tomorrow would bring. I wiped my face and looked at Mike and then my father.

'Listen,' I said, 'I am not saying that things will go back to being so good for us, but I am willing to try. Right now I have some place to be. Sista, Nikki, Brian and their family have been good to me and I need to be there for them.'

'Okay,' my father nodded and handed me a piece of paper, 'Here is my number when you are ready to call me.'

My father went to hug me but I stepped away. He picked up his hat and nodded and walked to the door. My father looked at me and I looked at Mike. My father left.

'Are you okay,' Mike asked.

'I'm good,' I replied.

Mike handed me my mother's key and we walked out the door closing it and locking it...

Sista

I applied the last of the makeup to Nikki and smiled at my handy work. I was doing the best maneuvering I could consider my condition. My stomach is huge. I could barely get around the bed. I looked at Nikki who was obviously weaker than before. Ms. Mae and I did a good job of dressing Nikki in a cream color head wrap and dress.

'How are you feeling?' I asked staring at Nikki as Nikki opened her eyes. She had been drifting off and on. Ms. Mae had gone to find the others to get the ceremony started. I sat next to Nikki on the bed.

'Tired from that radiation,' Nikki said out of breathe.

'Brian isn't going anywhere girl we can do this when you are ready.' I said holding Nikki's hand. She gave mine a slight squeeze.

'Sista, I have waited for this day my whole life. I have my grandmother here, my best friend and a man that I love dearly. We have to do this now. Before I lose my nerve.' Nikki attempted to smile but the fatigue overwhelmed her.

'I'll be right back,' I said stopping to kiss Nikki on the forehead. 'I love you. Just rest until I get back, okay.'

'Sista,' Nikki said weakly. 'I love you, too. Tell Brian to come here. Forget the superstition, I need to see him. Could you get him?'

'But,' I said. Then realizing the truth, I went out into the hallway. I fought back my tears as I walked into the hall. 'Brian,' I said in almost a whisper. Brian turned around and looked at me. 'Nikki is asking for you. She needs to see you.'

Sensing my concern, Brian looked at Eric and me and went into the room. Brian sat in the chair at Nikki's side. Brian grabbed Nikki's hand, which caused Nikki to open her eyes...

Brian and Nikki

'Hey,' Nikki said barely above a whisper. 'Boo Boo Bear. I am sorry. I know you have been waiting for this day for a long time.'

'Sorry for what?' I asked. 'I am a patient man. I can wait.'

'I will not be able to be the wife you want me to be though.'

'Shh, we talked about that. All that matters in that you are going to be my wife,' I said as I tried to fight back my own tears. I know some how that the end was near.

'You have been the best woman you could be. I know these last couple of years couldn't have been easy but I have been here because you needed me to be here. You needed me as much as I needed you. I'm here. Do you hear me, I'm not going anywhere.'

'I love you,' Nikki whispered.

'I love you more. Listen,' I said looking at my watch, just rest until everybody gets here. Then we'll get married and spend the rest of our lives together.'

I realized that Nikki didn't hear the last of my words as she drifted off again. I leaned over and kissed Nikki's forehead and stopped to look at Nikki breathing become slow and regular.

'We have all the time in the world,' I thought. Then I suddenly realized maybe I didn't. Eric stepped into the room and watched my face and he knew like I did. I don't know what is wrong with me, but I couldn't move. Maybe it was shock, but I couldn't move.

I couldn't think. Everything seemed to move in slow motion as I watched Eric run into the hall and called for help. As

Day and Sista walked back down the hall she saw Eric and me and then the doctors and nurses in the room. Sista made a dash for the room as the rest of the family came down the hall.

'Wait,' Eric said as Sista tried to move past him with determination. 'No,' Eric said more firmly. Sista stopped when he said this and looked at me. I didn't know what to do or say.

'What happened?' Sista asked. When we didn't say anything, she asked again only louder, 'Where is Nikki? What happened?'

Eric held Sista as I stood crying against the wall. I felt powerless, like there isn't anything I could do. 'We don't know. Let's just wait and see.'

Eric said as Sista stopped her struggling with him. Eric just held Sista as she cried. I felt a hand take mine and saw my mother standing there. It only made me cry harder.

I wiped my face with my handkerchief and looked back into the room just as AJ and Mike arrived. Nobody knew what to say. I fingered the ring in my pocket. I looked at the first doctor who emerged and sensed the truth. But he shook his head yes.

I looked at Sista and went back in with Sista close behind. I took Nikki's hand in my own and put it to my lips. I kissed it and Nikki stirred slightly.

For a minute, the room grew so still and so quiet. I felt like I stopped breathing, like all the air just raced out my body. Did I die? Did I somehow stop breathing?

It was only then that I realized it wasn't me. I'm still here. But how? Then I knew. It wasn't me that stopped breathing. It was Nikki...

A Year Later...

I tried to juggle the kids, the front door and the ringing phone all at once. I yelled for whoever it was to come in. I was happy when the door opened and Day walked in followed by Mike and took Nikki off my hands. She had been making a mess of everything.

Earl tossed the toys in front of him on to the floor and laughed. Both were as feisty as their mother. Ms. Lucy told Sista that one day she'd have a child to pay her back for all things she did as a child. Nikki and Earl would do that twofold. But what did I have to do with that? I was a good kid.

We decided when Sista first became pregnant to name our child after Nikki. If it was going to be a boy his name would have been Nicholas Earl.

We called him Earl though. Earl was named after Sista's dad. If it was a girl, we'd named her Nicole Cheryl, figuring Earline would upset our daughter when she got older. Nobody told us it would be twins. A boy and a girl.

'Uncle Day is here.' Day said to Nikki who laugh and grabbed at Day's face. Day looked at me as I was trying to pack the diaper bag and take the shoe out of Earl's mouth.

'Whoa,' Day said interceding and putting the shoe back on Earl's foot. 'Where is Sista? She left already?'

Mike took the bag and the car seat from me. Then I picked up Earl and I finally sat down. I was exhausted.

'Yeah, she went to visit Nikki,' I said finally catching my breath. 'Thank you both. These two are enough to drive a man to drink.' Mike took Earl from me.

'No problem,' Mike said. 'Earl is my buddy.' As Mike picked Earl up after putting down the car seat near the door. Earl laughed and then proceeded to spit up all over Mike. I jumped up to help Mike. Earl just laughed.

'Sorry about that,' I said taking Earl. I handed Mike a paper towel to clean himself up. I looked at Earl. 'Why you do that to Uncle Mike?'

Mike just laughed. 'It is cool.' Mike looked at his watch. 'Day, we need to get a move on it if we are going to get to the zoo. I want the kids to see everything before they have to get to their grandmother's'

'Yeah,' Day said, "I need to meet my mother later. My father is in town and we are going to try to do a family dinner.'

'That's good, Day. I am happy for you. Very happy. If you need help with the kids just call me before they get to their grandmother's. Hopefully, the two of you can tire them out. They waited until their mother left out before they started wilding out.' I handed Earl back to Mike and Day picked Nikki up from her walker. I carried the car seats to the car.

I looked at Day sensing that Day wanted to say something but didn't. Day knew that every Saturday, Sista spent her morning visiting Nikki and I was left with the twins.

Ms. Lucy, I really got to stop calling her that, she said to call her Mom, Brian, Eric, Mike and Day alternated on helping me out with the kids to make sure Sista could keep her visits. I kissed my kids once they were secure in the car and waved to Day and Mike.

'Tell Sista to call me,' Day said. I watched the car pull off before going back inside. It would be another hour before Sista would come home. But she rarely talked after her visits. I would be there all the same. Sometimes, I didn't know what to say or to do. But I was here if she did...

Sista

'Hey, girl.' I said as I sat on the bench. 'You know what day it is, I am here. I looked around trying not to cry. 'Going to my mother's later on. Day and Mike had the kids for the day. Who know that Day would finally get it together? Then again look what you did for my brother.' I smiled then paused.

'Loretta called my mother from Baltimore. She hasn't been around too much since my mother hit her. I guess she had that coming. She calls but never visits.' I took a deep breath. 'Girl, you should see Eric now. Eric got a good job now too girl.'

'He took me to lunch this week. Remember how broke he used to be. He even introduced me to his new girlfriend. He is getting so big dealing with her. Fat isn't the word. He eats so much. He was always greedy.'

I paused, 'I am going to bring the kids to see you when they get a little older. Let Nikki, Little Nikki, get to know where she got her name from. Girl, if you would have told me that I would be having two kids instead of one, I would have said you were lying. They are bad.'

'I don't like to call kids bad but girl.' I looked around and suddenly felt a strong breeze blow past me. I sat down the flowers I was holding and reached out my hand to touch the picture on Nikki's tombstone.

'Why aren't you here?' I cried. 'Why? I remember sitting there all those nights knowing that no matter what happened, you would be here. You'd be here and everything would be okay. But, I didn't think about what happened if you weren't. Sometimes the silence gets so loud and like my daddy I want to turn around and tell you about something and you aren't here. You ain't.'

'I did not think,' I began before clearing my voice. 'After my daddy passed away, I did not think I would be here again so soon. Not like this. I cannot help but to think about what my father once said. He said 'God do not make mistakes.'

'When you got sick again that last time, I got angry. I got upset. Not again, why her? I prayed that God would give you the strength to endure what you were going through. I never knew I would be here asking for the strength to go on without you.'

'We will all miss you Nikki. We will miss your smile, your style and your class. We miss your voice. We miss you.' I closed my eyes and I squeezed them hoping that when I reopened them, then all of this would be a dream. When I did reopen my eyes again, Nikki was still gone.

The doctors did all they could but nothing could stop Nikki's cancer from spreading this time. After months of prayer and holding vigil, Nikki died. Nikki was dead. She held on long enough to become Brian's wife.

I remember then that for the first time in a long time, I felt alone. I'm still hurting inside but still I tried to hold it together for the sake of my unborn child. But the loneliness, it began on the day that Nikki died and stayed with me.

The hurting felt like a blanket that never truly warmed me. On the day that Nikki died it seems the world stood still. It seemed like everything in the room stood still long enough that you know the color of air and understood its presence and purpose. I cried harder than I ever did.

At the funeral, Eric looked at Brian to see if Brian wanted to speak, but Brian shook his head. Brian, I guess had already prepared for this moment and felt he said everything he needed to say.

Just then an outburst erupted from the back of the room. Everyone in the church looked to see what was going on. I even wiped my eyes and looked and watched the man storm out of the church. I looked at Leonard who wasn't far away. It wasn't him. A chorus of voices erupted; each one questioned who the man was and why he made such a sudden outburst.

The minister looked at Eric who signaled for him to continue the service. I looked at Brian and suddenly we realized that there was one person that knew the pain that the two of us was feeling, besides Ms. Mae, he just left—Reggie.

I shook myself out of my daydream and looked around the cemetery. 'People always tell you, you should act like the person is still around. You never die if people are here to talk about you. But, they don't know the pain I feel. They don't know the hurt. They don't know what it is like to lose a good friend...'

I cried and allowed the tears flow. Suddenly, I felt a hand on my shoulder and turned to see my brother standing in the sunshine.

'Hey,' Brian said. I stood up. I started to speak but Brian shushed me. Brian hugged me. 'I know.'

'What time are you leaving? 'I asked wiping away my tears. I squeezed Brian's hand.

'In another hour. I stopped past to see the family. Mommy asked were you still coming over and I told her you would. She said Day would be dropping the kids off after the zoo.'

'I hope the zoo don't keep them. Those two are a handful like we used to be.' Sista nodded and then started crying again. 'I am going to miss you.'

Brian smiled. 'New York isn't that far away. You and AJ, you can visit any time you want with the kids. Without the kids.' he laughed. 'I just need a change of pace.'

Brian looked at Nikki's grave and placed the flowers he brought along side my twelve white roses. Brian closed his eyes and reopened them when I squeezed his hand.

'I thought after Daddy died that I wouldn't have to go through this again, not so soon. I thought I would never be in love, I never thought...'Brian's voice trailed off.

'We didn't know.' I said reassuringly. 'I remember when we first found out Nikki was sick, I thought we were through, and that we had fought this and won. We were wrong.'

I took a deep breath and looked at my brother who started to cry. Brian kissed my cheek. 'I haven't had a good day since she passed. I wished we could have had more time. I wish we could have had a chance to be together just a little longer.'

I knelt down and took Brian's hand again. 'Then don't go. Stay here. Do you really have to leave?'

'Yeah, it is my time. Too many things to think about here. My wife is gone. Family never goes away. I just need to breathe for a minute. Find what is going to take to make me happy again.'

I squinted as the sun suddenly became very bright, 'New job, New city. New life. Eric is home. I think he's ready to handle things while I am gone. He's already taking over for me with Mommy and Ms. Violet. They got him running errands and everything.'

Brian and I stood up. I hugged my brother. Brian smiled and walked me back to my car. As I buckled my seat beat and prepared to drive off.

'If you ever need me,' Brian said. 'Call me. I will not ever be that far away that you can't write me.'

I squeezed Brian's hand before getting into the car. I looked at my brother, afraid for that brief instance that this was the last time I would see him. He was right; New York is not that far away. I squeezed his hand before driving away. I needed to get home to my man, my husband...

310

Brian

I walked back to Nikki's grave. I kissed my hand and placed it the picture of Nikki's face on the tombstone. I looked long and hard at the picture and tried to muster up my strength to walk away. I couldn't.

Not yet, any way. I have been trying to find closure, a peace within myself and I don't think I will ever find it. I felt like I should say goodbye, something. Anything.

Nothing came out though. It was time to move on and I knew it. I felt it. I hated myself inside thinking about how quickly I went from celebrating my finally becoming Nikki's husband to sitting there at her bedside when quietly she passed away.

Lately, I got tired of people asking me if I was okay every time I got quiet. Like I wasn't allowed to have a bad day. How was I supposed to feel? Happy all the time? I just lost the woman that I loved.

Nikki was the woman I waited my whole life for. I loved Nikki in a way I would never believe I would love any woman every again.

Nikki was the woman I promised before God to love until death do we part. I promised, but she's gone and I still do. Death came and my feelings didn't change one bit. That's why I decided to leave. Not run away, but I needed to go away for awhile to clear my head.

I walked back to my car and looked at my watch. It was time for me to go. Maybe a new job, in a new city would be enough to end the depression I felt since the day Nikki died.

This morning, I asked God for a sign that I was doing the right thing. I'm patient. I could wait for his signal. I switched on the radio as I drove in the direction of the interstate highway.

On the radio, as the last few words of the song 'Superstar' faded, Luther Vandross reminded me, 'It is alright, alright now, alright now.' Somehow, I knew it would be. It was 2002 and anything can happen....then I woke up.

I was laying in my bed, but I was alone. Was I dreaming? I looked around wondering how much was really real. The only question was where was Nikki? Did she really die or was I just dreaming the whole thing? If she wasn't truly dead, answer me this, where was she now…

To Be Continued In Cold Summer Afternoon…

About The Author

Rasheed Clark, a native of Philadelphia, currently works and lives in Philadelphia. A graduate of the Peirce College, Philadelphia University (the former Philadelphia College of Textiles and Science) and Drexel University, Rasheed is currently hard at work on his next book, the sequel to 'Stories I Wouldn't Tell Nobody But God' entitled 'Cold Summer Afternoon.'

An Excerpt of Cold Summer Afternoon

An Angry Woman Says...

I sat in the dark of my apartment for over an hour. The only light came from the street lamp outside my apartment building. I looked around trying to figure out the number of times I wanted to burn this place to the ground just like Left Eye tried to do to Andre Rison. I was just that upset.

I thought about the times I wanted to poison his food and watch him gasp for his last breath. I would then just finish my untouched dinner and then plan his funeral. I wanted him to suffer as much as possible. Then, I'd be happy. Maybe.

I picked up my drink and swirled the ice around in the glass and then ran my hand across the gun. It was lying on the cushion of the couch next to me. I wanted to make sure it was still there. It felt cool to my touch.

Touching it, I thought about all of the arguments, the fights, the lies and the threats that came down to this one moment. I wanted him to die. In my mind, I already died several times inside. I wanted him to hurt just as much as I do now.

For far too long, I put up with his brand of drama like some people put up with a headache. The only difference is that now payback is a bitch. I didn't plan on killing him at first, but right now, I didn't have the strength to live with what he has done. At least what he did to me, I didn't even want to think about. My blood ran cold when I did.

Now, sitting here, I realized he could take everything from me. I realized that my happily ever after fairytale was all built on a lie. I looked around again and had to ask myself what would drive a woman to murder? How did I let it get to this point? I should have left. I should have been strong enough to walk away. It doesn't matter. I know how I planned to end it. I am going to finish it my way.

I put my drink down on the coffee table and ran my hand across the gun again. It was still there. Where was he? I took a deep breath and waited. Hold on. Wait. You hear that? I heard the familiar jingle of the keys to the front door. He's home.

I picked up the gun, stood up and aimed it at the door. I wasn't sure if he would turn on the lights. I prayed he wouldn't. My hands started to shake. I felt my palms grow damp under the weight of the gun. There were six bullets in the gun and every one of them belonged to him.

Slowly, the door opened. I heard a voice. Then, a brighter light washed over the room overtaking the light from the street lights outside. I closed my eyes and pulled the trigger. Boom. Boom. Boom. Boom. Boom. Five shots. I didn't want to open my eyes until the gun was empty and hopefully, he was dead...

From Rasheed Clark, the author of
'Stories I Wouldn't tell Nobody But God'...

From Rasheed Clark, the best-selling author of the explosive, debut novel "Stories I Wouldn't Tell Nobody But God" comes the most highly anticipated novel ever...

Love. Infidelity. Deception. Abuse. Lies. Shameful secrets. Hurt. Mistrust. For one of four women, it's enough to drive her to commit murder...

April... Trapped in a loveless marriage to a less than loving, abusive husband, she was alone until she meets Brian Robinson, who just lost the love of his life. Will she risk her marriage and make the ultimate sacrifice to find love again?

Renee... She made the transition from being the "other woman" to being one man's wife, but at what cost? She soon discovers what goes around truly does come around.

Blue... She must discover the hard way that you can't run from your past or yourself, especially when a man is involved? What will she do when she comes face to face with the man she promised to love forever?

Loretta...After destroying her own marriage through her own lies, infidelity and insecurities, she now holds the fate of another marriage in her hands. Wait until the man's wife finds out...

Brace yourself for a story you won't soon forget. Filled with more twists and turns than a rollercoaster, Cold Summer Afternoon is the book everybody will be talking about right up to its surprising ending...

Cold Summer Afternoon

Printed in the United States
138044LV00005B/129/A

9 780979 930201